Hannah sat up nearly dropping her t

There were photos of the familiar farmhouse, with a smiling young couple standing alongside the front porch, and another snapshot of the children with a big sheepdog, as the voice-over told the story of the accidental death of the father, coupled with the grave illness of the mother, causing the separation. Then suddenly a slender woman with dark hair and deep dimples was talking—the mother who'd never stopped searching for the three children taken from her so long ago.

Hannah blinked back a rush of tears, staring at the remembered features, scarcely changed by the years.

They told me you were dead. Oh, God!

Could this be happening?

Dear Reader,

Brides, babies and families…that's just what Special Edition has in store for you this August! All this and more from some of your favorite authors.

Our THAT'S MY BABY! title for this month is *Of Texas Ladies, Cowboys…and Babies,* by popular Silhouette Romance author Jodi O'Donnell. In her first book for Special Edition, Jodi tells of a still young and graceful grandmother-to-be who unexpectedly finds herself in the family way! Fans of Jodi's latest Romance novel, *Daddy Was a Cowboy,* won't want to miss this spin-off title!

This month, GREAT EXPECTATIONS, the wonderful new series of family and homecoming by Andrea Edwards, continues with *A Father's Gift.* And summer just wouldn't be right without a wedding, so we present *A Bride for John,* the second book of Trisha Alexander's newest series, THREE BRIDES AND A BABY. Beginning this month is a new miniseries from veteran author Pat Warren, REUNION. Three siblings must find each other as they search for true love. It all begins with one sister's story in *A Home for Hannah.*

Also joining the Special Edition family this month is reader favorite and Silhouette Romance author Stella Bagwell. Her first title for Special Edition is *Found: One Runaway Bride.* And returning to Special Edition this August is Carolyn Seabaugh with *Just a Family Man,* as the lives of one woman and her son are forever changed when an irresistible man walks into their café in the wild West.

This truly is a month packed with summer fun and romance! I hope you enjoy each and every story to come!

Sincerely,
Tara Gavin, Senior Editor

Please address questions and book requests to:
Silhouette Reader Service
U.S.: 3010 Walden Ave., P.O. Box 1325, Buffalo, NY 14269
Canadian: P.O. Box 609, Fort Erie, Ont. L2A 5X3

PAT
WARREN
A HOME FOR HANNAH

SPECIAL EDITION®

Published by Silhouette Books
America's Publisher of Contemporary Romance

This book is dedicated to B. J. Gifford
for a friendship I treasure

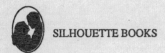 SILHOUETTE BOOKS

ISBN 0-373-24048-1

A HOME FOR HANNAH

Copyright © 1996 by Pat Warren

PAT WARREN

is a mother of four and lives in Arizona with her travel agent husband and a lazy white cat. She's a former newspaper columnist whose lifetime dream was to become a novelist. A strong romantic streak, a sense of humor and a keen interest in developing relationships led her to try romance novels, with which she feels very much at home.

Don't miss the second book in Pat's REUNION miniseries, MICHAEL'S HOUSE. This stirring, heartfelt story is coming to you next month in Silhouette Intimate Moments!

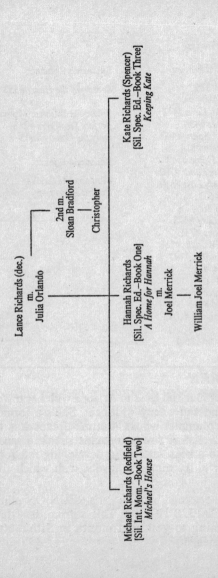

Lance Richards (dec.)
m.
Julia Orlando

2nd m.
Sloan Bradford

Christopher

Michael Richards (Redfield)
[Sil. Int. Mom.—Book Two]
Michael's House

Hannah Richards
[Sil. Spec. Ed.—Book One]
A Home for Hannah
m.
Joel Merrick

William Joel Merrick

Kate Richards (Spencer)
[Sil. Spec. Ed.—Book Three]
Keeping Kate

Prologue

He is such a good man, my Lance. He works so hard that he's always tired. I, too, am weary after a long day in the fields alongside him, then tending the house and cooking the meals, watching over the children. But I don't complain except occasionally here in my journal, where I pour out my thoughts while the house sleeps.

Lance is strong and determined to make a success of the farm he inherited from his parents. But two years of drought and poor crops have drained the little savings we had. Now we're mortgaged to the hilt, and I worry about that, about the effect on my family. The children are so sweet, such a help. Michael just started high school, yet he does the work of someone twice his age and still keeps up with his studies. Hannah's just turned eight, but her gooseberry pie's better than mine and she sews like an angel. Our beautiful Katie's only six, yet she feeds the chickens, gathers the eggs and has a smile for everyone. They're all healthy, thank God.

It's me who's been feeling poorly lately with this cough that won't ease up. Ah, but I'm young, barely thirty-two; I'll be fine come spring. This winter's been a harsh one. Mother says it's the last one she can handle. She needs sunshine, so she's returning to New Mexico. She hasn't been the same since Papa died. "Julia," she tells me, "I'm only half-alive without him." I understand, for I'd feel the same if I lost Lance.

The hour's late and I should be in bed. The house is asleep and peaceful, except for the wind moaning through the attic. Rex, the sheepdog, and I are the only ones still awake by the dying embers of the fire. I like the quiet, watching the snow fall outside, feeling safe. My constant prayer is that this year the spring rains will bring us an abundant crop so that we can get out of debt and Lance won't have to work so hard.

We married young, barely out of high school, but I've never regretted a day of it. So tall, so blond and fair, Lance is beautiful. So different from me with my dark hair and tan skin that he says he envies so. I tell the children that I believe in destiny, in fate. This is the life I was born for, to be mother to them and wife to Lance.

I love them all so. Nothing will ever part us.

Chapter One

The host of the national television show had just the right mix of charm and sincerity, Hannah thought. The program, "Solutions," was very popular, asking the viewing audience to call in to help solve a mystery or to assist in reuniting families separated for a variety of reasons.

In her Boston home, Hannah lay stretched out on the couch under an afghan, just getting over a bad head cold. Outside, an early-December snowstorm had marooned all but the truly adventurous. Glad to be inside where flames licked at the hickory logs in the fireplace, she took a sip of honeyed tea and turned her lazy attention to the silver screen.

The current search, according to the host, was for three children who'd been separated from their hospitalized mother over twenty years ago, taken from their farm home in Frankenmuth, Michigan, by the Child Protective Services. Pictures flashed on the screen of a fair-haired, long-legged boy who'd been fourteen at the time, a thin, sad-eyed girl of eight with dark hair and a pretty, blond six-year-old girl with huge blue eyes.

Hannah sat up quickly, nearly dropping her teacup. There were photos of the familiar farmhouse with a smiling young couple standing alongside the front porch, and another snapshot of the children with a big sheepdog as the voice-over told the story of the accidental death of the father, coupled with the grave illness of the mother, causing the separation. Then suddenly, a slender, mature woman with dark hair and deep dimples was talking, introducing herself as Julia, the mother who'd never stopped searching for the three children taken from her so long ago.

Swallowing around a lump in her throat, Hannah blinked back a rush of tears as she leaned forward, staring at the remembered features, scarcely changed by the years. *They told me you were dead. Oh, God!* Could this lovely person really be the mother she'd last seen being taken away in an ambulance? Could this be happening?

All too soon, the segment ended, and the announcer implored anyone who knew anything about the whereabouts of any of the three children to please call the number at the bottom of the screen. With trembling hands, Hannah reached for the pad and pen on the end table and scribbled down the number.

Struggling with a jumble of emotions, she sank back into the couch, picked up the remote and clicked off the set. Her mother, alive and searching for them all these years. Unbelievable. What had happened to big brother Michael and to little Katie? Over twenty years, such a long time ago.

Closing her eyes, Hannah let herself remember.

Boston—Three years earlier

With an eye on her rearview mirror, Hannah Richards made an illegal left turn into the narrow driveway leading to the parking lot behind the stately old brick building that now housed law offices. She'd gotten lost twice on the way over, despite the City of Boston map that lay in wrinkled abandon on the passenger seat. The snow that had been gently falling earlier in the day had changed, becoming wet and thick, delaying her further. If there was one thing Hannah hated, it was to be late.

Squinting around the nearly useless windshield wipers, she brought her Volkswagen to a screeching stop next to a red Mercedes convertible she wouldn't be able to afford if she worked ninety hours a week. One day, Hannah promised herself as she pushed her glasses higher up on her nose.

Pocketing her keys, she finished the last few bites of the apple that was today's lunch, along with a cinnamon roll she'd eaten as she'd searched for the address. Hannah was used to eating on the run, had in fact been doing it for years. She wiped her mouth with a tissue, wrapped the core in it and stuffed the mound in the already overflowing ashtray.

Perhaps she should have parked in the circular driveway by the front door, she thought, peering out and noticing that the back lot hadn't been shoveled except for the short walk leading to the stairs. Her new black boots were a bit slippery, not broken in yet. She hadn't thought to bring a hat, and the snow was really coming down out there. She hadn't seen her friend and mentor, Will Grover, since his wife's funeral two years ago, and she didn't want to show up looking like someone the cat dragged in. Hastily, she grabbed her shoulder bag, held it over her head and started for the back stairs.

The swirling snow, lifted by a chill wind, hit her the moment she stepped out. Head down, she circled a black van parked alongside the walk with its motor running and back doors open. She was nearly to the stairs when suddenly she collided with someone big and solid. Her feet flew out from under her, her shoulder bag went flying and she landed somewhat ungracefully on her backside with a yelp.

"Damn," Hannah muttered to herself, more annoyed than hurt.

The large box that the man had been carrying fell also, its contents spilling onto the snowy pavement. Embarrassment flooded her cheeks as Hannah saw heavy law books dropping into squishy snow piles with a wet thud. Chagrined, she looked up.

Lord, but he was tall, was her first thought. "I'm so sorry," she murmured, scrambling to pick up the books, hoping they weren't ruined. "I should have been watching where I was going."

"It's all right," Joel Merrick said, offering her a hand and helping her upright. She'd whirled into him so quickly he hadn't had a chance to dodge her. He reached for a heavy volume she rescued, and his hand closed over hers. Soft, small, almost delicate bones. His thumb at her wrist felt her pulse jerk in response.

He watched her remove snowy oversize glasses and noticed that her eyes were a warm brown, the color of good brandy. There wasn't a speck of makeup on her face that he could see. She didn't need any on skin the color of a freshly picked peach. He saw awareness register before she turned aside. "Are you always in such a hurry?" he asked.

"No, I..." Actually, Hannah knew she was the type who seemed to rush from appointment to appointment, always in a hurry, with never enough hours in the day. She saw no reason to tell that to this stranger. "I am running a little late today."

She'd told Will she'd meet him at one on Saturday afternoon at his office. It was half an hour past that, and now she'd be even later. She bent to pick up another book, her booted feet nearly slipping again.

Joel stopped her with a steadying hand, took the book and tossed it into the box, his eyes assessing her. Her auburn hair was pulled back from her face and wound tightly into something he'd heard called a French twist. The black leather boots and jacket looked new; the soft gray turtleneck and slacks she wore beneath seemed a bit prim. She stared up at him as his gaze skimmed her mouth, full and moist enough to set a man to fantasizing how she'd taste.

"I'll get the rest, Red," he told her, wondering what she'd do if he thrust his hands into all that thick hair and sent the pins flying.

Hannah took a moment to study him as she brushed snow from her slacks. Snowflakes dotted his curly black hair worn a shade longer than most of the proper Bostonian men she'd met so far. He was obviously not a law associate of Will's but rather a deliveryman loading books into the waiting van. Besides, he looked too rugged to be confined behind a desk with his climber's boots, jeans and plaid flannel shirt beneath his open sheepskin jacket.

"I'm holding you up," she said, nodding toward the van.

He grinned down at her, tightening his grip on her arm. "I think it's the other way around." Standing this close to her, he inhaled the unexpected scent of apples and cinnamon. He found it more enticing than a costly perfume.

His accent was more Western sounding than the broad *a*'s of the East Coast, so he probably wasn't from around here. Still, he had a killer smile, and Hannah thought he damn well knew it. His eyes were dark blue and challenging, with a hint of amusement. There was a stubborn slant to his square, unshaved chin. She usually didn't think much of that look, but found it oddly appealing on this man.

She gave herself a mental shake. What on earth was she doing standing here staring at a deliveryman as if she were interested in starting something? She shook his hand off. "I believe I can stand alone now, thank you all the same."

Still smiling, he cocked his head. "You're a feisty one, aren't you?"

Hannah decided not to respond to that. "I'll pay for any damage to the books," she told him, stepping aside and retrieving her shoulder bag.

"I'm sure they're fine." He reached to brush a snowflake from her cheek.

Her first instinct was to swat his hand aside, thinking the gesture a shade too familiar for two strangers. But she decided that cooly ignoring him would work much better. "Well, if you're certain..."

"Of course, you really knocked the wind out of me." Still grinning, he rubbed his chest. "Listen, Red, what do you say we go have lunch and talk over possible internal damage? I know this great little place around the corner. The clam chowder's homemade.''

''Thanks, but I've already had lunch. And my hair isn't red, it's auburn.'' She settled the strap of her bag on her shoulder as she again glanced pointedly at the van. ''I wouldn't want to be responsible for you losing your job.''

She thought he worked for a delivery service, Joel realized. He was about to correct her assumption, then decided to let the scene play itself out. Both as an attorney and as a man, Joel Merrick had learned that it gave you an advantage over your opponents if you retained a piece of knowledge they'd not yet discovered.

''That's very considerate of you.'' He nodded toward the two-story brick building. ''Are you looking for an attorney?''

''No. Actually, I *am* an attorney. I'm here to see Will Grover. We've been friends for years.''

Joel kept his features even as he mentally calculated who she was. Hannah Richards, Will's protégée. His partner had mentioned that Hannah was in town and would be stopping by to see if she wanted to rent their spare office. Privately, he'd thought that they didn't need the rental income, nor did they need another attorney around. They got along just fine. Knowing how fond his partner was of Hannah, he hadn't voiced his opinion. Now that he'd seen her, he was glad he hadn't.

''Will's inside. Want me to show you in?''

He was quite bold for a deliveryman. ''That won't be necessary.'' Again, she indicated the box of now-soggy books. ''You're sure I don't owe you for getting those wet?''

"Absolutely sure." Joel had cleaned out his library and was donating some outdated volumes to a bookstore that dealt in old editions, using their van.

"All right, then. So long." Hannah turned and headed up the stairs, more carefully this time.

"Say," he called after her, "I can't just go on calling you Red. Shouldn't we at least exchange names?"

Hand on the railing, she glanced back over her shoulder. "I don't think so. Chances are our paths will never cross again." Giving him a cool smile, she reached the landing and went inside.

Joel's grin widened. *Don't count on it, Hannah Richards.*

Seated behind his mahogany desk, Will Grover removed his rimless glasses and used a snow white handkerchief to polish them. "Change is good, Hannah," he said, his gravelly voice warm and welcoming. "Change means growth and adjustment. Without change, we'd all wither up and die." He spoke from experience. Hadn't he had to adjust to being without Emily after she'd died so suddenly a week short of their forty-fifth wedding anniversary?

Will narrowed his pale blue eyes at the young woman seated across from him. "I thought you agreed with me, that that was why you left Michigan and came to Boston."

"I do agree, in theory." Hannah crossed her long, slender legs. She'd arrived in town a week ago with all her worldly goods piled in her Volkswagen, checked into a motel and begun apartment hunting. She'd been lucky enough to quickly unearth a wonderful place to live, but finding an office was turning out to be far more difficult. It had been a frustrating seven days of searching.

"Leaving everything familiar and moving to a strange place is a bit unsettling. I don't know anyone here and . . ."

Will replaced his glasses and smiled at her. "You know me."

She couldn't help but return the smile. "Yes, and you're a dear."

Will sighed and rubbed his knuckles, his bones aching from the cold winter weather. A dear. Over the years, he'd gone from being called a handsome rascal to an impressive presence in the courtroom, and apparently was now viewed as an elderly *dear*. Where had the time gone? The crusading attorney in him wanted to live every moment of it again, but the seventy-year-old man he'd become just wanted quiet time to sit, to read, to fish.

Hannah studied her old friend, wondering why Will looked so melancholy. "Are you feeling all right, Will?"

He heard the concern in her voice and felt a rush of warmth. It had been a long time since someone had expressed an interest in his health and well-being. "I'm fit as a fiddle, for an old geezer."

Perhaps her lack of enthusiasm for the city he loved had saddened him. She honestly liked Boston. It was big enough, yet not too large. She'd had it with small towns and even smaller minds, where she'd never felt as if she fit in. "Boston's wonderful, and I don't mean to sound ungrateful that you want me here. I've known for a long while that it was time for a change. You and I have been talking about this for months, by letter, by phone. I've been working toward this, saving for the move for months. When I took the Massachusetts bar exam last fall, I set things in motion for quitting my firm in Michigan. But now that I'm here, things aren't falling into place as quickly as I'd hoped, I guess." She sent him an apologetic glance.

Will reached for his pipe. "Patience was never your strong suit. I remember in class when at times the questions tumbled out of your mouth before I'd finished my lecture."

She remembered that his had been her favorite class. Professor Grover had made the law sound exciting and challenging, had made it come alive for her. She nodded, acknowledging her own youthful impatience. "I must have been a real pain in the butt."

Will packed his pipe with tobacco that smelled deliciously of cherry. "Not at all. Bright students are never a pain." And Hannah had been one of the brightest, having skipped two grades ahead as a youngster, graduating college at twenty and entering law school immediately. She'd managed a 3.9 average in her studies, but her personal life hadn't gone as well. Which was one reason why he'd urged her to try Boston, where he could keep a fatherly eye on her.

Will reached for a match. "Are you finding your way around town all right?"

She'd spent only that one week in Boston last fall to take the bar exam. Passing it had been the final step in her decision to move. "I bought a map, but I still get lost now and then. I'm learning."

"I imagine you've been busy since you arrived. Have you found an apartment yet?"

"Yes, and it's wonderful."

Hannah couldn't know that her brown eyes took on a special light when she spoke of something she found exciting.

She continued, "It's on one of those narrow, winding streets off the Common, an old house converted into apartments. And I've got the entire top floor with my own entrance in back."

A place of her own, something she'd longed for ever since she could remember. In Michigan, she'd rented a small furnished apartment for the past couple of years while she worked for the prestigious law firm of Schlessinger, Robbins and Carmichael. She'd put off buying furniture because she'd suspected that one day she'd move from the state of her birth. "I bought a bed and a kitchen set, but I'm going to take my time putting together the rest." There was no rush, to say nothing of not enough money in her bank account to get everything at once.

Will puffed on his pipe, getting it going, then leaned back in his ancient but comfortable chair. "I'll come over one evening, bring a bottle of wine and we'll christen your new home."

A real home, something she could scarcely remember ever having. Hannah swallowed around a sudden lump in her throat. It was about to happen, all the things she'd dreamed during the long, lonely years. And this dear man had set her in motion. "Absolutely," she told him. "You'll be my first guest." Her *only* guest, since she knew no one else in Boston.

"Wonderful." He watched her chin come up a notch and saw the determination that was as much a part of Hannah Richards as her wonderful hair and big brown eyes. She didn't consider herself beautiful, Will knew from observing her closely over the years. She was proud of her brains, her quick, agile mind, but considered her looks unimpressive. She was wrong, but she would have to discover that for herself.

He knew that, at twenty-eight, she'd had a man or two in her life. Even knew of one who'd hurt her badly.

Which was probably why Hannah Richards was a difficult woman for a man to get close to. Had he been a younger man, he never would have gotten past all the barricades she'd thrown up around herself over the years. He wondered if any eligible man ever would, so wary was she that she trusted very few. "Did you have any luck finding an office to rent?"

Hannah sighed, unable to hide her disappointment. Funny how in this great big city, there were so few suitable commercial rentals. Especially since she knew exactly what she wanted. An older building, not all modern steel-and-glass. Quiet elegance, a good location and the right price. Did all three ever come in the same package?

She'd called on ads, walked the neighborhoods that were her first and second choices, inspected half a dozen possibilities and dismissed them all as being too far out, too ordinary, too expensive. In their many conversations, Will had offered her a space in his building, but she'd deliberately put off looking at it until there seemed no alternatives, wanting to do this on her own.

But time was running out. She was already getting referrals from Sanctuary, the women's shelter she'd contacted upon her arrival, the one she'd been corresponding with from Michigan. Some of the troubled people there couldn't wait. She needed a place to meet with them so she could get started on their behalf.

"No, I'm afraid not," she said in answer to his question.

Will almost smiled. He'd tired of Michigan and returned to his home five years ago. He'd kept his Boston town house all these years and he knew the city well, knew that good office rentals were rare. And he knew

Hannah's taste. "So what do you think of my building?"

It was perfect. With pride, Will had shown her around before escorting her into his office. The foyer with its slate floor, richly paneled walls and twin leaded-glass windows framing the heavy, carved front door was where his secretary, Marcie, had her desk. They'd walked through the archway and down a hall with thick gray carpeting and wallpaper in a conservative stripe, past a small lounge, a rest room, a storage area.

Will had given her a peek into both lower-level offices, then led her up the spiral stairway to the second floor, where an impressive law library had dazzled her. It was a fantastic room with eastern exposure to the sun, two round tables, comfortable leather chairs and an Oriental rug in shades of blue and gray on the polished floor. Floor-to-ceiling bookcases on three walls held a collection of law books that would take Hannah a lifetime to accumulate. As it undoubtedly had for Will.

Then he'd shown her the available office, and she'd fallen in love at first sight. The room was a good size, yet somehow managed to look cozy. A small, reclaimed brick fireplace with a distressed-wood mantel was on one side across from built-in bookcases that appeared to be of solid oak. The carpeting was a Wedgwood blue, and here the wallpaper was white-on-white silk and smelled newly hung. Three long, arched windows looked out on snow-covered treetops and a cloudy sky. There was even a private bathroom. Hannah had been mentally imagining furnishings she would buy to decorate the office as she'd followed Will down to his office.

She'd been quiet so long that Will couldn't help but wonder what she was thinking on so hard. "You don't care for it?"

"It's beautiful and just what I've been looking for, but..."

"The rent?" He knew she wasn't exactly flush, knew she'd need money to live on until she got a client list going. His affection for Hannah was similar to what he might have felt for the daughter he'd never had. He wouldn't insult her by offering free rent, but he named a figure that, from the surprised expression on her face, he knew was far less than she'd been expecting.

"Oh, I can't accept that...."

"Certainly you can. My needs are few. The building's free and clear, and so is my home. You would please an old man by joining me here where I could see your lovely face every day."

Hannah felt affection for Will swell inside her. She blinked rapidly, her eyes suddenly moist. "No one who knows you would consider you an old man. Not with that quick legal mind."

"Then take advantage of my experience all you wish. Talking over your cases will keep my mind sharp." Will set his pipe into the large glass ashtray. "I don't take but a few cases these days, the ones that interest me. Joel handles the rest."

Ah, now they'd come to it, the real reason for her hesitation. She sat back, unsure how to approach the subject with Will. "It seems nearly everyone I've run into knows Joel Merrick," she began carefully. "I've heard some interesting tales about your partner this week."

When Will had first told her about his vacant office, he hadn't mentioned a partner. She hadn't found out until the last couple of letters and even then, Will had been oddly vague. After making the rounds, Hannah thought she knew why.

Will leaned forward, his eyes taking on a humorous glint. "Don't tell me you believe everything you hear, Hannah."

"No, not everything." But surely they couldn't all have been wrong. From the law clerk at the courthouse, who'd taken the time to show her around to Lee Stanford, who ran Sanctuary, to the grocer on the corner, they'd all had something to say about the Merricks. An old family dating back to the Pilgrims, to hear some tell it. And the maverick youngest Merrick named Joel.

A Harvard graduate, a brilliant attorney, a killer in the courtroom. And a killer in the bedroom, or so she'd been told repeatedly. After growing bored with corporate law, he'd left the family law firm headed by his father and begun by his grandfather, and had gone to live for quite a spell on a Montana ranch owned by his uncle. Last year, he'd returned unexpectedly and teamed up with an old family friend, Will Grover. These days, he specialized in criminal law, and the waiting list for his services was long and monied.

Some labeled him arrogant, others cocky, while a few said he was a playboy who enjoyed winning cases by unorthodox methods. Most agreed he didn't take the law, himself or anyone else very seriously.

Joel Merrick sounded exactly like the sort of man Hannah went out of her way to avoid.

"What have you been hearing about Joel?" Will asked, curious about her pensive expression. He was aware of Joel's reputation, but he also knew the real man, the one seldom seen by many.

Hannah decided to level with Will. "That his family's got money, so he takes only cases that challenge him. That he doesn't care if his client's innocent or guilty if he thinks he can win. That his clients are usually women and they all fall in love with him. That he's arrogant and sometimes ruthless.''

Leaning back, Will linked his hands over his portly belly. ''There's truth in some of that, but not much. Emily and I were houseguests of the Merricks the weekend Joel was born thirty-two years ago. I've watched him become the man he is and, as with all men, he's made some mistakes. But I know him to be a good and decent man, despite what you may have heard.''

Will watched her face and thought to reassure her. ''Your cases would be strictly independent of either of us. You can have as little or as much to do with Joel as you choose. It's up to you.''

He'd always seemed able to read her mind. She knew that Will must care for Joel Merrick or he'd never have agreed to partner with him. She felt a bit chagrined at having revealed what amounted to mostly rumors. Still, she'd needed him to know that she had her misgivings about his partner. ''On that basis, if the two of you can put up with me, I'll be happy to accept your offer.''

''Good, then it's settled.'' Will stroked his white mustache, thinking that Joel hadn't been too enthusiastic about renting out their spare office. It would be interesting to see his reaction to Hannah.

Hearing the back door bang shut, Will checked his pocket watch. ''That's probably Joel now. He had some errands to run earlier, but he said he'd be stopping back. The office isn't usually open on Saturdays, though sometimes we come in to do paperwork. Marcie works Monday through Friday. You can get your own secretary or use her if you like. She's not only a great legal secretary, she brings me homemade cookies.''

"That'll be fine." She'd talk to Marcie on Monday and determine if they could work out some arrangement.

Across the hall, a door opened.

"Joel," Will called out. "If you've got a minute, come on in." He got to his feet, wondering what Hannah's first reaction to his partner would be.

Shrugging out of his sheepskin jacket, Joel Merrick stepped into the doorway. Noting the shock on the face of the woman seated opposite Will, he gave her his killer smile. "Well, hello, Red. Looks like we meet again."

Chapter Two

"Have you two met?" Will interjected into the sudden silence.

"Sort of," Joel answered, coming into the room.

Noticing Hannah's surprised expression and Joel's cat-that-ate-the-canary look, Will decided to sit back down and watch round one.

From long habit, Hannah recovered quickly, swallowing her dismay at having misjudged the man she'd bumped into out back. She met his bold gaze and gave him a chilly smile. "You could have introduced yourself earlier."

He raised his eyebrows. "What, and spoil the fun? Besides, if you'll recall, I suggested we exchange names, and you told me it wasn't necessary." He watched the memory stain her cheeks as he hung his jacket on Will's antique coatrack. "An attorney who readily jumps to conclusions." He shook his head in mock seriousness. "That could be a problem."

Hannah crossed her arms over her chest in a defensive pose, which was exactly how she felt. She hated being tricked, and he'd done it deliberately. "Your accent distracted me. You don't sound Boston born and bred."

Joel brushed snowflakes from his dark hair. "Probably because I spent a lot of time in Montana." And often wished he were back there, though he'd never said the words aloud.

"You had me at a disadvantage, knowing I had an appointment to see Will. But then, I imagine you enjoy having the advantage on your side, Counselor." She should let it go, Hannah thought, but some perverse instinct told her that if she let him get away with putting one over on her this time, he'd do it again.

Joel folded his long limbs in the chair alongside her. "That's true enough. What attorney doesn't? You can learn a lot about someone if they don't know everything you do."

Well, at least he was honest, Hannah decided. Manipulative but honest. "And have you learned a lot about me?"

She wasn't wearing her glasses. Earlier outside, he'd thought her eyes were a deep brown, but sitting close alongside her, he noticed flecks of gold and lighter amber in their depths. Her lashes were thick, incredibly long and dark against her fair skin. Joel felt that unmistakable sensual tug of attraction and determined he would keep her from noticing. Any good attorney knows that an expression-free face and a motionless body are often his or her best weapons. Something told him that he'd need every weapon at his command in dealing with Hannah Richards.

"Not yet," he said in answer to her question. "But I will."

Fat chance, she thought, but managed a slightly warmer smile for Will's sake. Undoubtedly Joel Merrick thought he was God's gift to both women and the courtroom. No matter. He would learn in short order that Hannah knew exactly how to discourage unwanted attention. She'd been doing it for years.

Will cleared his throat, deciding it was time to break the obvious tension in the room. "Hannah's agreed to rent our upstairs office, Joel," he said, watching his young partner's face. "Of course, she'll have her own practice, and we'll all be business associates only."

Joel grinned at Hannah. "Of course."

He wouldn't be a problem for long, Hannah told herself. He doubtless had a long waiting list of available women all susceptible to his charms. She was hardly the type to interest a playboy. And she had little interest in a man to whom life seemed one big joke.

Rising, she turned to Will. "I've got to run. It's wonderful seeing you again." She walked around to his side of the desk and bent to kiss his leathery cheek.

From his top desk drawer, Will extracted a key and held it out to her. "May you be happy and comfortable here."

Her smile held a wealth of warmth. "I'm sure I will be. See you on Monday." Hannah picked up her jacket and handbag.

Joel rose, blocking her exit. "If you need any help moving your things upstairs, I can get a van or a truck and give you a hand."

The last thing she wanted was to owe someone a favor, especially Joel Merrick. "Thanks, but I can manage." Moving around him, she left the office.

Noting Joel's surprised scowl, Will hid a smile. It would appear that round one was a draw.

Hannah flipped her long single braid back over her shoulder, dusted her hands on the legs of her jeans and stepped back to the doorway to get the overall effect. The delivery van had left some time ago, and she'd been rearranging her office furniture ever since. Tipping her head to one side, she studied the room.

Her distressed-cherry-wood desk and the Queen Anne chair with the delicate blue cushion she'd done the needlepoint work on herself sat just in front of the three arched windows so the light would be at her back. She'd decided that the beveled windows were too pretty to cover up with drapes or curtains. The like-new Tiffany lamp she'd found at a garage sale last year seemed to belong on one corner of her desk. Her books were all neatly arranged on the shelves along with a couple of unusual pottery pieces. Off to one side of the room, she'd placed a settee and matching chair with two low tables to form a relaxed conversation corner. Her clients would need an atmosphere of trust, a serene environment, soft colors and warm woods.

Hannah glanced to the right at the box of toys and children's books she'd gathered, knowing many of her clients would come with little ones. It was important to keep them busy while she talked with their mothers.

The antique filing cabinet in the opposite corner had been a real steal at a "gently used" furniture outlet. On the fireplace mantel, she'd placed a chunky vanilla-scented candle, a Waterford clock given to her for her college graduation by the last foster family she'd lived with and a sprig of violets she'd picked up on her way in and stuck into a cut-glass vase. Satisfied with the look of things so far, she drew in a deep breath and caught the faint aroma of rich wood polish.

Yes, the place was shaping up, taking on a personality, one Hannah knew she'd be comfortable with. She'd spent quite a lot on the few pieces she'd purchased over the past two days, a bit more than she'd planned. But the effect was well worth it. After all, she'd gone without lunches for months in Michigan, walked to save gas and done without in many ways in order to accumulate enough to make her office just perfect. And welcoming.

Most of her clients wouldn't have much monetarily. The least she could do was to provide a relaxed atmosphere in which to discuss their troubles. She only hoped she'd be able to help the people referred to her by Lee Stanford, the woman who ran Sanctuary. She already had two appointments set up for tomorrow.

Hannah glanced at her watch as footsteps sounded on the stairs. After five. Her visitor had to be Marcie, who'd begun to stop in each evening before leaving for the day. She moved to stand behind her desk as Marcie appeared in the doorway wearing a broad-brimmed navy hat on her blond beehive hairdo reminiscent of the sixties.

"I'm leaving, kiddo, and..." She stopped, her generous mouth forming a broad smile. "Oh, my! Isn't this lovely!"

Hannah had liked Will's secretary from their first meeting. In her midfifties, divorced with two grown daughters and two and a half grandchildren, Marcie Goodman was everything Will had said—efficient, knowledgeable and a marvel in the kitchen. Along with her usual apple, Hannah had had one of Marcie's huge oatmeal cookies for lunch. "You like it?"

"Oh, hon, I love what you've done with this room." Marcie's eyes took inventory as she walked to the desk and ran her hand along the smooth wood. "Your clients must be in the bucks for you to want to impress them with all this."

Nothing could be further from the truth. "Not really, but I think we all feel good among pretty things." And most of the women she'd met at Sanctuary had far too little prettiness in their lives. Absently, she picked up the red marble apple from its prominent place on her desk.

"I noticed that earlier when you unpacked it. Must mean something to you, right?"

Hannah rubbed the smooth, cool surface with her thumb. "Yes. Will gave this to me. When I was in law school, I was working two part-time jobs, but I still just barely got by. I practically lived on apples and cereal. I used to run into his classroom chewing on an apple. When I graduated, he gave me this as a permanent reminder of those lean days."

Marcie smiled. "Will's a wonderful man. He sweet-talked me into coming to work for him when he moved back from Michigan. For no one else would I have come out of retirement. But I'm glad I did. I was getting fat lazing around the house all day." She patted her rounded waistline. "Trouble is, I like to cook."

Hannah loved puttering around the kitchen, too. But she had so little time to indulge in trying new recipes from her cookbook collection. "I want to thank you for getting my business cards printed up so quickly."

"No problem, honey. Fred over at the print shop always puts my orders through with a rush." Marcie adjusted her hat. "We used to be an item."

Hannah wasn't quite sure if Marcie's tales about having dated half the eligible men over forty in the Boston area were true or figments of her imagination. The first conversation they'd shared, the older woman had given her a rundown on her disastrous but thankfully brief marriage, her girls—whom she adored—and her current love life, which was both vast and varied.

"I don't know how you keep up with all your men," Hannah commented.

"Scorecards, hon," Marcie said with a hearty laugh. "Just kidding. Fred's happily married now. That was years ago." Pushing up the sleeve of her white wool coat, she checked her watch. "If you don't need anything else tonight, I'll run along. Bob's taking me to the Ice Capades. Front-row seats."

"Thanks for asking, but I'm fine. Have a good time."

"I always do." She turned toward the door, then swung back. "Bob knows a lot of guys, all ages. When you're ready, hon, just give me the word and we'll double. See you in the morning."

Hannah set down the apple, smiling at Marcie's retreating back. Double date. No, thanks. The last thing she wanted was to get involved with some man who would undoubtedly be looking for vastly different things from life than she was. No, she'd go it alone, the same way she'd been handling things for years. Alone, where she need answer to no one.

Of course, she was scared to death about this long-distance move and this whole new venture, Hannah admitted to herself.

Never mind, she'd do it. She'd conquered a score of fears in the past and would again. She was a survivor with unwavering determination, a woman focused on specific goals. Finally, she was in charge of her career and her life. She'd never again have to dance to someone else's tune.

Removing her glasses and placing them on the desk, Hannah walked over to gaze out the windows. She'd take comfort in the fact that Will would be nearby if she needed advice or someone to talk over her cases with. She would let the high-profile, hotshot Mr. Merrick take the courts by storm and charm juries. She'd establish herself as an attorney who fought for the rights of the underdog and the often disenfranchised, women beaten up by men and beaten down by life.

She watched a cold wind rearrange the snowdrifts down below as the streetlights came on, and shivered. Her office was warm, but her thoughts caused her to tremble. She'd already met with several of her new clients at Sanctuary. Half the battle she faced was in convincing these women that the law could help them, that they need no longer be afraid, that she could win for them.

It wasn't that she was against men, Hannah acknowledged. Just those men who didn't respect women and their rights. Before leaving Michigan, she'd represented a young man who wanted custody of his son over his drug-addicted wife. She'd gotten that for him in an area of the law that also seemed to be finally recognizing a father's rights.

Hannah sighed. So many wrongs to try to make right. She watched a small winter wren hop onto a barren limb and cock his head as he stared in at her. Then he glanced around at the swirling snow, the ground devoid of anything to eat, the trees offering little protection from the cold. But, fluttering his feathers first, he spread his wings and bravely flew off.

She could relate. It was a big world out there, often cold and offering little comfort or friendliness. The survivors stepped out anyhow and faced the unknown, if not bravely, then at least putting on a good front. Those who were lucky made it. She didn't want to think about the ones who didn't.

Turning from the view, Hannah was startled to find a tall, lean figure filling her doorway, his lazy smile in place as usual.

"Your office looks great," Joel said, strolling in to inspect the contents of her bookcase. Checking out her collection, he nodded approvingly. "Impressive." Swiveling to face her, he found himself wondering why she always wore her hair tightly contained in some way, today in a long braid. "You've done a lot in a week."

He'd managed to surprise her that day in Will's office and twice since, sneaking up on cat feet and suddenly appearing in her path as she was coming or going. It was unnerving. "I'm seriously thinking of hanging a cowbell around your neck so I'll be forewarned of your arrival." The thick carpeting throughout the building would muffle a noisy herd of buffalo, Hannah thought crossly. She intensely disliked surprises.

He grinned at her suggestion. "They don't do that anymore, you know," Joel said as he walked over to pick up and examine the marble apple. "Hang bells on cows, I mean. Oh, maybe in Switzerland they do, where cows can get lost grazing along a grassy mountain. But with all the cows in Montana, they'd have to order bells by the carload."

Curiosity overcame Hannah's reluctance to prolong their discussion. "I believe you said you lived in Montana for a while. Must be quite a change from this area." She knew from Will that Joel had two brothers and a sister, all married and living near their parents, who had a big place in town and an even larger home on the Cape. A close-knit family, Will had called the Merricks. Yet Joel had wandered off, and she wondered why.

Joel shrugged as he hefted the apple, measuring its weight. "Couldn't seem to get along at home when I was a teenager, so they sent me to Uncle Bart, hoping he'd straighten me out."

Hannah sat down at her desk, needing the little shred of authority that gave her. Why did he have to be so handsome, so beautifully dressed in gray slacks and a Glen plaid jacket, his jet black hair curling onto his forehead and those midnight blue eyes that studied her so intently? "And did he?"

"I suppose, much as anyone could have." He strolled over to the settee and tried it out, sitting down in the center and stretching both arms along the seat back. "Rising at five every morning and working till you drop tends to take the starch out of even overactive fourteen-year-olds."

He spoke calmly, but there seemed an underlying anger carefully camouflaged. "Were you hyperactive?"

"More like mischievous. Restless. Unmanageable maybe. Or so Dad said." Again came the slow smile. "Nothing serious. A couple of fights I got into. One stolen car. Boyish pranks."

Hannah raised a brow. "Stealing a car isn't exactly a boyish prank."

Joel leaned forward, bracing his forearms on his knees. "Well, not to worry. Daddy got me off. Clean record. And Uncle Bart straightened me out. Now I visit him and Montana because I like the open country. So here I am, law-abiding, taxpaying, registered voter. I rescue kittens, help little old ladies cross streets and never even jaywalk. Pretty boring, eh?''

"I don't know. You tell me. Are you bored?''

Bored. Not the same thing as boring. He wondered why she'd deliberately changed the meaning. To learn more? "Some of the time, like most everyone. Didn't Thoreau say that most people lead lives of quiet desperation?'' Restlessly, Joel rose and went to inspect the watercolor in pastels she'd hung over the fireplace. "This is nice. Do you know the artist?''

She did, quite well. It was a painting she'd done last year, a hobby she'd taken up years ago to fill her weekends when she wasn't researching a case or studying. "I'm glad you like it.''

He swung to face her. "How old are you, Hannah Richards?''

What now? she wondered. "Twenty-eight. Why?''

"I'm wondering how you managed to find time to graduate college, earn a law degree, work at a very reputable firm and still know so much about antiques and fine furniture and good paintings.''

Hannah thought she knew where he was coming from. "Not just people born with the proverbial silver spoon can recognize fine things. It's all out there for the learning if someone cares enough to bone up.''

He stepped closer, and the scent of apples drifted to him. He saw the core in the wastebasket, and yet the smell lingered around her as well. The women he dated all wore expensive cologne. He was surprised to find such a simple scent more intriguing. He brought himself back to what she'd said. "You don't much care for people born with that proverbial silver spoon, do you?''

She shrugged, took a step back and dropped her eyes to his tie. It was a study in red, gray and black slashes on a white background, vibrant and eye-catching. It suited him perfectly. "I haven't known enough to form much of an opinion."

"You'll get to know more after your practice gets going." His fingers ached to uncoil her braid, to thrust his hands into the thickness of her hair, to watch those brown eyes widen in shock.

"I doubt that." Naturally, he would assume she was out for the big bucks. Apparently, Will had told him very little about her, which suited Hannah just fine. Sidestepping the desk, she moved to tug at the settee, adjusting its position a fraction.

"Here," Joel said, walking over. "Let me help you with that."

Hannah straightened, a look of annoyance on her face. "I don't *need* your help. I'm used to doing for myself, thank you."

Joel was honestly taken aback. "I was only trying to lend you a hand. Is that so hard to accept?"

"It is for me." She knew she sounded ungrateful, but maybe if she let him know how she felt, he'd back off. "I don't like to be beholden to anyone. I pay my own way, I do for myself. That way, I owe no one. I hope you'll respect my feelings."

He frowned, perplexed. "I would if I understood them. Is this some women's thing?"

Exasperated, Hannah drew in a deep, calming breath, keeping her temper in check. "No. It has to do with independence, and it doesn't apply to just women. Dependence weakens a person, makes them vulnerable to others. I don't ever want to be in that position."

She was a piece of work, Joel decided as he shoved his hands into his pants pockets. Certainly, he'd never encountered a woman quite like her. Why was she pulling this tough act with him? "I'm not quite sure why you're so strong on this, but I have to say that you're beautiful when you're angry, Hannah Richards."

Such a tired old line. And one she knew had no basis in truth. She'd never been beautiful and she no longer cared. Brains could take you much further than looks any day.

Joel grew thoughtful as he watched her expressive face register several emotions. He wasn't looking for a woman, never was. There were plenty around if a man wanted one. He wasn't even sure why this woman with her cool eyes, chip on her shoulder and prim hairdo interested him. There was something about the flash of vulnerability, mingled with her fiercely individualistic stance and the wholesome scent of apples, that fascinated him. Everything about her seemed to issue a challenge.

He'd never been able to resist challenges.

He watched her zip up her briefcase, trying desperately to ignore him. He swallowed a smile. "Do you want to go ice skating?"

Thrown off balance, Hannah looked up. "What?"

"Ice skating." Joel glanced outside at the darkening evening. "I know this great outdoor rink not far from here. Music and lights, even a hotdog stand. What do you say?"

"You plan to go skating dressed like that?"

"I've got a change of clothes downstairs and skates, too. Come on, Hannah. It'll be fun."

Fun. When was the last time she'd taken the time to just have fun? She couldn't recall. But spending the evening with Joel Merrick would be a mistake. "Thanks, but I have work to do." She needed to do some research on how best to represent Ellen Baxter, her first case on her own. She didn't have time to waste having fun. She reached into the closet for her leather jacket and slipped it on.

He'd seen the flash of regret in her eyes and wondered why she'd turned him down when she obviously wanted to go. He wouldn't press. He could tell she would hate being pressed. "All right." At the doorway, he turned back. "You know what they say about all work and no play, don't you?"

Belting her jacket, she met his unwavering gaze, but didn't answer. Finally, he turned and left.

Hannah listened to his muffled footsteps going down the stairs, then moments later, heard the back door close. Slowly, she walked to the windows and saw him march to his Mercedes, the collar of his black overcoat turned up.

It was cold, but a beautiful evening, the sky clear and the snow no longer falling. Probably, stars would be visible soon. It would have felt good to be outdoors, to free her mind and skate with the wind. To laugh, maybe have a hot chocolate later.

The revving of Joel's powerful engine caught her attention. He'd cleaned off the windshield and was backing out. He swung the little car around and headed down the driveway more cautiously than she'd have guessed. He'd revealed some telling things tonight. She got the impression that his childhood hadn't been as happy as she'd imagined. Maybe he wasn't so bad after all and...

Hannah shook her head. What was the matter with her? Whatever he was, she had no business thinking about Joel Merrick or any other man.

Grabbing her briefcase, she walked out the door.

* * *

"That's it, sweet lady," Joel said into the Dictaphone mike. "Don't forget to add love and kisses from their favorite attorney at the end of each letter. I'll sign them sometime late Monday afternoon. See you then and thanks, Marcie." He turned off the machine, sat back and rubbed the tense muscles at the back of his neck.

It was past six on a Friday after a long week that he was glad to see end. He had a trial beginning at nine on Monday that would tie him up for quite a while. Murder for hire, a messy one. The *State of Massachusetts v. Amanda Fowler,* his client.

Amanda had been arrested after a part-time gardener had told the police that she'd paid him ten thousand dollars to kill her wealthy, ailing husband, Blake Fowler. The newspapers had had a field day crucifying the pretty blond young woman who stood to inherit an estate of over seven million. Blake's two grown sons kept popping up on the six-o'clock news condemning their scheming stepmother, crying for justice.

But Amanda had told Joel she was innocent.

After six months of interviews and research and preparation, Joel wasn't sure whom he believed. He had his suspicions, his theories, but would he be able to prove them in court? That was the question.

Rising, he walked to stare out the window. His office was in the front of the building and looked out on the circular driveway and snow-covered shrubs beyond. The streetlights were on, and most sane people were either home or on their way.

Hurrying home didn't appeal to Joel tonight. He liked his apartment on Beacon Street in the Back Bay area. The building was old but recently renovated, his place on the tenth floor overlooking the Charles River Basin. A good location, a great view. He'd spent time, money and energy decorating his living space himself.

And still it felt lonely.

Annoyed with himself and his own discontent, Joel frowned out at the darkening evening. By all standards, he was a success, if success could be measured in status, money, position. He knew how to win cases, to garner large fees, to finally succeed after leaving his father's firm because corporate law had bored him. Criminal law was arduous, exacting and demanding, but rarely boring.

At thirty-two, he had plenty of money, a great place to live, a super car, work he enjoyed most of the time, a family and lots of friends. He even had an impressive list of women he could call, most of whom would be eager to spend time with him. Last year, he'd been voted Man of the Year by the Massachusetts Bar Association. He seemingly had it all.

Why, then, did he feel this vague restlessness, this feeling that something was missing?

Joel ran blunt fingertips through his hair, wondering if he was just one of those men who would never find contentment, who'd always be striving for something just out of reach. He'd been like that since boyhood. The trouble was, he didn't even know what that something was. Unlike some people, who seemed to have been born knowing exactly what they wanted.

Like Hannah Richards.

His mind had drifted to their new tenant more than once over the past week. He'd caught glimpses of her in the courthouse halls, rushing to some appointment, buried in research books in the upstairs library, brushing snow from her Volkswagen in the back parking lot before hurrying off. He'd scarcely said ten words to her since the evening she'd finished putting together her office, yet she bounced into his thoughts more often than he liked.

She was so focused, so intense, so energetic, such a fierce workaholic. What had made her like that? he wondered. What did she do to unwind, to relax? Surely she had a life outside her work. And what was she working on for such long hours since she'd just arrived in town? Was she just putting on a good front to keep Will from being concerned about her? Joel knew Will worried anyway, hoping Hannah would make it, since he'd been the one who'd convinced her to move to Boston.

Maybe he should try to help her, Joel thought. She was temperamental as hell about anyone lending her a hand. But surely she wouldn't turn down clients. He had an overflowing case load, one he could easily share with her. Some of the easier, lighter cases. They'd help get her established in town, get her started, and then if she did well, referrals would follow.

Yes, that's what he'd do, Joel decided. Only, he'd have to handle her with care. God knew she offended easily.

At the back door, he checked the parking lot and saw that Hannah's car was still there. He climbed the stairs and saw that her door was open, but her office empty. He walked on to the library next door.

She was seated at the largest table, head bent as she wrote on a legal pad, law books spread out before her every which way. She was too absorbed to have heard him approach. She was wearing a classic navy suit with a white blouse, a pencil stuck into her red hair, which was coiled into some sort of a twist as always. Her oversize, dark-framed glasses were perched low on her nose, giving her oval face a whimsical charm. Joel felt a smile form as he leaned against the doorframe and cleared his throat.

"How's it going, Counselor?" he asked as she looked up in surprise. He saw a trace of annoyance flicker across her features as she removed her glasses and leaned back.

"So-so." She'd been avoiding Joel Merrick and now felt the guilt of it. He made her uncomfortable, so, from long habit, she solved the problem by evading him. However, for Will's sake, she could at least be polite. "How are things with you?"

"Tough one coming up Monday." He turned serious, strolling in, pulling out one of the chairs and sitting down. "Murder One."

"I guess they don't get any tougher than that." She really couldn't spare the time, but there was something different about Joel tonight. Almost as if he were worried, when so far, every time she'd noticed him, he'd been smiling and confident. "Want to talk about it?"

It was the first interest she'd shown, the first opening for a conversation she'd given him. He decided to grab it. "If you're sure I'm not interrupting."

He was, but she could make up the time later. After all, there might come a day when she'd need a willing ear. Will, she'd discovered, was seldom in. Besides, she felt just the tiniest bit flattered that Joel would want to talk over a case with her.

Hannah put down her pen and set aside her legal pad. "It's all right. I'd like to hear, really."

Joel didn't think she could offer much insight with her limited experience, but often just talking out loud with another attorney helped clarify things in his mind. Will hadn't been in for days, gone ice fishing with a couple of pals.

He leaned forward and began explaining his case, inordinately pleased at the thorough way she listened, inserting a question now and then, totally absorbed in what he was saying.

"Blake's two sons, Kent and Peter, I don't feel are as innocent as they're trying to make themselves appear to the media. Kent's a heavy gambler, and Peter's been in trouble with the law over minor skirmishes since he was in his teens."

Of course, Hannah had read about the high-profile case in the papers. Odd how she'd missed noticing that Joel was representing the beautiful widow. "Did they resent their father marrying such a young woman after their mother died?"

"Probably. But their mother had been dead for ten years before Blake married Amanda."

"She's a nurse, isn't she? Came to take care of him after he had a stroke?"

"Yes, that's right. I know how suspicious it looks. A young woman moves in on a vulnerable old man who just happens to be filthy rich. He marries her, changes his will and the kids are suddenly out in the cold. When he dies, she's the first suspect."

Hannah picked up her pen, toying with it as she thought of possibilities. "Who else would have hired the gardener to kill the old man? One of his sons?"

"Possibly. But there's more. Blake's sister, who's never married and was totally dependent on him, also lived with them. And he's got a penniless brother who moved to Boston just months before the old man died. Word was that Blake disliked him and had had him barred from his home. Lots of suspects."

"Just goes to show you being rich isn't worth the aggravation. Even your relatives are willing to kill you for your money."

"I've never thought money bought happiness." And he should know, since his family had it by the bucketful. Some of them were happy, he supposed. But certainly not all.

Hannah studied Joel from under lowered lashes. Gray seemed to be his favorite color, for he had on charcoal slacks with a pale gray shirt and paisley suspenders, his matching tie hanging loose. His hands, resting on the table, were large and strong, the fingers long and lean. Lost in thought, he stroked the jacket of the book in front of him, and had her wondering how his touch would feel on her skin.

Hannah sat up, clearing her throat. What was it about this man that always had her thinking uncharacteristically? "Do you think Amanda Fowler is innocent?"

"I don't honestly know."

She frowned at that. "Doesn't it bother you, representing someone, trying to get them off, when they might be guilty of murder?"

"Everyone's entitled to fair representation. As an officer of the court, I'm sure you know that. I'm there to protect the rights of my client. The rest is up to the jury and the judge."

"I'm not terribly comfortable with that."

It was Joel's turn to frown. "Are you so sure that all of your clients are in the right?"

."Fortunately, yes. The women I represent have been wronged. Unquestionably wronged."

He found that hard to believe unequivocally. "Give me an example."

"All right. Take Ellen Baxter. Her husband has been physically abusing her for years. She finally went to a women's shelter and, after some convincing, she's going to take action against him."

"You mean get a restraining order?"

"More than that. She's pressing charges. No matter what differences the two of them have, there's no excuse for a man hitting a woman." Hannah sighed. "Of course, I've done some of this type of work before. The problem is that all too often, women say they'll press charges, but later, they change their minds. The abuser threatens her or their children, and they drop the charges. It's *so* frustrating."

"So why do you specialize in women's rights, then?"

She looked up at him, honestly shocked. "Because there's such a need. There are too few attorneys willing to work in this field, and the need is huge."

Joel leaned back. "I'll bet I can guess why lawyers steer clear of those cases. You get to collect very little if any fees. While I applaud what you're doing, I'm wondering how you're going to make a living representing these people, most of whom are close to indigent."

"Not all of them. Custody battles, for instance, are often between a man with money and a wife with none, but if he loses, he has to pay attorney fees. And rape can happen to anyone, regardless of income. The others, well, I'll manage."

He had to admire her, though he truly doubted that she'd make it. He wondered if she knew just what she was up against, and knew his face reflected his doubt.

"Don't say it," Hannah told him, raising a hand. "I can tell you think I'm crazy. But this is important. Someone has to help these people."

Joel sighed. "I don't doubt that you're right. But a body has to eat." He hoped he would be able to word his offer so as not to offend. "Maybe I can help. I've got a couple of cases in the early stages, not terribly time-consuming ones. You'd still have time for your work. But they pay well and they'd tide you over until you got going. I'd refer these clients to you and—"

"Thanks, but no thanks." Picking up her glasses, Hannah put them on, then hurriedly began straightening the books she'd spread out. "I don't need your help, nor do I want it. I thought I made that clear. I already have a large referral base from Sanctuary, with several more on a waiting list, actually." She got up and turned to replace the books on the proper shelves.

Touchy, touchy. Damn, but he hadn't meant to offend her. "Listen, I didn't mean . . ."

"I know." Hannah shoved the books into place with more force than was necessary. "And I appreciate your offer. But please, I need to do this my way, on my own."

"All right. I respect that." Joel stood, wondering why anyone would get so huffy over an offer of help. Hannah Richards had to be the most difficult-to-understand woman he'd ever met.

"Thank you." Scooping her papers up, she moved toward the doorway.

He stopped her with a hand on her arm. "Could I ask you one more question?"

Warily, she looked up at him.

"You have such beautiful hair." His hand reached to touch a small strand that had escaped the tight control of the twist. "Why don't you ever wear it down?"

What an odd question. The man certainly knew how to keep her off balance. Hannah stared into his eyes, wondering if this was one of his little put-ons. But she saw only interest and an unnerving awareness. "I . . . I'll think about it."

He dropped his hand and gave her his lazy smile. "Thanks."

Hastily, she went to her office and closed the door.

Still smiling, Joel stuck his hands in his pockets and began to whistle as he made his way downstairs.

Chapter Three

Sanctuary was housed in a converted three-story brownstone that had been standing years longer than its residents had been alive. The two top floors each had one bath and several bedrooms, some double, some triple occupancy, with an occasional crib or trundle bed stuck here and there. The lower level was dominated by a large, airy kitchen, a big dining room, a good-sized TV room, an enclosed porch that ran the width of the back of the house and a small anteroom by the front door.

There, the front desk was presided over by Daisy Jones, a small, energetic black woman of indeterminate age who proudly displayed one gold front tooth and had a huge heart made of the same material. One of the "graduates" had found the time and money to have a nameplate of sorts made for her, which sat on her desk. It read If Daisy Ain't Happy, Ain't *Nobody* Happy.

Daisy clucked over and cared for all the residents like a mother hen. She dispensed Band-Aids and hugs to the little ones, and tea and sympathy to their mothers. It had taken Hannah only one visit to realize that Sanctuary couldn't operate without Daisy, who manned the phones and screened visitors, releasing a series of locks only if they passed muster.

On Monday morning, Hannah stomped snow from her boots on the small front porch and rang the bell. Recognizing her, Daisy buzzed her in. "Can you believe it's snowing again?" Hannah asked, setting down her briefcase and unzipping her leather jacket.

"Not only that, but it's the full of the moon," Daisy commented. "All the crazies are out en masse."

The tempting smell of bacon and onions lingered in the warm air, and the drone of a television game show could be heard along with the insistent cry of a very young baby. Stuffing her coat into the small hall closet, Hannah frowned. "Did you get some new admittances?"

Daisy nodded. "Four, to be exact, since Friday—two women, two babies."

Hannah nodded toward the kitchen. "Is Lee back there?"

"Sure is. She's working on the week's menu plan so Cookie can go to the store." Daisy lowered her voice. "That always puts her in a bad mood 'cause there's never enough money for all we need, so you might want to tippy-toe around her."

"I thought Father Ray was supposed to help out last week." Hannah had been told that a local Catholic priest was wonderful about getting his parishioners to contribute food and clothing, as well as obtaining financial donations.

Daisy shrugged. "Father says there's a recession and donations are down across the board."

The same old story, never enough money. Hannah didn't know how Lee managed to keep a cheerful attitude most of the time when she was always having to stretch a dollar until it cried uncle.

"You just visiting or here to see someone special?" Daisy asked.

"I need to talk with Ellen Baxter. She's here, isn't she?"

"Oh, yeah, she's back. But you're not going to like the shape she's in." Daisy knew that Hannah had been working with Ellen, preparing to file charges against Rod Baxter.

A frisson of apprehension ran up Hannah's spine. "What happened?"

Daisy decided she might as well prepare Hannah before she went upstairs to see Ellen. "On Saturday, she went back to their apartment when she thought Rod was at work, just to pick up some of the kids' clothes. He came in and...well, it was pretty bad."

Hannah felt like groaning out loud. She'd specifically warned Ellen not to go back home, that a restraining order alone wouldn't keep Rod away. "Thanks, Daisy. I'll see you before I leave." Grabbing her briefcase, Hannah went through the swinging doors to the kitchen.

Three walls had had to be taken out in order to make the kitchen big enough to accommodate the twenty or more folks usually in residence. Three years ago, when Lee Stanford had started Sanctuary, she'd quit a lucrative job at the *Boston Globe* to do work she'd thought far more important. Her connections at the paper had resulted in much publicity and many donations, which was why she'd been able to secure the house, get the re-modeling done and buy badly needed furniture and supplies. Since then, contributions had slowed as people had moved on to other favorite charities.

Undaunted, Lee never lost hope or quit fighting. Hannah found her sitting at the far end of the large oak table alongside Cookie, the chief cook and bottle washer, who'd been with Sanctuary from the start. Cookie was in her forties, weighed well over two hundred pounds and could make nutritious meals seemingly out of nothing, which she was called upon to do on a regular basis.

"That should do it, Cookie," Lee said, handing her the list. "Keep track of what you put in the cart so you have enough money to pay for it all at checkout." She handed the woman several folded bills. "Hopefully, next week, we'll be able to do better."

It was something Lee said every week. "Don't worry, Lee," Cookie told her. "We'll manage. We always do." She heaved her bulk out of the chair and waved to Hannah. "There's fresh coffee in the pot. Can I get you a cup?"

Hannah had met these people a few short weeks ago. Once they learned she'd come offering legal help to anyone in need, they'd all treated her with respect and admiration, surprising her with their enthusiasm. Every day, she vowed not to let them down.

"Thanks, Cookie. It's cold out there."

Hannah watched Lee rub her forehead and knew it to be an unconsciously weary gesture. Lee Stanford was thirty-eight, a tall woman, five foot nine and solidly built. She was strong yet motherly, which made her perfect for her chosen line of work.

Hannah slid onto a chair. "I hear it's been an interesting weekend."

Lee held out her mug for a refill as Cookie came over with the pot. "Yes, indeed." As they sipped coffee, Lee filled Hannah in on the new admittances and updated her on Ellen Baxter.

"I think I'd better go talk to Ellen," Hannah said. She rose, glancing into the next room, where two small children were sitting on the floor watching television and a young pregnant woman was dozing in a rocking chair.

"I have another problem," Lee said with obvious reluctance. "I don't know if you want to take this one on."

Quickly, Lee told her, then got up and went to the sideboard, returning with a piece of paper she handed to Hannah. "Here's her name, address and phone number. I hope you can help her. She's just a kid."

Hannah looked at the note. Lisa Tompkins. Date rape. "I'll look into it." She drained her coffee and picked up her briefcase. "First things first. I'll go find Ellen."

Stuffing her hands in her jeans pockets, Lee smiled encouragingly. "Good luck."

"Naturally, everything you tell me will be confidential," Hannah said into the phone.

The voice at the other end was soft, almost muffled. "I don't know. I just don't know what to do."

Of course, the girl was confused. Only nineteen and a freshman at Boston University, Lisa Tompkins had told Hannah she'd been thrilled when the handsome senior had asked her out. He'd been a perfect gentleman on their first date, then had turned into someone she didn't recognize on their second.

"I understand how difficult this is for you, Lisa." Hannah leaned back in her desk chair, trying to sound reassuring. "Did you tell your family?"

The yes that followed was so low Hannah barely heard her. "How do they feel about...about the young man?" The shame was deeper because Lisa's uncle was friendly with the young man's father, she'd just been told.

The answer was hesitant and slow in coming. "My mom said that if my dad were alive, he'd kill Lyle with his bare hands. We haven't told Uncle Bill. I just know he won't believe me. The trouble is, Lyle's family's got so much money. They know everyone in Boston. Who's going to believe me over them?"

Hannah suspected she had her work cut out for her. "We need to discuss this in person, Lisa. Can you come to my office or would you prefer that I go to your home so we can talk about what happened in depth?"

The young woman took her time deciding. Finally, she spoke, her voice a bit stronger. "I'll come to you, I guess. I don't want to talk about this in front of my mom and my sister anymore. It's too upsetting, for all of us. Where are you located?"

Hannah gave her the address and directions. They agreed that tomorrow at ten would be best. Hannah hung up with a frown, wondering if Lisa would show or talk herself out of working with an attorney. Rape victims were frightened and unpredictable, often feeling as if they'd somehow caused the violation. Still, Lisa's family seemed to be behind her. That was important.

"Working late again, Hannah?" Will asked from the doorway of her office. "It's nearly seven, and Marcie told me you beat her in this morning. Don't you need food and sleep like the rest of us, or are you still living on apples and four hours of snooze time a night?" His words were teasingly affectionate but laced with concern. In the three weeks she'd been in town, two since moving into his building, he'd scarcely seen her except coming and going.

"Work keeps me out of mischief," Hannah said, removing her glasses and smiling at Will. He was so kind to check on her, such a nice man.

"You, mischievous? Highly doubtful."

"Did you catch any fish last week?" she asked, changing the subject.

"Enough to share some with Sanctuary. Didn't Cookie tell you I hauled over a mess of 'em couple of days ago?" Ever since learning of her interest in the shelter, he'd lent a helping hand whenever he could. "She's some cook, that lady. Fried up some on the spot and made me stay for lunch."

Her smile warmed. "That was sweet. Thank you."

"Hell, I'm not sweet," Will protested. "Just can't eat that many fish at one time." Unbuttoning his suit coat over his vest, he sat down on Hannah's settee. The fragile-looking furniture in the room made him feel big and clumsy, but he wouldn't tell her so. Instead, he thought he'd probe a little. "How are you getting along with Joel?"

Hannah busied herself packing her briefcase with the files she'd been working on to look over later. "Fine, I guess," she answered. "Our paths haven't crossed much. He's pretty involved in a court case right now."

"Yes, Amanda Fowler. I wonder how it's going."

Hannah had wondered, too. She'd almost stopped in to listen for a while when she'd been at the courthouse earlier filing some motions. It would be interesting to watch Joel in action. "It's a tough one. She's not the only one who had a motive."

Will raised a craggy brow. "Did Joel discuss the case with you?" That surprised him.

Hannah locked her briefcase. "Some. He seems a little worried about the outcome. I hadn't thought him to be the worrying kind."

"We're all the worrying kind, Hannah. Some more than others." Slowly, he got to his feet, grimacing at the arthritis that made straightening painful. "Joel's like an iceberg. He only shows ten percent of himself to most people."

Downstairs earlier, she'd heard Marcie take a message for Joel from someone named Bubbles. She doubted that he lacked for a friendly ear if he felt like confiding in someone. "That's why icebergs are so dangerous, Will," she told him with a smile.

"Joel's a pussycat when you get to know him," Will insisted.

"Really? I guess his friend Bubbles thinks so. She was hunting him down today. I overheard Marcie take a message."

Will chuckled. "Bubbles. That's a good one." He stuck his thumb in his vest pocket and turned to Hannah. "Women like that are after only one thing."

"Yes, and I'll bet I can guess what."

"His money."

"Oh, that." Grinning, she slipped on her jacket.

"You got Joel figured out all wrong, Hannah. I doubt he even calls those girls back. Why, last summer, he spent more time going to the ballpark with me than dating."

Hannah picked up her briefcase and shoulder bag. "Is that a fact? Well, you're good company, Will."

He decided to give it up—for now. "So, you're finished for the day?"

"Yes." A quick stop at the market, a long soak in the tub with a glass of white wine, followed by a seafood salad. Then she'd look over tomorrow's files before an early lights out. "And are you calling it a day?" She followed him out into the hall and down the stairs.

"Just got to clean off my desk, then I'll head home." And how he wished someone other than Benjie, his aging cat, would be there waiting for him.

At Will's office door, Hannah squeezed his hand. "I'll see you tomorrow." At his nod, she headed for the back door.

And collided with a tall form in the dim back hallway. Hannah let out a yelp as her briefcase went flying. Stepping back, she looked up into amused blue eyes. "I might have known. Were you lurking in the shadows just waiting for me to come around the corner?"

Joel laughed as he reached for her briefcase and handed it to her. "Actually, I was coming to get you. We have to hurry or we'll be late."

Puzzled, Hannah frowned. "Late for what?"

"Dinner. The reservation's for eight. If we leave right now, we can stroll through Faneuil Hall on the way over."

Was she losing her mind? "I don't recall making plans for dinner." She'd been so preoccupied, but surely she'd remember a dinner engagement.

Opening the back door, Joel hustled her out. "You didn't, exactly. But you have to eat—and look!" He waved at a clear sky. "It's a beautiful night. I'll bet you've never even been to Faneuil, Boston's famous marketplace."

He was railroading her, and she didn't have to go along with it, she reminded herself. "No, I haven't. But I've got too much work to do yet tonight and..."

On the landing, he turned to her, his eyes beseeching her in the soft overhead light. "I personally stopped at Cherrystones and reserved a table by a window looking out on the harbor. Their fish is so fresh it thrashes on the plate when they bring it to you. Surely, you wouldn't be cruel enough to subject me to eating dinner all alone?"

He was a charmer. She felt herself weakening. How long had it been since she'd gone out for a quiet dinner in a nice place? Forever. "I don't believe you ever need to eat alone. I understand Bubbles was looking for you earlier."

Joel looked momentarily chagrined, then smiled. "Nice girl. Met her at the library. Deep philosophical thinker. But I'd much rather eat with you. Come on, it's a great evening for a stroll." He held out his hand. "Stash your stuff in the car and let's go."

Maybe because it was a cold, crisp night with a sky full of stars. Maybe because she'd put in a long day and was more than ready for a little relaxation. Or maybe because Joel Merrick was just too hard to resist.

She did as he requested.

It was chilly inside the two-story granite marketplace known as Faneuil Hall, but the tantalizing bakeshop aromas mingling with freshly brewed exotic coffees gave off a warmth of their own. Visitors and locals elbowed one another along the aisles, peering through glass cases at delectable fudges and tangy Greek souvlaka, as well as raw oysters. A ragtag band at one end played not well but loudly, and a variety of peddlers could be heard hawking their wares.

Hannah was enchanted.

"Mmm, it smells wonderful in here." She inhaled deeply. "There's nothing like this where I come from."

Joel took her hand and threaded it through his arm as a rowdy group of teenagers, laughing at their own nonsense, pushed past them. "We'll have to come back and eat here one night. Just about any ethnic food you like is here."

Hannah paused to stare at a display that claimed to be the largest selection of New England scrimshaw jewelry plus rare engraved whales' teeth and original Nantucket lightship baskets. "Now, who would ever think to engrave a whale's tooth? And how would you ever obtain them in the first place?"

"Very carefully," Joel said as he moved them along to the next storefront, featuring a vast variety of puzzles from jigsaws to mazes to brain teasers. "Look at this collection."

Hannah all but pressed her nose to the window. "Oh, I love puzzles. My brother used to let me help him sometimes and..." She stopped, shocked at her own comment. Memories of those early days so seldom popped into her mind anymore. Or was it that she'd pushed them back for so long that they'd stopped coming?

Joel looked down at her face, her expression disturbed. "I didn't know you had a brother." Will had told him very little, but he had said she had no family left.

"I did, once. A long time ago." She'd adored Michael. He'd been fourteen when she'd last seen him, all long legs and gangly arms. And he'd been crying.

"What happened to him?"

Hannah cleared her throat. "Isn't that pottery lovely?" she asked, dragging him on to the next shop, effectively changing the subject.

All right, so her family, dead or alive, was off limits. He could handle that. But it was puzzling.

They moved to the upper level, where it was less crowded, walking on past wind chimes and unique scented candles and a store that featured every imaginable kite. "Too bad it's winter," Joel commented. "We could get one of those red-and-yellow sailfish, take it out by the harbor and let her rip."

Hannah studied him as he gazed at the kites like a little boy. He was wearing his usual boots, jeans and sheepskin jacket tonight. He'd explained that court had let out early and he'd gone home to change before looking for her. There was such a look of longing on his face that she wondered at it. "Didn't you fly kites when you were growing up?"

"A couple of times. Dad took us out, but he was always in charge of the kite, unwilling to let me or my brothers handle it alone. It wasn't much fun that way." Suddenly serious, he met her eyes. "Ever know anyone like that? Hell of a nice guy, but he has to run every show."

She was beginning to understand why he'd rebelled at home as a boy. "I've met a few. Control freaks, I think we call them these days."

"Yeah, I guess you're right. Back then, we just thought of them as bossy and demanding." He was saying too much again, revealing things he hadn't intended. There was something about Hannah that caused him to open up. Joel decided he should watch that.

A light breeze coming through the open double doors at the far end caught her hair and whimsically rearranged it. He reached up to brush it back and found his fingers lingering in the thick waves. "I love your hair.

It's such a great color. Did you inherit it from your mother or your father?''

"Neither, really. My mother was dark and my father very blond." So long ago. Such a short time to know even a small measure of happiness. "They're both gone now," she heard herself say, then felt her thoughts skitter and slide as his fingers touched her scalp.

He saw her eyes meet his, then slowly darken with awareness. Her hand still rested in the crook of his arm, and he felt her fingers tighten as she stared up at him. What was she thinking, feeling? he wondered.

Something there, Hannah acknowledged. Something in his eyes that told her he was more than she'd originally suspected. Handsome, certainly. Self-assured, definitely. But something more, something that hinted of vulnerability and even loneliness. Odd how she hadn't noticed that before.

And that something reached out to her.

She'd warned herself not to let Joel Merrick get too close. She'd told herself repeatedly that no good would come of any alliance between them. He was Beacon Hill, Harvard and Hyannis, teeming with family and friends, Man of the Year. She was small-town, no family and few friends, a stranger in a strange town. If he wanted her, it was only temporarily, as a plaything, to be discarded when he tired of her.

Hadn't she been through that already? Wasn't she way too smart to stick her hand into the flame twice?

Why, then, was her heart beating much too rapidly as his hard, strong fingers massaged her scalp and his deep blue eyes caressed her face? Why did she want him, she who had no business wanting a man? Why wouldn't she learn that giving in would mean getting hurt?

Hannah pulled her gaze from his and, with a trembling hand, brought his arm down. "I think we should leave. Our reservation..."

Stepping back, Joel swallowed hard. He wasn't mistaken. He was too experienced to be mistaken. He recognized a look in a woman's eyes that told him she was attracted to him. Hannah had that look. Yet she'd slammed on the brakes and turned from that attraction as easily as she'd turned from a display window full of jewelry she couldn't afford. What was it about him that made her turn from him so often so easily?

He meant to find out.

Cherrystones Seafood Restaurant sat on Commercial Wharf on Atlantic Avenue, a short walk from Faneuil Hall. The aroma as guests entered was overwhelmingly of fish, though the menu was varied. By the time they were ushered to their window table, Hannah's mouth was watering.

"Do you know I haven't had fresh seafood served in a restaurant since I arrived in Boston?" She took the menu from the waiter with a smile. "I can hardly wait."

"Good. I'd about decided that you lived on apples." Joel picked up the wine list. "Would you like a drink?"

"White wine would be nice. Chardonnay is my choice, if they have it." She perused the menu while he ordered their wine, then turned to gaze out the window. The harbor looked icy and cold but still fascinating. "There's something about the sea, isn't there? Mesmerizing."

Joel leaned forward so he could watch her stare out at the sea. "Oh, I don't know. There's a lot to be said for open land, acres and acres of it, filled with hundreds— no, thousands—of cattle and horses that belong only to you. And endless blue, blue sky like nowhere else on earth."

She was smiling when she turned to him. "You love Montana." It wasn't a question.

"Yeah, I guess I do. My father doesn't understand, but ranching sort of gets in your blood. Out there, you're in charge of you, you know. No one else to tell you what to do. You have to make the decisions, to take the blame and enjoy the credit. Both ways. Bart loves it as much as I do. Dad went once, said he couldn't stand the loneliness."

"But you can be lonely in a city full of people." Of course, she'd denied that she'd been lonely since arriving in Boston. The truth was, she hadn't realized she was until this evening.

Joel smiled, pleased at her perception. "That's exactly how I feel. There's a difference between being alone and being lonely."

The waiter brought their wine, then took their order before withdrawing. Joel lifted his glass. "Thanks for coming with me."

Hannah raised hers. "Thank you for dragging me along. I think maybe I needed this." The wine, cool and tart, slid down easily.

"Bad day?"

"Oh, not necessarily. Just long."

"How are things going with that battered-wife case? Ellen somebody, didn't you say?"

"Ellen Baxter, yes." She set down her glass, feeling a mixture of anger and disappointment. "Her husband hit her again and scared her so badly that she wound up in Emergency. I thought I had her convinced to press charges. But he threatened to really hurt her if she involved the police, so she went back to him."

"He threatens to kill her, so she returns to him?"

"Unfortunately, yes. That's often the way it is with battered wives. Fear rules their every thought and action."

"Do they have children?"

"Yes, a boy of six and a girl who's just seven."

"Why do you suppose she stays?"

Hannah took another sip of wine before answering. "It's so hard for those of us not in such a relationship to understand. The whole thing has to do with self-image. These men manage somehow to convince the women that it's all their fault, that she makes the man so angry he has no choice but to hit her."

"Unbelievable. How is it possible to get them out of these potentially deadly relationships?"

"That happens usually when the man goes too far. Nearly kills her, and she finally agrees to prosecute. Or he hurts the children. Or, all too often, he actually kills her."

"It sounds as if you've handled cases like that."

"Only one. It was awful. She died, kids became wards of the court and he's in prison for life. It's all so sad and so unnecessary. We need more family counselors trained in this specialty."

Their food arrived, baked halibut for Joel and stuffed flounder for Hannah. By mutual, unspoken agreement, they talked of lighter things while they ate, sights around Boston that Hannah hadn't yet visited, some funny stories about Will and a comment or two about Marcie's many boyfriends. By the time the check arrived, they were both full enough to welcome the mile stroll back to their cars. Their footsteps crunched on the snowy walk, the sound loud as they turned onto a side street. Someone had a fire going, the woodsy smell tantalizing in the crisp air.

Halfway there, Joel slipped his arm around Hannah as a chill wind whipped at them. "It's gotten quite a bit colder," he commented to explain the familiarity.

Was she mellow from one glass of wine, sated from the best dinner she'd had in weeks or did she just *want* to be closer to him? Hannah wondered as she found herself not objecting. She no longer knew the answer herself.

She only knew that it felt good to be up against his strong, solid body, to have his warmth drift to her along with a most pleasant masculine scent. Only until she got to the car, she told herself. What, after all, was the harm?

"Do you ski?" Joel asked, his mouth close to her ear.

"No, I've never tried. But I love to ice-skate." On the farm, each winter her father had flooded a section, and all of them had had skates. She'd been rather good, if memory served correctly. Some memories at least were good.

At the back parking lot of Will's building, Joel stopped alongside Hannah's car. "Will you go skating with me soon?"

"I don't know, Joel." Suddenly, her heavy briefcase on the passenger seat, containing work yet to be done, brought her back to reality. "This has been nice, but I can't afford to play again so soon. I'm new in town and . . ."

"You can work days. Evenings, you need to relax. Or don't you enjoy being with me?"

There was that hesitancy again, that guileless look. Did he know she was particularly susceptible to it? "I do enjoy being with you. But . . ."

"No buts, then." He placed his hands on her upper arms, his eyes serious in the parking-lot lighting. "Listen, being an attorney is tough, demanding, difficult. You need to regroup regularly or you're doing your client a disservice. A rested, relaxed mind is more able to defend and represent."

She smiled at that. "I'll bet you're hell on wheels with a jury."

He didn't answer but shifted even closer, his hands moving around her back. He watched the smile slip from her as she read his intention. Her dark eyes were in shadow, so he couldn't read her thoughts, but she didn't push him away. With that small encouragement, he lowered his head and captured her lips.

She was hesitant, letting him lead the way, getting used to the feel of his mouth on hers. Slowly, after long moments, she responded cautiously, almost as if against her will. Gathering her closer, Joel felt a sharp tug of desire he hadn't experienced in some time.

Hannah had seen the kiss coming and could easily have pulled away. She hadn't, curious about his kiss. Yet she hadn't been ready for the rush of awareness that had her blood heating, churning. She hadn't thought his mouth would be so soft, so careful, as it moved over hers, so sensitive when she'd not expected gentleness from this confident man.

But most important, she hadn't expected that her arms would creep up around his neck, pulling him nearer and nearer still. She hadn't anticipated the soft sigh of pleasure that escaped from deep within her as she opened her mouth more fully to his. In short, she hadn't expected to feel so much.

Joel shifted slightly, deepening the kiss. One hand moved up into the silkiness of her hair, while his other hand slipped low on her back, aligning her more perfectly with his body. Drawing in a deep breath, he saw her eyes drift open, looking surprised yet hazy with desire. With a soft moan, he dipped to taste more of her.

Hannah had thought she'd prove to herself that she was one of the few women immune to Joel Merrick's kisses. She'd been wrong, she realized. Dangerously wrong. She felt her breath catch in her throat as his tongue moved into her mouth. The sensual, smoky taste of him, remnants of wine lingering, had her senses swirling as, unbidden, her hands caressed his nape. This kiss was even more potent than the first, an awakening, an exploration, and it had her blood racing.

Equally stunned, they drew apart slowly. Joel's arms remained loosely around her as if reluctant to let go. Hannah had trouble finding her voice even as she wondered what to say.

"Look, I don't want to get involved," she finally said, thinking she sounded as inane as she felt.

"Me, either. I can't say I didn't want to kiss you, but I had no idea you'd pack such a wallop, Red." Releasing her, he stepped back when what he really wanted to do was pull her back and do it all over again.

Hannah licked her lips and tasted him, then felt the heat rise in her face. It was chemistry, that's all. It had to be. She had to leave, to be alone, where she could think more clearly. Her reaction to him had jolted her to her core.

"You're something of a puzzle, Hannah. You have many sides, it seems. So cool, so controlled. Then wham!"

Opening her car door for her, he gave her his killer smile. "Like you, I just love puzzles."

* * *

I take my pen in hand to write tonight, and my hand trembles. How can our lives fall apart so completely in just six short months?

He's gone, my Lance. We buried him last week, but I've been too sick at heart to pick up my journal. He'd repaired the old tractor, trying to hold it together since we have no money to buy a new one. Then he climbed up, and something went terribly wrong. It bucked and tossed him off, then ran him over. Michael and I found him there on the hard ground, no longer breathing.

My heart died with Lance, I think. My cough is no better, and now I ache, both physically and clear through to my soul. I must keep on, for the sake of the children. There is no laughter in our house now. Only sadness, tears and pain. We're trying to keep the farm going, to tend to the animals and ourselves. But we only go through the motions. Lance was our strength and he's gone. With him went our hopes, our dreams.

Michael does a man's work now, but his schoolwork suffers. Hannah helps with the meals and washing the clothes, but she grows thinner. Even bright-eyed little Kate no longer smiles. The pain in my chest as I lie in bed at night makes me want to join Lance. But I must keep going, must find strength somewhere.

What will become of us?

Chapter Four

Lisa Tompkins was a slender young woman who was probably quite pretty when her face wasn't red and blotchy from crying, Hannah thought as she took the chair opposite the settee in her office. She'd found that most of her clients felt more comfortable in that cozy corner rather than facing her across the desk.

She'd started a fire in the grate to make her office more inviting, as well as to add warmth, and she'd poured Lisa a cup of coffee from the small pot she kept on the counter in the bathroom, but the nervous girl hadn't touched it yet. Hannah crossed her legs and balanced a legal pad on her lap. "Can you tell me what happened, Lisa?"

Lisa tasted her coffee, perhaps for courage, but kept her eyes downcast as her hands shredded a tissue during her recital. It was brief and oddly unemotional, some of her statements quite disturbing.

Hannah worded her questions as gently as possible. "Why did you agree to go to Lyle's apartment after the concert, Lisa?"

"He told me he'd just gotten a new painting and he wanted my opinion on it. I'm an art major, so I didn't think his request was unusual. Several friends have asked me about colors and textures." Her tone was wary. She was obviously bright enough to realize that agreeing to go with him to his home had been a cardinal mistake.

"It never occurred to you that he'd try anything?"

"No!" Lisa looked up, her attitude defensive. "I knew that my Uncle Bill and Lyle's father were friends. I sure never thought he'd make a move on someone with a family connection. Besides, he's a straight-A student, you know. On the student council. A respected senior and...and..." She tried to hold back tears that suddenly began flowing like a dam that had sprung a leak. "I hear myself say all this and I know how stupid it sounds. I was stupid to go." She shuddered over a sob.

Hannah reached over and touched the girl's folded hands. "Not stupid, Lisa. Innocent and trusting. That's not a crime. Unfortunately, he took advantage of that trust." Like someone had once done to her. She hadn't been physically raped like Lisa, but he'd destroyed her trust forever.

She waited until Lisa wiped her eyes and got herself under control. "Since we talked, have you told your uncle?"

Lisa pressed her lips together. "I did, but I shouldn't have. Uncle Bill went right over and confronted Lyle in front of his father. Lyle denied everything. He said he'd asked me in to check out his new painting, then he'd driven me back to my dorm and hadn't even kissed me good-night." The tears began again in earnest.

"He said that he has a steady girl and only took me out because he knew my family and felt sorry for me because I was so shy. He...he said if I was raped, it had to have happened after he dropped me off." Blinking, she looked at Hannah. "Lyle's father was furious, and Uncle Bill told me I'd only make a fool of myself if I took on Lyle and his family. I told you no one would believe me."

"*I* believe you, Lisa. And so will the judge." Hannah leaned forward, intent on convincing the young girl. "We can and will prove this. You need to trust me. Do you, Lisa, because that's paramount?"

Lisa took another tissue from the box Hannah had placed on the table and blew her nose. "I trust you, yes. I know you mean well and all. But I just don't know if I can get up there and tell...tell everyone what happened. Especially since I don't know if they'll believe me."

Hannah folded her hands over the yellow pad. "I believe they will. You didn't do anything wrong and you shouldn't be the one to pay." Uncapping her pen, she began her notes. "Now, I want you to go over everything and leave out no detail. Can you do that?"

Taking a steadying breath, Lisa dried her eyes. "I think so."

"Okay, start at the beginning, your first date with Lyle." As Lisa began her recital, Hannah took notes.

The session lasted two hours, and Hannah could see that by the time they finished, Lisa was exhausted from having to recall every emotional detail. Hannah felt that they had a strong case. She'd have to go to the hospital and meet with the rape counselor. Thank goodness Lee had seen to it that Lisa had been examined immediately after. That was always crucial.

The clock on the mantel showed that it was nearly noon when Hannah stood up. "I know this has been tiring, but you'll have to go through some of it again. You have to go to the police station to report the rape." At the look of shock on the girl's face, Hannah hastily rearranged her afternoon schedule mentally. She'd ask Marcie to make a couple of calls for her. "I'll go with you, if you like."

Lisa's lower lip trembled. "I . . . I thought you could handle that part for me."

Lord, but she was young, Hannah thought. Had she ever been that innocent? "I'm afraid not. But I'll be right there with you." Provided the cops let her stay in the room. Sometimes they did, and other times, they took a hard-nosed attitude. No point in mentioning that until they got to the station.

"We might as well get it over with." Hannah went to the closet for their outerwear. "Would you like to stop for some lunch on the way?"

Lisa took her coat from Hannah. "I don't think I could eat a thing. I'm hoping this coffee stays down."

Hannah could empathize. Slipping her arm around the girl's shoulders, she led the way downstairs. "This will all be behind you soon, Lisa. Then you can get on with your life."

The man on the witness stand was no kid. Kent Fowler, the dead man's son, was somewhere in his mid-thirties, Hannah guessed. Just a few years younger than his stepmother, Amanda Fowler, who sat at the defense table accused of the father's death. Kent had a bad complexion and a receding hairline, but he wore expensive çlothes and a pinkie ring that looked to be several carats from where Hannah sat in the gallery.

She really couldn't spare the time to sit in on Joel's case, she'd told herself as she'd hurried down the courthouse hallway the afternoon following Lisa's visit. But curiosity had had her checking the docket book and slipping into courtroom C for just a few minutes.

That had been half an hour ago. She found herself fascinated by Joel's carefully planned interrogation of Kent Fowler, the son he'd told her had a gambling problem that could indicate a motive for murder. Joel didn't pace or get theatrical. He held no notes in his hands. He simply stood slightly to the side of the witness box and stared at Kent with those piercing blue eyes as he patiently fired questions.

"What do you do for a living, Mr. Fowler?" Joel asked.

"I work in my father's business."

Blake Fowler had made his fortune building a chain of sporting-goods stores. "In which store do you currently work?"

Kent shifted on the chair. "It varies."

Hannah listened intently as Joel hammered away at the son's alibi for the night of the murder, at his poor relationship with his father and his jealousy of his stepmother. The softer Joel spoke, the angrier Kent became, until he finally lost control.

"Are you accusing me of arranging the death of my own father?" Kent yelled out.

"Did you?" Joel asked quietly.

"No!"

"Objection!" The prosecutor was on his feet.

Judge Eaton banged his gavel as the gallery began buzzing. "Order. I will have order." He looked toward the prosecutor. "Overruled. I'll allow this line of questioning, but make your point quickly, Counselor."

"Thank you, Your Honor," Joel said. "Now, then, Mr. Fowler, are you familiar with a bar on the waterfront called Eddie's Place, where offtrack bets can be made?"

In the back row, Hannah listened in admiration. Joel was good. She'd give him that. He was moving in for the kill, and there seemed little Kent Fowler could do about it.

And he looked so at ease up there, as if no one or nothing could throw him. If he was nervous, it didn't show. She wished she had that kind of confidence. Maybe one day.

He looked every inch the well-to-do, Harvard-trained lawyer in his pin-striped navy blue suit. How could she have thought, even fleetingly, that she could fit into his world?

Glancing at her watch, she rose. She hated to leave, but she had an appointment. As she glanced one last time to the front, Joel turned and caught her eye. She tipped two fingers to her forehead in a salute to his expertise, and gave him an encouraging smile. He winked back.

She left the building, her emotions jumbled.

"You are going to make me fat," Hannah told Marcie as she gazed at the generous piece of lasagna the older woman offered. Located on the lower level, the small lunchroom had been added when Will realized their long hours often had them missing meals. There was a refrigerator, microwave, sink and small table with four chairs. Despite her protests, Hannah took the dish and sat down.

"You could use a few pounds, if you ask me," Marcie answered, joining her at the table. "You're on the go so much you don't take the time to eat properly."

Swallowing a delicious mouthful, Hannah was glad she'd accepted Marcie's luncheon invitation. "Got to strike while the iron is hot, or so they say."

Through the open doorway, Marcie saw that Joel's office was empty though it was almost two. "I thought Joel said he'd be in this afternoon."

"That Fowler trial is taking longer than he expected, I'm sure. I'm beginning to think that Amanda didn't do it." She took another fragrant bite.

"Did you stop in and watch Joel in action?" Not waiting for a reply, Marcie went on, making an educated guess. "He's something, isn't he? That man could sell ice cubes to the Eskimos."

"He was doing a great job of establishing reasonable doubt in the minds of the jurors by giving several family members a motive to have killed Mr. Fowler. I wonder who really did do it."

"We'll probably never know. But I'll bet Joel will get Amanda off."

Finishing, Hannah frowned. "Even if she may be guilty?" That still didn't sit right with her.

"I suppose that could happen." Marcie rose and took both paper plates, throwing them in the trash can. "It's not like in the movies where someone rushes in in the last five minutes and makes a dramatic confession, now is it?"

"Would that it were so. Where's Perry Mason when we need him?" Hannah got up and reached into the fridge for the bottled water she kept there. "Thanks for lunch. It was great."

"Anytime. Tell me, what do you think of Joel now that you've been here a month?"

Wondering why Marcie wanted to know, Hannah shrugged. "He's all right. A good attorney." A good kisser, came the thought, and she felt heat rise into her cheeks.

Marcie eyed her shrewdly. "He's very attractive, too." When Hannah didn't answer, but instead busied herself pouring a glass of water, she decided to plunge on. "About that double date I mentioned a while back, are you interested? Bob knows this nice CPA, in his thirties, never married, drives a Jag."

Shaking her head, Hannah picked up her water. "Thanks, but I'm just too busy getting my practice established right now to date anyone."

"Some other time, then," Marcie offered, loath to give up.

"Possibly." Hannah escaped the lunchroom, hurrying upstairs. Marcie was a great secretary, but a persistent matchmaker. Well, if she turned her down often enough, the older women would finally have to get the message. They all would, including Will. Hannah simply wasn't interested.

As she reached her office, her thoughts suddenly drifted to the dinner she'd shared with Joel and the stroll around Faneuil Hall. The kisses she'd had trouble forgetting.

It had felt good, being with someone interesting, talking about the things they had in common. Like the law and a love of seafood and puzzles. It had felt even better being in his arms, feeling the need swell inside her. It had been so long since a man had openly wanted her, since she'd felt like a woman.

Sitting down, Hannah sighed. But, nice as all that was, none of it was for her. She simply couldn't put herself through all that turmoil. Temporary pleasures could bring on a lifetime of regrets. She'd been young back then, foolish and eager to taste life. She was older now, hopefully wiser. No man and all he offered were worth the pain he so often left in his wake.

She would have to keep that firmly in mind, Hannah thought as she opened the file folder on her desk. She had a custody hearing at three and she needed to go over a few facts.

It had been a tiring day. Tie hanging loose, Joel rubbed the back of his neck as he shut the front door and walked to his office. It was past seven in the evening, and apparently everyone else had gone home hours ago. He'd been in court all day, then had spent a grueling hour and a half going over things with Amanda Fowler in preparation for tomorrow.

Things were proceeding slowly but nicely. Amanda, unused to court proceedings, was understandably nervous. The outcome was far from a sure thing, but Joel felt they had a good chance. Still, it was her life, and he didn't blame her for the case of nerves that had her losing both weight and sleep.

He would have liked to have gone straight home, poured a couple of fingers of Scotch and grilled a steak. But he'd promised Marcie he'd stop in and sign the letters from last evening's dictation. He flipped on the light in his office, tossed his coat onto a chair and sat down at the desk.

Efficient as always, she had them lined up for him. He scanned them quickly, signed them all and scribbled Marcie a note of thanks. Turning out the light, he remembered he needed a reference volume. Wearily, he climbed the stairs.

And stopped halfway up when he heard the sound of glass shattering.

Taking the steps two at a time, Joel reached the open doorway of Hannah's office and found her with one arm braced on the mantel, her back to him as she stood facing the fireplace. Cautiously, he walked in, not wanting to alarm her. "Hannah?"

He'd expected her to swivel about, surprised to find she wasn't alone. But instead, he saw her spine straighten, but she didn't turn around. "Hannah, are you all right?"

When she didn't respond, he stepped closer and saw the glass shards in the fireplace, scattered over the ashes in the grate. "Hannah, what's wrong?"

"Nothing. Go away."

The hell he would, not until he learned what had upset her so. No one else was on the premises. She had to have thrown the glass into the fireplace. It seemed so unlike the controlled woman he knew. He touched her shoulder lightly. "Talk to me."

She jerked from his touch. "Leave me alone. I...I need to be alone."

Joel had had enough. Taking hold of her shoulders, he turned her, his eyes on her face. Her cheeks were drained of color, and her eyes were dark and haunted. Her hair was mussed, as if her angry fingers had combed through it. She didn't look up at him, just stood with her lips pressed into a thin line.

"Tell me. It's okay. You can tell me."

"No, it's *not* okay." She struggled out of his hold and moved to stand at the window, her back to him.

Frustrated and getting angry, he followed her. "I'm not leaving until you talk to me. Obviously, someone hurt you and..."

"Hurt me?" She whirled about, and now he could see frustration redden her cheeks. "No, no one hurt me. *I'm* the one who hurt someone. I let her down. Because of me and my inadequacies, she lost her children." Hannah's voice ended on a dry sob as her hand went to her throat. "Oh, God, *why* couldn't I have won for her?"

Joel reached to pull her to him, wanting to comfort her, but she shoved away from him.

"Let me go. I need to leave." Moving to her desk, Hannah grabbed her shoulder bag and fumbled for her keys.

Joel took them from her. "You're not going anywhere until you calm down. You're in no shape to drive. If you don't want to talk to me, fine. Then let me hold you, just hold you." Gently, he eased her into a light embrace.

She moved aside. "I don't want you to hold me. I'm not a clinging female who turns for help to a man every time something goes wrong." She wasn't going to break down here in front of him. She hated the very thought of it, hated anyone seeing her as weak and ineffectual. She'd been struggling with a myriad of feelings—anger, disappointment, helplessness. So she'd thrown a drinking glass into the fireplace, but even that hadn't been enough.

The pressure, the need for release, was still there. It had been bubbling up inside ever since she'd returned from the court hearing. Ever since she'd seen the look of utter devastation on Jenna Nichols's face and the triumphant smile that Brad Nichols flashed her. She'd wanted so badly to punch him in his perfect nose right there and then.

"It's not a weakness to accept comfort when you're upset," Joel said, aware she was fighting an inner battle and had thrown the glass as a release.

"I'll be fine after I drive around awhile and get this out of my system. Driving always distracts me." Again, she reached for her keys.

Joel shoved them in his pocket. "I have a better way to distract you." Bracketing her face with his hands, he took her mouth.

He'd been prepared for her to fight him, to pull away, but instead, she moaned deep in her throat and wrapped her arms tightly around him, opening her mouth more fully. This wasn't the gentle kiss they'd shared the night they'd walked back from Cherrystones. Nor was it the hazy, passionate kiss that had followed the first.

This was raw emotion, turbulence, restless seeking. She wanted to forget whatever had upset her and was using him to empty her mind. He willingly allowed her to, his hunger matching hers. He reveled in her hands bunching in the material of his jacket at his back, glorying in the way she pressed her body to his. Her response was pure instinct, wild need, a storm thrashing and swirling them into the eye.

He let her lead, mating his tongue with hers, meeting her thrust for thrust, his hands slipping under her blouse and stroking soft skin hot to the touch. He took her under, certain that at the moment, she knew only him, thought only of him, wanted only him.

When finally he released her, Hannah took a step back, feeling unsteady, her knees weak. Her breath hitched as she fought for the control she'd somehow handed away. He'd made her forget, if only for a short time. The power he held over her had her heart thundering still. What on earth was happening to her?

Taking her hand, Joel led her over to the settee and sat down opposite her, giving himself a little breathing room. He didn't want to think about how badly shaken he was, how quickly she could make him forget his own name. "Are you going to tell me what happened, or do you want to go another round with me?"

She would tell him, if only to get him to leave her alone. "I lost a case today," she answered, and locked her shaking hands together in her lap.

There was more, he was certain. "Is it the first you've ever lost? Must be to cause such a reaction."

"Hardly. It's just that I failed my client, and now, she's lost custody of her two little girls. Their father doesn't really want them. He just wants to get even with Jenna for dragging him into court last year over child support. God, it's all so unfair." She drew in a deep, steadying breath. "I usually don't fall apart so badly. It's just that, the way Jenna looked at me, I felt so damn helpless."

"You and I both know that custody is always temporary, that you can petition the court again for another hearing. If the father's as bad as you say, he'll soon tire of those kids and gladly give them back."

"Yes, but Jenna feels that even one night without her girls is too much. He's a playboy, goes out every night, leaves them with sitters."

"As long as he doesn't hurt them, they'll survive this. Kids are resilient, and their mother will handle it, too." He reached over to tip up her chin. "As for you, are you aware that the world won't stop spinning if you personally don't rescue every woman and child in need?"

She wasn't ready to admit that. "That judge made me so damn mad. He absolutely would not listen to all the evidence we had about what a lousy father Brad Nichols is. He has a chauffeur drive the girls to school and back, never taking the time himself. I'll bet he's never read to them or played a game with them or..."

He thought he knew where this was coming from. "I take it he's got money and she doesn't. Is this the rich bastard versus the poor underdog female? Is that why you're so vehement?"

"No, it certainly is not. Jenna is a referral from Michigan and is far from poor. I wouldn't care if Brad was a Rockefeller if he'd just pay attention to his children, be a real father, not a vindictive ex-husband who's using his own kids to hassle their mother."

"Give it a few months, then try again. You'll get them back for her."

Hannah drew in a shuddering breath. She was embarrassed that he'd seen her lose control. However, he had found a new way to divert her. Yes, he surely had.

Remembering the shamefully intimate way she'd kissed him back, she rose with cheeks flaming and walked to the fireplace. "I sure made a mess in here."

"I'll get the janitor to clean it out tomorrow." He walked over to her. "Maybe we could get a punching bag and hang it in that far corner. Might be easier on the glassware."

"Very funny. Tell me you've never thrown something in anger."

He placed his hands on her arms. "And the next time I get the urge, will you sacrifice yourself and come calm me down as I did with you?"

She touched her warm cheeks. "At your service, sir."

"Maybe we should give that a practice run." Before she could pull away, his lips were on hers again, his arms drawing her close.

She could have struggled, could have moved back, now that she was once more in control. Or was she? Hands trapped between their bodies, she could feel the erratic beat of his heart. Hannah felt the sensual pull dragging her under, just like the last time. Just like the first time.

Hands on his chest, she pushed, extricating herself. Annoyed that her pulse was furiously pounding, she frowned at him. "I don't think you need further practice, Counselor." Walking to her desk, she gathered up her things.

"Want to stop for a bite to eat before going home?" he asked. He was tired yet reluctant to let her go in her present mood.

Food was the last thing she wanted. And to make matters worse, she felt as if she might be coming down with a cold. "I really am beat tonight, but thanks anyway."

A good man knew when to back off. Joel waited for her to lock up, then followed her downstairs. He paused in the foyer. "My car's out front. I'll wait until you come around the drive to make sure you're all right."

Why did his hovering annoy her so? She only knew that it did. "There you go again. I've been managing to get around on my own for quite a few years now and..."

"Yeah, yeah. I know. Humor me. You might not always be so lucky. There are a lot of crazies out there."

Chagrined at being reminded, Hannah had to agree. "All right. Good night, then." She went out the back, locking up, checking the deserted parking lot before going to her Volkswagen. After the car warmed up, she drove around and saw Joel waiting for her. As they went their separate ways, he tooted his horn in farewell.

Hannah hated to admit even to herself how pleasant and brand-new it felt having someone worry about her.

Chapter Five

A vicious winter storm with frigid winds hit the Boston area the week before Thanksgiving and had the residents shivering. The snowfall was minimal, but the wind-chill factor took the temperature down into the single digits, unusual for this early in the season. Joel decided to stop for a few items at the small grocery near the office rather than fight the crowds in the large supermarket near his apartment.

His coat collar turned up, he sprinted to his car, a frown on his face. The Fowler case would soon move to closing arguments, and he was far from confident about the outcome. He had his own theories, the circumstantial evidence and obvious motivation pointing more toward Kent than his stepmother, but Joel hadn't a clue what the jury was thinking. He'd called Blake's elderly brother and sister to the stand, as well, but neither seemed a good suspect, although each had a motive of sorts. The younger son, Peter, a high-school dropout with a juvenile record and two divorces behind him, appeared too unfocused to have plotted his father's death.

That left Kent as the prime candidate. Unless, of course, Amanda Fowler was lying, which he really didn't believe.

Joel pulled into the parking lot of The Bread Basket just as the streetlights popped on. Still pondering his case, he skirted the icy patches and hurried through the swinging doors. He grabbed a cart and started down the dairy aisle. Haphazardly gathering easy-to-prepare fast foods, since he didn't eat at home all that much, he found himself distracted enough to have swung down the baby aisle by mistake. Turning around, he nearly ran into another cart.

Standing behind it was Hannah Richards.

He hadn't seen her in several days, not since the incident in her office when he'd tried to comfort her over losing a case. And had wound up kissing her instead. As she met his eyes, he thought by her flushed face that she might be remembering that evening, too. "Haven't seen you around lately. How are things going?"

Hannah had known she'd have to face Joel again after behaving so childishly over losing Jenna Nichols's custody case last week. Trying to dispel his opinion of her as overly emotional, she decided to act as normal as possible. "I've been around. You're the one who's hardly ever in. How's Fowler coming?"

Joel unbuttoned his coat in the warm store. "I wish I knew. The jury's hard to read. A real stoic bunch."

"I've never had much luck in figuring out how a jury will go." She wiped at her nose with a tissue. "Marcie thinks you'll get her off, one way or another."

"I hope it'll be because she's not guilty." He studied her face more closely and realized she hadn't been blushing, that her cheeks were unnaturally flushed. "Are you feeling all right?"

"I've got a cold. This weather doesn't help. Michigan never seemed to get this wintry this early." She hadn't taken the necessary precautions, Hannah admitted to herself, dashing to the car with her coat open, not getting enough rest or eating right. She had only herself to blame. But it was just a cold, and she wouldn't let it get her down.

"Maybe you should medicate yourself and get to bed." He glanced down at her basket, then smiled as he took inventory of the contents. "Diapers and baby food? Is there something you haven't told me?"

Hannah swiped at her red nose irritably. "They're for Dawn Carruthers. Her children, actually. One of my clients."

"You do her shopping?"

She was in no mood for these questions, Hannah thought. Just her luck to run into him when she was in a hurry. Yet she knew that Joel wouldn't give up until he got all the information he wanted. Lord, all she wanted was to drop these things off at Dawn's place, go home and sleep for the next twelve hours. "Not usually. But her deadbeat husband is so far behind in child support that Dawn can scarcely afford to put food on the table with her minimum-wage job. I'm just helping her out until we can get her ex to court."

How often, he wondered, did she do this kind of thing? Hannah tried to appear tough, but Joel knew how much these women with their many problems got to her. More than to most people. He wondered why, but today wasn't the day to ask questions. She looked all done in as she checked her list and reached for another package of diapers to add to her cart. "Can I help you deliver the stuff? You look ready to drop."

"Thanks, but I can manage. Dawn doesn't live far." Grateful that he hadn't launched into a bleeding-heart lecture, she gave him her best effort at a smile. "Good luck in court tomorrow."

Of course she'd refuse his offer of help. Didn't she always? "Thanks. See you later, then." He moved on, wondering what on God's green earth it would take for Hannah Richards to accept a modicum of help from anyone. And, more important, what had made her so damn obstinate and independent?

Just three more blocks, Hannah thought as she maneuvered the Volkswagen over an icy patch in the street. She'd be home in a few more minutes, where she could take something for her pounding head, her stuffy nose and the persistent cough.

Snow had begun to fall as she'd left Dawn's tiny apartment, where her two- and three-year-old had to sleep in their mother's bedroom and the cupboards were bare most of the time. Anger had her gripping the wheel. Adam Carruthers, the children's father, worked for his father's automotive-parts company on the outskirts of Boston. An only child, spoiled since boyhood, Adam was irresponsible to a fault, quitting his job frequently, getting in one jam after another and letting his folks bail him out. Small wonder he didn't support his children. You'd think the grandparents would have a conscience, but apparently not.

How to get blood from a turnip was the problem, Hannah thought as she at last turned into her driveway. How can you garnishee wages when the man claims he doesn't work? Adam lived with his parents, wore expensive clothes and zoomed around town in a new BMW. Where was the money coming from, and how could she get some of it for Dawn? Go after the grandparents, maybe? She doubted there was a precedent for that sort of action.

Climbing out of the car, Hannah almost fell back as a great gust of freezing wind slammed into her. Lips trembling, she grabbed her shoulder bag and briefcase, closed the VW's door and made her painstaking way up the back stairs to her apartment. Her cold fingers could barely get the key in the lock. Inside, she didn't know if she had the energy to undress.

This was a bad time to get sick, Hannah thought with a moan she couldn't suppress. She had so much work to do, so many people counting on her. Tomorrow, she had to meet with Lisa Tompkins's rape counselor, then file a contempt charge against Adam Carruthers so she could get him back into court and show cause why he hadn't been paying support. And she needed to stop in at Sanctuary for another referral Lee had called about.

She couldn't afford to let anyone else down. She'd taken an oath to defend these people, to help them. She couldn't get Jenna Nichols's stricken face from her mind. She couldn't let that happen to another client. She'd just have to get over this cold by morning. She simply had to.

Somehow, she managed to get herself into a long flannel nightgown she'd had for years. A comfort item, one she loved. She turned up the heat, took a cold capsule and removed her makeup while the water for tea boiled. She'd meant to buy some whiskey but hadn't gotten around to it. Honey and lemon would have to do.

Walking slowly, she carefully carried the steaming mug into her bedroom and placed it on the nightstand.

She turned back the covers, drank half of the tea and, still shivering, crawled under. She was asleep in seconds.

Joel sat at his office desk at four in the afternoon, his thoughts as restless as his hands as he doodled on a legal pad. He'd been working on his closing argument in the Fowler case for two hours and still wasn't satisfied. Something wasn't right. If only he could get a handle on what it was.

In a separate trial, the gardener, Toby Woods, would face his own jury. But who had hired him? Amanda, as he'd claimed, or someone else? Amanda was a cool one, showing little emotion publicly over the length of the trial. He hadn't put her on the stand for that very reason. She came across as cold and calculating. But was she?

And where the hell was Hannah? Surprisingly, he would have liked to have talked over his case with her. He'd found during the past weeks that her views were more insightful than he'd originally suspected. Or did he just enjoy talking with her, being with her?

True, she was feisty as hell at times and stubborn enough to flare up his temper regularly. But she was also beautiful and caring, a woman with a loving heart. Like his mother, only far more independent. And, in his arms, though her lips would deny the attraction, Hannah responded almost instantly to his touch.

At first, he'd thought she might just be working from home or taking a few days off. Apparently not. It seemed that her cold had hit her harder than she'd admitted to him the other night at the Bread Basket. She'd checked in with Marcie but hadn't shown up at the office in two days. That didn't seem like Hannah, to let a mere cold keep her away from her work. Unless she was sicker than he thought and...

The ringing phone interrupted his thoughts. Absently, he picked it up.

"Hey, Joel, glad you're in." The deep voice of Tyler Brent, one of Joel's best investigators, came on, sounding rushed and excited. "Finally, I have something for you."

"Your timing's perfect," Joel told him. "What've you got?"

"The guy's on his way in to see you. Name's Harry Templeton. He used to work with Kent. And does he have a story to tell."

Joel sat up straighter. "Let's hear it." When Ty finished, Joel let out a low whistle. "Think he's legit?"

"You bet. I've checked him out. But don't take my word. See for yourself."

"Thanks, buddy." Joel hung up. He didn't really believe in eleventh-hour breaks. But maybe, this once...

Twenty minutes later, when Harry Templeton walked into his office, Joel remembered seeing him in the visitors' gallery in court. The man was in his late twenties with curly brown hair and a wispy mustache that drooped over his upper lip. He wore a turtleneck sweater over cords and a heavy denim jacket. After shaking his hand, Joel asked him to have a seat and waited.

"I wasn't gonna come in," Harry began. "I don't need any hassle from cops, you know. But I been following the case, listening every day in the back row, and I think the wrong person's gonna get put away." Harry shifted in his chair, stroking his mustache in what was probably a habitual gesture. "I'm no saint, but I can't let that happen. When that fellow Tyler came into the store asking questions again today, I took him aside, told him I got something might interest you."

"I appreciate your coming to me. Tell me what you know."

Harry crossed his legs. "First, I want to know if the cops are gonna want to question me over this. Tyler didn't say."

"That depends on what you know. Are you in trouble with the police?"

"Nah. I had a little juvie record years ago. Nothing since, 'cept maybe a couple of parking tickets. I'm just not real fond of John Q. Law, you know."

"I understand. If what you say is pertinent to the case, most likely the prosecutor would want to hear it directly from you. Unless you're directly involved in something illegal, the police probably won't bother you." He watched the nervous fellow digest that, then decided to nudge him along. "What's your connection to the Fowlers?"

"I work at the Bay Village store. Kent used to work with me, and we got to be friends. We took a couple of fishing trips together and one jaunt to Vegas. He really likes to gamble."

"So I gather. Do you?"

"I can take it or leave it alone. Not Kent. He'd bet on what time the sun comes up tomorrow. His favorite's the track. His dream is to own a racehorse."

"That takes quite a bit of money."

"Yeah, sure does. But that's his plan. Soon as his old man's estate's settled and he gets his share." Harry looked over his shoulder to make sure the office door was closed and then leaned forward, lowering his voice.

"He kind of made sure he'd be coming into money, you know."

Joel felt an adrenaline rush, then tamped it down. Tyler had never sent him false leads before, but it would be wise to be cautious. "And how did he do that?"

"He took every dime he could scrape together and hired that gardener to knock off his old man and frame the wife. He purely hates Amanda Fowler. Toby's not real bright, you know. His IQ's real low. Kent poured a couple of drinks into him and got the poor stiff to agree. Damn shame."

"And how do you know all this?"

Suddenly looking confident, Harry leaned back. "'Cause he told me the whole story. He's a guy who likes to brag, you know. About the places he's been, how much his old man's worth. He even asked me if I wanted a piece of his horse, so I could make money, too. I told him I didn't make enough to invest like that."

Joel reached for a yellow pad and picked up his pen. He checked his watch. Ten to five. He'd have to call the prosecutor tonight, make an appointment for early morning. If Harry's information checked out, they'd have to inform the judge and request a recess until they could work this out. "When did this conversation take place and where?"

As Harry told his story, Joel began to write.

Sprawled in the chair across the desk from Will, Joel grinned at his partner. "I wish you'd have been there. Everything went the way it's supposed to and rarely does. Harry didn't waver on the stand, and then I recalled Kent. I got in about two questions, and he fell apart. It was beautiful."

Will puffed on his pipe, as pleased for Joel as if it had been his own case. "So you got the lovely widow off, just like she knew you would. Correction. The *rich* lovely widow. She may want to show her gratitude in more ways than merely paying her fee."

Joel quickly shook his head. "Nope, not my type. I have to admit I wasn't a hundred percent sure I believed her story right up until Harry came into my office. Amanda told me something surprising afterward. She really loved Blake Fowler. He was the father figure she'd never had, a man who was kind and generous to her."

"And does she stand to inherit all his millions?"

"He didn't leave Kent and Peter out of his will entirely. But Kent will need every cent for his own defense trial. Goes to show you, you never know how these things will play out." The adrenaline was still pumping throughout his system.

And the one person he wanted to share his victory with still wasn't back.

"Have you talked with Hannah? She can't still be out with a silly cold."

Will adjusted his rimless glasses. It was a question he'd been expecting. Marcie had mentioned that Joel had been inquiring about Hannah daily. "I spoke with her this morning. She sounded terrible. Said it's moved into her chest. I suspected this might happen. She let herself get run-down."

"She has to be pretty sick to stay away from her desk this long." Coming to a quick decision, he got to his feet. "I think I'll go see her, maybe take her some chicken soup. From the deli, of course."

Setting down his pipe, Will shook his head. "I wouldn't if I were you. She's a very private lady. She won't thank you for dropping in when she's not up to par.''

At the doorway, Joel swung back. "Then again, I might be just what the doctor ordered to cheer her on to recovery." He shot Will another grin. "I'll let you know."

Listening to his partner grab his coat and rush off, Will sat back in his creaky chair and smiled. So Joel was going off to offer tea and sympathy, and chicken soup. Interesting. Will wished he could be a little bird on Hannah's windowsill when Joel arrived.

She was having a hazy dream, one where her feet were dragging through thick snow and a winter wind whipped at her face and blew her hair all about. Step after grueling step, she struggled on, her teeth chattering and her limbs aching with the cold. And somewhere in the distance, there was a pounding sound that wouldn't quit. Her head thrashing on the pillow, Hannah moaned aloud.

She awoke with a start when a voice called out her name. Had she been imagining the sound? With shaky hands, she shoved off the heavy covers, suddenly hot all over. This going from freezing cold to burning up was wearing her out. And the damn pounding was back.

Blinking in the dim bedroom, she tried to sit up so she could see the nightstand clock. Three o'clock. Through the slanted blinds on the window, she saw light creeping in. It had to be daytime, though which day, she couldn't be sure. It seemed to Hannah as if she'd been in bed fighting this cold for weeks. Then she heard her name called again, a male voice.

Oh, Lord, did she have the energy to go to the door? She made an effort, finally sitting up. Her gown was damp, though she remembered changing it a while back. From the foot of the bed, she picked up her chenille robe and struggled into it, nearly falling back onto the bed twice.

The pounding grew louder, the voice more insistent. Not Will's voice, she decided as she shoved her feet into her slippers. Suddenly, she knew exactly who her uninvited visitor was. No one else would be so loud, so persistent.

With shuffling footsteps, she made her way to the door, shoving her hair back with fingers that shook. "All right," she called out, wondering if her weak voice could be heard through the thick wooden door. "I'm coming."

The pounding stopped, thank goodness. Hannah opened the door, leaving the chain on, and peeked out.

Sure enough, Joel Merrick in all his handsome glory stood on her landing, a scowl on his face. Just what she needed.

Joel's frown deepened. Her face was so pale, her eyes dark and bruised looking. "You look like hell," he told her.

"Thank you. So nice of you to come and tell me that."

"What are you doing in there?" he asked, trying to figure out what was wrong with her.

"Hosting a dinner party for twenty of my closest friends. You're not invited. Go away." She made as if to shut the door, but it rammed into his big-booted foot. She raised impatient eyes to his. "I'm not up to fencing with you, Joel."

"You're sick. Open the door."

"I like to be alone when I'm sick. Go away." She shoved the door against his foot, but found it solidly planted.

"I'm not leaving. Open the door. I want to take your temperature and check you out. If you don't let me in, I'll break the door down."

He probably would, too. Hannah felt what little strength she had left drain out of her. Without another word, she nodded. She waited until he moved his foot, then shut the door, slid back the chain and opened it again.

He came bustling in, bringing in a rush of cold air, causing her to shiver all over. Slowly, she made her way to the kitchen, thinking another cup of tea might taste good. She'd had several over the past hours—or was it days?—but never managed to finish one. At the counter, she paused, steadying herself. She couldn't pass out in front of this man. Hadn't she already shown him enough of her weaknesses?

Joel flung his coat onto a chair and followed her. "Have you eaten lately?" he asked, gentling his voice. Even so, she flinched as he touched her arm.

"I'm not hungry. Some tea, maybe."

He found the teakettle, filled it, turned the burner on. Then swung back to study her. Dark shadows under her eyes, eyes that looked a little glazed, flushed face, damp brow. Reaching over, he touched the backs of his fingers to her forehead. "You're burning up. Have you got a thermometer?"

Did she? She thought so. But where? "Maybe in the bathroom medicine chest."

Hannah hobbled to a kitchen chair and sat down, propping her head in her hands. Wouldn't it have to be the one man she'd found attractive in years who'd come to see her looking her absolute worst? At her best, she wasn't a beauty, but now! She had to look a sight. And felt even worse.

He returned with the thermometer and shook it down. "Open up." He waited until she did, then popped it in her mouth. The kettle was whistling, so he moved to the counter to make her tea. When he took it over, he saw that her eyes were closed, her head leaning heavily on her hand.

He removed the thermometer, and his eyes widened. "A hundred and four. You've got more than a simple cold here, lady."

Hannah rolled her aching shoulders. "I get a bad cold once a season. Then it goes away, and I'm fine the rest of the year."

"I come from a big family. I watched my mom take care of all four of us. You don't spike that high a fever with just a cold." He looked around, spotted the wall phone and went to it.

Her head was throbbing again. Where'd she leave the aspirin? Through squinting eyes, she looked over at him. He was dialing her phone. "Who are you calling?"

"Information." Joel removed a pen and notepad from his jacket pocket, spoke into the phone, then jotted down the number they gave him. He quickly dialed the new number.

He was doing it, taking over. Hadn't she told him repeatedly that she didn't want someone taking over her life? He was talking with someone now, arranging heaven only knew what all.

Hannah placed her hands on the table and pushed herself upright. The room spun around. She held on, closing her eyes, until finally it stopped. With determination, she walked over to him as he was hanging up. "Who'd you call?"

Joel wanted to pick her up and carry her to her bed. She shouldn't be up. But he knew she'd fight him. "My cousin, my uncle's son, Terry. Dr. Terrence Merrick, actually. Another family rebel. Turned his back on the law and went into medicine. He has a practice not far from here. I caught him just as he was leaving. He's coming over to take a look at you."

Hannah was trembling all over, from fever, from her impotent anger. "Who asked you to come here? Who gave you the right to call a doctor for me? I'm a grown woman. I can take care of myself."

"Hannah," Joel said, swallowing his temper, knowing it would only make things worse, "everyone needs help sometimes. Are you trying to kill yourself? You have an infection probably. Or worse. You could go into convulsions with such a high fever, here all alone. Let me help you, please." He reached out and touched her arm, steadying her.

"I don't need help." A sudden coughing spell shook her, but she brushed off his hand. "How do you think I've survived all these years? Alone mostly, that's how. And I...I will again. I..."

Suddenly, the room began spinning, weaving, dark swirls in front of her eyes. She shut them tightly, her hands reaching out to grab him, grab something. If he hadn't caught her, she'd have slid to the floor.

Gathering her into his arms, Joel shook his head. "All right, Wonder Woman. You can let go now."

"It's probably a combination of things, really," Terry told Joel. "As you mentioned, not enough rest, meals on the run, working too hard. Along comes a virus she could easily fight off under ordinary circumstances when she's in top shape. But not when she's run-down." Straightening from the couch where Hannah lay, he reached into his medical bag. "Make sure she takes one of these every four hours. Aspirin, too, for the fever until it's normal. If it climbs, she'll need a sponge bath." Terry grinned at Joel. "How well do you know her?"

Joel shrugged. "A man has to do what he has to do." He smiled and shook his head. "There's no way she'd let me give her a bath if she's aware of what's going on. I'll call someone."

"She'll be in and out of it for a while. That shot's pretty powerful, and I'd guess she hasn't eaten in days. Get some liquids into her, all she'll tolerate. Twenty-four hours should make a big difference." He snapped his bag shut.

Joel clapped him on the shoulder. "I can't thank you enough for coming over. She's so damn stubborn."

"She's got a nasty bug, all right. Could have turned into viral pneumonia. A chest X ray might be in order when she feels better. Some things a body can't fight without help."

"*Help* is a four-letter word to Hannah." He walked to the door with Terry. "Send me your bill."

Terry gave him an admonishing look. "Hey, don't insult me. Just be careful you don't catch the bug yourself. There's quite a bit going around."

"I'm healthy as a horse." He opened the door. "You and Gretchen going to Hyannis for Thanksgiving?"

"Yeah, probably. You?"

"Oh, yeah. Command performance, you know. Otherwise, Mom won't speak to me until Easter. I'd really like to go to Montana, but I probably won't be able to until after the holidays. Have you talked with your dad lately?''

''Last week. He's the same as ever. He wants us to visit, but I can't make it right now, either. Probably not until spring. If you go, it'll appease him until then.''

''Glad to help out. Thanks again, Terry.'' He watched his cousin leave, then closed and locked the door.

Back in Hannah's living room, he saw that she was sleeping soundly. He found her room and snapped on the light. There was a big brass bed, a chest of drawers that looked like an antique, a cheval mirror and a bentwood rocker. The impression was tasteful coziness, as with her office. On the wall, another watercolor by the same artist, this one in blues with touches of ivory. Soothing.

As he'd guessed, the bedclothes were damp and mussed from her previous wrestling bout. Joel removed his tie and jacket, and went to work.

Hannah had no idea of time passing, only of little snippets of wakefulness. She opened her eyes once to find herself in her own bed with clean, sweet-smelling sheets and her comforter covering her. The room was in semidarkness, and someone she couldn't quite make out was in a chair by the foot of her bed. She was too tired, her brain too foggy to figure out who. Before she tumbled back into sleep, the person made her swallow some pills and drink some ginger ale. Then she slipped back into oblivion.

She drifted, dreamless, floating. The cough would wake her now and then, but her chest didn't hurt as badly as before. And the headache was thankfully gone. Yet this lethargy, this heaviness of limbs where raising a hand to smooth back her hair was a monumental effort, was so annoying. She'd never felt like this before. She closed her eyes, not wanting to think.

Each time she awoke, the shadowy person was in the chair. Once, she thought there were two of them, whispering together. Sometimes, they didn't move. Other times, they forced liquid down her until she had to turn her head aside. She thought she felt a cool cloth on her head once, but when she opened her eyes again, it wasn't there. Time drifted and so did she.

Hannah's eyes opened slowly, and she blinked against the glare. Finally, she managed to look around and saw that her window blinds were slanted to let in a weak winter sun. Then her gaze shifted to the foot of her bed. Slumped on her bentwood rocker was Joel Merrick, his unshaved chin resting on his chest as he slept.

How long had he been there? She remembered vaguely arguing with him in the kitchen about some phone call he'd made, then the blackness had claimed her. Gingerly, testing for a lingering headache, she angled to look at the bedside clock. Ten after four in the afternoon, since there was daylight. Had to be the day after she'd apparently passed out. Had he been here all that time?

Her bedclothes were clean and dry. Moving slowly, she turned back the coverlet and saw that she was wearing her long, pale blue nightshirt. Her eyes widened. Who had helped her out of her gown and into this? Heat moved into her face. Oh, no.

She would worry about that later. She must have been a lot sicker than she'd realized. She'd lost a whole day and night where she couldn't remember things. Joel had come, insisting that she let him help her. She'd resisted but, weak as she'd been, she'd had to accept. There were times, Hannah supposed, when illness forced a person to accept assistance, much as she hated to admit it. Fortunately, she rarely became that ill.

Her mouth was so dry. On the nightstand was a decanter of ice water, a glass and a pill bottle. Carefully, she swung her legs over the side of the bed. The room swayed a bit, then straightened. Thank goodness. She picked up the decanter and poured water into the glass.

He heard the sound of ice clinking in a glass and woke with a start. "You're awake," Joel said, rising. "Here, let me do that."

"It's all right. I've got it." She set down the pitcher shakily. Lord, but she was weak. She drank thirstily, then turned to him. "I believe I owe you many thanks."

Joel drew his hand across his face, brushing away the remnants of sleep. "You don't owe me anything. How do you feel?"

"Like I wrestled a tiger and he won." She saw him smile. "Was I really terrible?"

He sat down beside her as she put aside the glass. "Yeah, you were. You're the stubbornest female I've ever met. You won't let anyone help you unless you pass out."

"Are you sure you didn't knock me out?"

"A virus knocked you out. Terry said if you'd have gone without treatment much longer, you'd have had to be hospitalized." Her color was much better, though she was still pale. But her eyes were clear, and her hands shook only a little. She'd given him one hell of a scare.

Hannah frowned, trying to recall. "Terry. Who's Terry?"

"My cousin. A doctor. I called him and he gave you a shot, then some pills. Told me to keep stuffing them in you along with lots of fluids. Do you remember any of it?"

She wrinkled up her forehead, trying. "Only snatches." She glanced down at her nightshirt. "Did you...? I mean, I wasn't wearing this, I know, and..."

He smiled. She had to be better if she was worried about modesty. "No, not me. I called Marcie and she came over. She gave you a sponge bath and changed your gown. She also brought over a pot of chicken soup and gave me strict orders to give you some as soon as you felt up to it. Are you hungry?"

She felt better knowing Marcie had been the one, not Joel. As if on cue, her stomach gurgled. "I guess I could eat a little."

"Great. Let me prop you up and I'll go heat some soup."

"I'd like to go into the bathroom first." She touched her tousled hair. "I must look terrible."

"Honey, you look wonderful compared to the day I found you."

"What day was that?"

"Yesterday, early afternoon. You've been sleeping on and off over twenty hours." He held out his hands. "I'll walk you to the bathroom in case your legs are wobbly."

His grip was solid, his arm slipping around her waist so strong. Her knees nearly gave way once, but she managed.

"Don't lock the door in case you pass out, okay?" Joel asked, still worried.

She sent him a tolerant look. "I'll be fine, honestly." He was worse than a mother hen. Hannah closed the bathroom door.

He watched her eat, making her self-conscious. At least she'd brushed her teeth and hair, rinsed her face.

She never wore much makeup, but she could sure use some today. The cool water helped bring back a little color. She'd just settled herself against the pillows propped at the headboard when he'd returned with a tray. Apparently, he had no qualms about searching through her cupboards until he found what he needed.

She finished the whole bowl, then leaned back, her energy drained from the small effort. "That was so good. I'll have to tell Marcie, call to thank her for everything."

Joel removed the tray, took it away and brought her a tall glass of orange juice. "Doctor says you need liquids."

"In a minute." She'd get her second wind in a minute, Hannah thought, closing her eyes. "I can't believe how weak I still feel. A virus, you say?"

"Actually, it could have worked into viral pneumonia if neglected," he said, sitting alongside her on the bed. "You're not real good at taking care of yourself, are you?"

Hannah raised her head. "Usually, I am. It's just that I had so much to do and..." Suddenly, her clients came swimming back into her mind. "Did Marcie call about...?"

"Yes, she took care of everyone. Will notified Lee at Sanctuary and filed the contempt charge on that deadbeat dad. Everything else can wait until you're a hundred percent better."

"Everyone's been so nice. I..." Tears pressed against the backs of her eyes. Oh, God, would she further humiliate herself and end up weeping? She pressed her lips together, struggling for control.

Joel took her hands into his, caressing the soft skin with his thumbs. "You scared me, Red. You honest-to-God scared me."

"I'm sorry." She blinked up at him. His hair was mussed, and he needed a shave. His clothes were rumpled and his wonderful blue eyes worried. No man had ever looked so good to her. "Thank you, for all of it."

He squeezed her hands. He knew how hard it was for Hannah Richards to accept help, to thank people for help she hadn't asked for. "You'd have done it for me. Hell, you help your clients above and beyond every day. You don't need to be Wonder Woman to prove anything to me. I think you're pretty terrific just as you are."

She couldn't let herself believe him. He was only saying that because he was kind and a good person. He'd have tried to help a transient on the street. She mustn't make too much of his words, considering he'd had very little sleep lately. However, she couldn't not say anything. "I happen to think you're pretty terrific, too."

She couldn't know how much her eyes said that her lips refused to acknowledge. She was grateful, he knew. But there was more there. Something more that she was fighting with all her being. "I need to know something, Hannah. Why is accepting help so difficult for you?"

Her defenses were down. Perhaps, if she explained, he'd understand and not push this subject with her again. "I was orphaned at a pretty early age. I went from one foster home to another. I was never mistreated, but love and affection weren't part of the picture, either. The last one was better than the rest. I learned that the only person I could truly rely on was myself. If someone does something for you, they want something in return. Always. So I stopped accepting help. That way, I don't owe anyone. Can you understand that?"

More than she knew. "Yes. Thanks for telling me. Now let me tell you something. I don't want anything in return for helping you through this. Nor do Will or Marcie. It may take you a while to believe that, but it's true." He leaned closer so he could see right into her eyes. "What I want from you, Hannah, has nothing to do with gratitude or repayment of favors."

A frisson of apprehension raced up her spine. "What *do* you want from me?"

He smiled at her. "Friendship, for now."

Hannah thought that over. "For now. What about later?"

"Let's worry about later later." He got up and shook out a pill from the small bottle, then handed it to her with the juice. After she'd finished, he slipped off his shoes.

Hannah looked up in surprise. "What are you doing?"

"Getting ready to rest. You're getting tired, and I haven't slept much, either. Do you need anything else?"

She'd figured he'd leave now that she was on the mend. But apparently, he was going to sleep on the couch. She could hardly fault him after all he'd done. "No, nothing, thanks. I am a little sleepy." She sat up, poking at the pillows mounded behind her.

"Scoot down and I'll fix 'em," Joel said. When she did, he arranged the pillows more comfortably, then walked around the bed and lay down beside her, his back propped against the headboard.

Hannah's mouth flew open. "What are you doing?"

"I told you. I need to rest and so do you. Come over here and snuggle up against me. I'll hold you and you'll sleep better."

She couldn't keep the shock from her voice. "I don't think so."

"Yes, you will. Now, stop fighting me on every little thing." He shifted until he was quite comfortable, then scooted her until she was stretched out with her head resting on his chest, his arms loosely around her. "There. Now, go to sleep."

She could feel his heartbeat beneath her ear. Her own was hammering away. How could she sleep wrapped this way in his arms? She hadn't been with a man in...good Lord!...in years. Joel was too attractive, too masculine, for her body to ignore the male-female thing. She might be sick, even feverish, but she wasn't made of stone.

Hannah squirmed about, trying valiantly to do as he requested. After all, he'd been so good to her. She'd wait it out a little longer, then she'd sit up and tell him this wasn't working and he'd have to leave. She needed rest, not stimulation.

Hannah settled her hand on his solid chest. His heartbeat had slowed, his breathing evening out. She sighed and closed her eyes. She had to admit it felt good to be held. He was so big, such a comfort. She felt protected, as if no harm could come to her with his arms around her. Wasn't that ludicrous?

She was getting drowsy. The medication, probably. Another couple of minutes and she'd rouse him. After all, this was ridiculous. They were co-workers, not lovers. And she'd been sick. She might be contagious. He shouldn't be here, so close to her, where she could feel his breath softly ruffling her hair. She should tell him to go, to...

Hannah slept.

Holding her, Joel sighed. He hadn't felt so relaxed, so comfortable, in ages. He closed his eyes.

Chapter Six

Hannah stood in front of her bathroom mirror brushing out her hair. It had gotten quite long. She really should get it cut. Or did it just appear longer because she'd taken to wearing it down more these days? It was less bother, she told herself. A French twist took time. The way she chose to wear her hair had nothing whatsoever to do with Joel Merrick. Absolutely nothing.

The Merricks. She was about to meet them all for Thanksgiving dinner at the family home in Hyannisport. How had she ever agreed to such a thing?

Ever since her bout with the virus and all Joel had done for her, she found it difficult to turn down his smallest request. It was an odd turn of events, something she'd never encountered before. Even though he'd said she didn't, she felt she owed him. And he'd been so boyish asking her, saying how much it would mean to him.

Since when had that become important to her? she wondered.

Oh, he'd made it sound like such a fun day. His mother would be cooking a traditional turkey dinner, and his father would do the carving. His two brothers and one sister, their spouses and children would all be there, as well as the doctor who'd attended to her, Terry Merrick, the one she couldn't recall meeting, and his family. And Will, of course. An all-around fun day.

She was scared to death.

They were to drive there in his Mercedes. A quick check of her watch told her he'd be by to pick her up in twenty minutes. Even the weather was cooperating, with plenty of snow still on the ground, but the skies were fair and the temperature was in the midthirties. Great weather for snowmobiling. She'd never even seen a snowmobile up close.

Hannah drew in a shaky breath. It seemed she was stepping out of her comfort zone in a lot of ways for Joel. And all because of that sneaky virus.

She'd awakened in his arms late that evening, a first for Hannah. He'd slept on as she'd eased out of his embrace to study him. Such a nice face, that stubborn chin, those ridiculously long lashes. That black hair falling forward, begging her fingers to touch the dark curls. She'd had to struggle not to, knowing it would wake him. And then what would she say, caught with her hands caressing him?

He must have felt her examining him, for he'd awakened and just lay there, giving her that killer smile. "Didn't I tell you you'd sleep better with me?" he'd asked. She couldn't have denied that one. And then he'd said some things that had had her thinking ever since.

"Do you know why I wanted to sleep with you like this, Hannah?" he'd asked. "Besides the obvious reason that I like holding you, of course. Because I wanted you to know you can trust me. I've noticed that in most of your legal cases, you represent clients who've been abused in one way or another by men. A daily dose of that and you're bound to be affected. Maybe you have something in your own background, as well, that has caused you to mistrust men. I wanted to show you that not all men are like that. Certainly not this man. You can trust me. I wouldn't hurt you."

He'd given her a lot to mull over, Hannah thought as she stepped into her forest green slacks. Trust was an issue that was near and dear to Hannah's heart. Or the lack thereof.

Slipping on her matching cowl-neck sweater, she had to admit that if there was a man she would consider trusting—other than Will—it would definitely be Joel. He'd fed her again that evening, then left her with a gentle kiss on her forehead. She'd gone back to the office for a few hours the next day and found that he'd run interference for her with a couple of clients, handled several calls and placated a few impatient people rather than disturb her.

That had been a week ago, and the only way she'd figured out how to thank him was by accepting his Thanksgiving invitation. Shaking out her hair, she ran a brush through it, then stepped back to check her mirror image. Joel had said to dress casually and warmly, as they'd probably wind up outdoors with some activity or another. The Merrick compound apparently had a great deal of adjacent snow-covered property ideal for winter sports. Fortunately, she felt well enough to eagerly look forward to being outdoors again.

In the bathroom, she was reaching for her mascara when she remembered that enhancing her appearance to attract a man was the last thing she usually did. Still, after being ill, she needed a little help or she'd resemble a just-released prisoner of war. Ignoring the small voice of reason, she did her eyes, then picked up her blush. Just a little, she told herself.

She'd just finished zipping up her boots when she heard the knock on her door. She opened it to find Joel standing there holding a single long-stemmed red rose.

"The last rose of summer," he said, walking in.

"Sure it is." She took it nonetheless, burying her nose in its lovely fragrance. "Thank you."

What a difference a week made. She was still a little thinner, but beautiful as ever. He took her hand, tugged her close to him. "Green is really your color." Inhaling her fragrance, he smiled down at her. "And you smell better than freshly brewed coffee."

Hannah laughed. "I guess that's a compliment."

"You bet it is." He cocked his head. "Tell me, are you one of those women afraid to kiss a man because it might ruin your makeup?"

That was a new one. If she said yes, he'd probably hand her a tissue. "No, should I be?"

"Either way, I'm going to kiss you." He'd wanted to for weeks now, but he'd given her room to recover, to let the need for him build inside her. Now, he could see it in her eyes, could read it in the tiny trembling of her full lips.

Reversing their positions, he shifted her until her back was to the door before covering her mouth with his. She could taste determination in this kiss, as if he wanted to set the tone before they set out. Wanted to stamp his indelible imprint on her. She would have fought against him if he'd used the slightest bit of force. Instead, he was gentle, and Hannah found herself surrendering to that simple need that so thoroughly matched her own.

Desire. It swam to the surface, making him edgy, making him reckless. He hadn't intended to devour, but found he had to. Had to. If he would have but this one kiss before leaving, he would make it one she would remember. One she would think back and recall at odd moments each time she looked at him. He drew her closer, then closer still, and heard the soft sound she made deep in her throat.

Passion. She was awash in it, lost in him. Her body throbbed with it, ached with need, clamored for more. This was what she feared when she thought of getting too close to him, this delirium he could take her to so readily, this mindless leap into passion. One touch, one taste, and he ignited feelings in her she'd been running from for most of her adult life.

Hunger. She awoke in him such a hunger that Joel wondered if it would ever be satisfied. Unable to be content with half a loaf, he ran his hands over the soft wool covering her arms, then slipped around back, his fingers tunneling beneath and touching soft flesh. There, he caressed and stroked, feeling her skin grow warmer as his mouth continued to make love to hers.

Her arms went around him as if they'd kissed like this many times before. Caught in the whirlpool, Hannah strained against him, sanity rapidly slipping from her foggy mind. She hadn't really known, hadn't truly believed, she could feel this much, want this badly.

Before she lost all reason, she stepped back from him, breaking the kiss. She blinked, staring at him, struggling with an incredible yearning to be one with him. His hands trailed down her arms, and she felt her pulse scramble as his fingers curled around her wrists. Breathing hard, Hannah fought to understand the feelings that awakened such a need.

Even a little distance from him plunged her back into a reality she hated to face. She couldn't, wouldn't, give in to the wanting. She'd been down this road before, and it was filled with potholes. Joel might be a better man than any she'd known. But he was still a man and could hurt her badly without intending to.

With a shudder, she turned aside and straightened her sweater. ''I guess maybe you did rearrange my makeup a bit,'' she said, needing to make light of it. She walked to the hall mirror to make some hasty repairs.

She'd rearranged a few things, too, Joel thought, turning aside and drawing in a deep breath. Like his plans, his dreams. He'd never met anyone who had such complete power over him, who could bring him to his knees with one touch from her small hand, one taste of her lips.

Crazy. It was crazy. He'd never been one to fall apart over a woman. He liked them, sure. In his bed, in his company, in his life. But this one had him tangled in knots. He hoped to hell he could keep her from finding out.

Clearing his throat, he adjusted the knot of his tie. Mom liked everyone to dress for holiday dinners. He zipped up his leather jacket and turned to Hannah. ''Ready to go?''

She bent to pick up the forgotten rose she'd dropped. She didn't know if she was ready, but go they would. With a shaky smile, she walked through the door he held open.

* * *

Hannah stood leaning against a fence surrounding the Merrick compound's adjacent acreage, up to her ankles in snow, the sun shining on her coppery hair. The compound comprised his parents' home and several others along the shoreline belonging to the younger Merricks. Lord, but it was intimidating.

The main house was of white clapboard with a wraparound porch that seemed to go on forever. It was three stories high with gables and wings and add-on garages and covered walkways. A sloping lawn, green in summer and cloaked in white now, led to the sea, which looked gray and forbidding on this day, with mammoth chunks of ice visible for what seemed like miles out.

And the Merricks. There was white-haired Jason, the patriarch, puffing on a pipe along with Will on the heated, glassed-in porch, setting up a chess game yet taking the time to greet her. And Lois, looking too young to have given birth to such a brood, her face red cheeked from the oven, stopping nevertheless to give her a big hug. Hannah thought that Joel resembled his father most, yet exuded his mother's warm personality.

Then there were the brothers, Todd and Sam, and their wives, whose names she likely wouldn't remember, and their collective children, two boys for Todd and a daughter belonging to Sam. Or was it the other way around? Regan, his sister, was easy to pick out of the crowd. She looked about ten months' pregnant, and her husband, Roger, hovered around her as if she might deliver momentarily—an event Hannah was certain the resilient Merricks would have taken in stride.

Maybe this is the way we'd have been, Hannah couldn't help thinking. If her parents had lived, if she hadn't been separated from Michael and Katie. Maybe then they'd all be gathering at the farm on holidays, together with their mates and maybe a child or two, cooking and laughing and just being together. She swallowed around a lump in her throat, swallowing down what never could be.

She watched a golden retriever scamper along the shoreline, enjoying the day. She found herself wishing she had a place with a yard so she could get a dog. A big sheepdog like Rex. Nostalgia. She was consumed by it today.

"Duck, Hannah!" one of the Merrick boys called out, and she did, dodging instinctively. Looking up, she saw Joel, who'd been helping build a fort in the snow, scooping up another handful, his grin wide. As she watched, he made his way toward her, carefully packing his snowball, mischief in his eyes.

"You wouldn't dare," Hannah said, stepping backward along the fence. "Not in front of your entire family."

"Oh, no?" He took aim.

She turned her back to him and waited. When nothing happened, she peeked over her shoulder. That's when she got a faceful of cold, fluffy snow.

"Oh, just you wait!" Sputtering, she rebounded, grabbing a handful, going on the attack.

Joel pretended panic, walking backward. But he misjudged the snow's depth and went down in a heap.

Hannah launched herself on him, rubbing snow on his face, ears, neck. "Say uncle. Say it now, or be prepared for more."

"Uncle, uncle!" Joel called out, then grabbed her upper arms and rolled her over onto her back until she was looking up at him, laughter in her dark eyes. "Now who's got the upper hand, my fair lady?"

"All right, you win. Not fairly, but you win."

"Not fair? Why not?"

"You outweigh me by a ton. Is that an even match?" Suddenly, a sneeze shook her.

Joel inched back. "I'd better take you in before you get sick again."

She tugged on his sleeve. "Ease up, Merrick. I'm fine."

He leaned on his propped elbows. "Then the very least I can do is warm you." Lowering his head, he kissed her.

There it was again, that instant rush, that familiar heat. Hannah let herself enjoy for a long moment, then pushed at him. "Hey, this is a little public here."

"Ashamed to be seen kissing me?" he asked.

She saw that he wore a smile, but his eyes were serious. "Of course not. I'm just not used to an audience."

He glanced over at his nephews, niece and brothers. "No one's looking," he told her.

Somehow, this seemed to matter to him. She wouldn't let him down. "Then, come here, big fella." And she opened to him, the kiss long and dreamy. When he lifted from her, his smile was genuine. Letting him help her up, Hannah wondered what all that was about.

"Ready to go in?" Joel asked. "Or do you want another ride on the snowmobile?"

He'd taken her when they'd first arrived, flying with the wind while she'd held on to him for dear life. It had been exhilarating, but once was enough. "No. I think I should offer to help your mother."

"Mom has plenty of help. Let's go sit by the fire." Joel took her hand and led her inside.

* * *

"What kind of law do you practice, Hannah?" Jason Merrick asked as he passed her a dish of golden yams.

Seated next to Joel, Hannah felt him tense at the question, and sensed a strained subject being introduced. She turned to Joel's father, seated on her right at the head of the table, and smiled. "Pretty much general practice at this point."

Jason helped himself to hot buttered peas. "I see. No specialty like criminal or divorce or personal injury? Or perhaps you've considered corporate law? We're always looking for bright young lawyers in our firm."

Hannah felt rather than saw Joel set down his fork. Since the man persisted, she wasn't about to lie. "I'm interested in women's rights, actually. Child support, battered wives, custody cases, that sort of thing."

"And she's very good at what she does," Will, seated across from Hannah, interjected.

Jason poured gravy lavishly on his turkey. "That's an interesting field, but it doesn't pay very well, does it?"

She was his guest; nonetheless, Hannah wasn't too happy with Mr. Merrick's line of questioning. "As I mentioned, I've only just arrived. Time will tell." She turned to his wife at the far end of the table. "Your dressing's wonderful, Mrs. Merrick. Everything is."

"Thank you, dear." Lois had apparently heard enough of her husband's conversation to send him a warning look, but he wouldn't look up to meet her eyes. Other conversations buzzed about the table, the children chattering, food being passed and exclaimed over.

Jason wasn't a man easily warned off or diverted. He shook his head as he thoughtfully chewed a bite of salad. "Young people today don't seem to know where they belong. They don't want to go along with the tried and true. Their elders have carved a path for them, taken out the kinks, so to speak. Smoothed the way. Yet some just turn their backs on all that and walk off. Doesn't always work out, would be my guess.''

Again, Will came to the defense, this time of Joel, who'd been the target of his father's ill-disguised remarks. "Now, Jason, we forged our own path. Young people have the right to do the same. And who's to say their way won't work just as well? Maybe better." He peered over the top of his glasses at Joel and winked.

"Maybe so," Jason agreed, to a point. "Experimenting to see where you fit in is fine. When you're young, fresh out of law school, testing the waters. But by the time you move into your thirties, you ought to settle down and find your niche."

Now she could see why Joel had left home in his teens, why he spoke with hesitancy about his father. Jason Merrick undoubtedly loved his youngest son, but he couldn't overcome the need to control him. For his own good, of course.

She could be still no longer. "Did you hear that Joel won a very difficult case recently? Amanda Fowler, who'd been accused of hiring the gardener to murder her husband. He uncovered the real killer and got a confession." Beaming, she turned to Joel. "We're all very proud of him, aren't we, Will?"

And Will was proud of Hannah. "Yes, we most certainly are. That case was as tough a one as I've seen."

Suddenly, Jason had nothing more to say, digging into his dinner, eyes downcast.

Not a gracious loser, Hannah thought as she sipped her wine.

* * *

"He's not a cruel man, ordinarily," Joel said in the quiet intimacy of the car as they drove back to Boston that evening. "He was a good father when I was young. The trouble is, he can't handle anyone who doesn't think like he does."

"None of your brothers or sister ever rebelled against his wishes for them?"

Hands loosely on the wheel, Joel shook his head. "Not really. Todd and Sam are in the family firm. Even Regan passed the bar but, before she could be sucked in, she got married. And probably got pregnant real quick so she could avoid Dad's long reach. You noticed, I'm sure, that they all live around Mom and Dad. It's been Dad's lifelong dream to have his kids all live nearby and work together in the firm. Trouble is, he never stopped to wonder if it was *our* dream."

"Amazing. You're all in law. You'd think that would be enough for him. And your mother? Does she ever take an opposite stand?" It had surprised Hannah that Lois Merrick hadn't stood up for her son. Was she afraid of Jason or just too well mannered to jump into the fray?

Joel sighed. "My mother's a wonderful woman, loving and kind. But she's never bucked my father on anything he says or does. That's just the way she was raised, I guess." Her quiet acceptance bothered Joel, but it didn't stop him from loving her.

Hannah was still thinking about Jason. "Why would your father care what type of law any of you practice?"

"Because he didn't choose it for us. Because if you don't want to work in *his* company, it's as if you're turning your back on *him*. That's why he barely stays in touch with Bart, his only brother. Because Bart quit the law early on and moved to Montana. Dad takes that as a personal rejection. He doesn't honestly think he's trying to control everyone, just doing what he genuinely feels is best for us."

"I hope you'll forgive me if I don't agree."

"Obviously, I don't, either, and it's caused a lot of friction between him and me."

That was why his father referred to Joel as his maverick son. Will had told her that. What he hadn't mentioned was the way Jason Merrick put down his own son in front of others.

Hannah continued, "Everyone's entitled to live his own life, make his own choices, as adults. I should think he'd be proud he raised four fine adults, each able to make their way in the world with a sound occupation and all living nearby. So many families are... are scattered to the wind. Some even lose touch." Hannah shifted her gaze out the side window into the dark night. The holiday, coupled with the wine, was causing her to be overly sentimental, she decided.

Hannah had told him she'd been orphaned at an early age, Joel remembered. He could scarcely imagine how that would feel. Despite his feelings of frustration with his own family, he cared about them. Still, when he married, he'd not make the mistakes he felt his parents had. At least, he hoped he wouldn't. "When I have children, I'm going to do things a lot differently. How about you?"

Eyes averted, Hannah blinked. "I don't intend to have children, so it's a moot point."

That surprised him, coming from a woman as caring as Hannah. "Oh, I think someone might come along and persuade you otherwise." He reached across the console and took her hand in his. "You're too beautiful to wind up alone."

Flattery again. Why did he do that? She wasn't beautiful. She was the smart one, and Katie had been the pretty one. People had always said so. "I do all right alone." Yet already, his fingers laced with hers were making her pulse race. Oh, Lord, now that she'd had a taste of being in his arms, how was she going to be able to fight those feelings?

Joel downshifted to pass a lumbering station wagon, then signaled before exiting up the off ramp. But his mind was on the mostly pleasant day they'd shared. And on one particular incident that would belie her odd statement about not wanting children. "I noticed you and Mandy with your heads together in the library."

"Yes. She's very bright, you know." And reminded Hannah of the girl she'd once been. Mandy was nine, his brother Sam's daughter. She was a sweet girl, almost painfully shy. Hannah thought that one day she'd be a beauty, but for now, she was all long legs and would soon need braces for a bad overbite, which made her even more self-conscious.

"Don't tell me she showed you her journal?"

She turned to him. "How did you know?"

"Just a guess. She's shown it to very few, actually. She must have really taken to you."

"I could relate to her. I used to keep a journal when I was her age." And she still had them, one for every year from eight through twelve. The children of the foster family where she'd been living at the time had made fun of her because she was always scribbling in her notebooks. She'd stopped then, not wanting to give them more reasons to criticize her.

Hannah had quickly learned, even at an early age, that the best way to get along was to not make waves, to do what was asked of her unquestioningly and not draw attention to herself. That philosophy had effectively subdued her personality during those difficult years.

Joel turned onto her street. "And what did you write in your journal? About all the boys who wanted to kiss you?"

She had to smile at him. Men sure had a different way of looking at things. "A girl of nine or ten, at least back when I was that age, and I'd guess the same applies to Mandy, isn't thinking about kissing boys. That's a guy thing."

He had to agree. "If I'd have kept a journal, I'd have had it full of the names of girls I wanted to kiss."

"And I imagine you kissed them all in time."

"My fair share." He swung into her driveway, coasting all the way to the back stairs, and stopped the car. "However, Miss Richards, my conquests have been greatly exaggerated." He angled toward her, suddenly serious. "Do you believe me?"

The moon reflecting on the snow allowed her to see his features quite well. Did she? Maybe a little. "I'm not sure. Joel, you have everything, always have had. Good looks, charm by the barrelful, a great family that also happens to be wealthy, an exciting occupation. What girl could resist you, then or now?"

He reached over to place his hand on her shoulder. "You resist me. Why?"

"*I* resist you? Who was that kissing you right up those stairs before we left? And in the snow in front of half your family?"

"All right, so you kiss me occasionally. But inside, you resist me, or at least you want to resist me. I can tell. Why?"

Hannah brushed back her hair. There was no point in denying the obvious. "It's a long story, one we don't have time to go into right now."

Joel checked his watch. "It's only nine. We have lots of time."

"It's been a long day. I really need to get some rest." She gripped the door handle. "Thank you for a wonderful day."

He shifted closer, his hand tightening on her, inwardly cursing the damn console. "Why can't we talk about this? I think you know by now that I want you, Hannah."

She let out a shaky breath. This was about the last thing she wanted to go into right now. "Now, you do. For a while. But I'm not looking for a quick fling."

"It wouldn't be quick," he said, his lips twitching.

"Cute. But I'm not joking. You want me perhaps, for a short time. But later, you'd find reasons to leave. Everyone moves on."

"I'm not like that, Hannah. I've tried to tell you that."

"*Everyone's* like that, Joel. I can't go through that." Her voice was beginning to tremble, as were her hands. Why couldn't he have just let it go?

He was quiet a long moment, studying the stubborn set of her chin, the troubled eyes. "He must have hurt you badly," he finally said, taking a guess.

Hannah looked down at her hands, now nervously grasped together in her lap. "Yes, he did. And I'm never, *ever* going to let another man hurt me like that again." She had to get out of there, to be alone. Hurriedly, she opened the door and rushed up her back stairs.

He wasn't going to let her go like that. Joel went after her, his long strides reaching the top landing even as she did. "Wait a minute." As she fumbled for her keys, he pried them from her hand, opened her door and followed her inside. "We're not going to leave it like this."

Hannah tossed her shoulder bag on the nearest chair, then yanked off her leather jacket. She was too warm, too upset, to think clearly. "Please, Joel, I don't want to talk any more tonight."

"Fine, then let's not talk." He pulled her to him roughly and took her mouth, her stubbornness fueling his anger. Why was she comparing him to another man, one who'd obviously hurt her? Why wouldn't she listen to him, believe that he wasn't the run-around she thought he was? Why wouldn't she give them a chance?

His arms crushed her to him, and for the first time in recent memory, he chose physical persuasion over a verbal jousting. She wouldn't pay attention to his words. Maybe she'd respond to this.

He knew he was being unreasonable and he didn't care. He only knew he had to make her see. That they were good together. That they were explosive together. Already, her taste had him drowning in her special flavors, his mind emptying of anger and filling with her. Only her. And he believed that she felt the same, though she denied it.

First surprise, then anger had Hannah rigid and unresponsive. Her first instinct had been to fight him, push him away. She knew enough about Joel to know he wouldn't force her. But she also knew enough about herself to realize she couldn't push him away, not after that first moment, that first heady taste.

He was behaving recklessly, and she gloried in it, craving his passion to make her forget all the unhappiness of the years before she'd met him that had surfaced unexpectedly on this holiday. She needed him to chase away the memories, the demons who lived inside her and wouldn't allow her to be like other women. She wanted him to make her feel like a desirable woman, not a ragtag child no one wanted, abandoned, alone and forgotten.

She needed to feel loved, if only for a moment. She wound her arms around him and let him take her deeper.

Joel felt the change in her, the gentling that was less surrender than acceptance. Her body entwined with his felt right, as if they belonged together. Couldn't she see that; couldn't she feel it? Possessively, his hands moved between them, then under her sweater to cover her breasts. He wasn't sure the moan he heard came from her or himself.

She let him stroke her yearning flesh for just an instant, the unfamiliar touch taking her breath away. Then she stepped back, pulling his hands from her, knowing that if she let this go on, she'd soon be leading him into her bedroom.

"All right," she said unsteadily. "You wanted to prove that you could make me want you. You win. You can."

He didn't feel like a winner as he saw her struggle for control. He felt like a rat. He raised a hand to her cheek, his voice thick with regret. "Hannah..."

She moved aside. "Please, I need to be alone."

Joel dropped his hand and stepped back. "I'm sorry."

She felt crushed inside, unable to fight him and herself, too. For the moment, she hated him for making her face her own needs. "No, you're not. Maybe you're more like your father than you think."

He sucked in a painful breath. It did no good to tell himself she was hurting and wanted to hurt him back. Without another word, he turned and left, closing the door quietly behind him.

With trembling fingers, Hannah slid home the dead bolt. She hadn't cried in years, not the soul-shattering sobbing that came from deep inside, having schooled herself while living in the homes of strangers to lock away her feelings. But as she ran to her bed and flung herself onto it, she let the tears come.

Antiseptic hospital smells surround me as I lie in my solitary bed. Time has little meaning, and I'm not sure how long I've been here. The pain in my chest is constant, like a living thing, and the coughing weakens me even more.

But the ache in my heart is even worse. Where are my children? Daily, almost hourly, I relive the afternoon the ambulance came for me. I see their faces—Michael trying to be so brave, Hannah struggling to hold back her tears and little Katie openly weeping—standing by the porch railing as they whisked me away. Social workers told me all three would be well taken care of in foster homes. But since then, no one tells me anything.

My mother is old and not well herself. She had to move back to New Mexico, for I could not take care of her. I've failed everyone—Lance, the children, my mother. I couldn't keep up the farm, and now that's gone, sold to pay the expenses. I wouldn't care about that, if only I could see my children, know that they're all right. I wouldn't even care about the tuberculosis that keeps me here, a prisoner in this hospital in the contagious ward. If only I could hold my babies again.

Who is there to help me? I feel so alone. I grieve still for Lance. I need my children, need a reason to get well, to fight this disease that keeps me helpless and frail. But there's no one, no hope to cling to.

I want to die.

Chapter Seven

Lisa Tompkins's thin shoulders shook as she wept out her relief. She ignored the tears flowing down her cheeks and hugged her attorney in the hallway outside courtroom A. "Hannah, thank you. I was so scared, but you did it."

"*You* did it, Lisa," Hannah told her, holding the young woman at arm's length. "You had the courage to press charges and follow through."

Lisa turned to accept her mother's tearful hug before facing her uncle. "Are you still angry with me, Uncle Bill?"

A muscular man in his midfifties, Bill Tompkins seemed to wear a perpetual frown. Since the untimely death of his brother, he'd felt responsible for Aaron Tompkins's small family, and it often weighed heavily on him. "I wasn't so much angry as concerned, honey. I didn't want them to make you have to say all those terrible things on the stand. I know it wasn't easy."

"Not easy, but necessary. Maybe now, Lyle will get the help he needs so no other woman will have to go through what I did."

Just then, Lyle Freeman, flanked by his parents and a deputy, stepped out into the hallway. His father's face was flushed, his mother was crying and Lyle's eyes were downcast. The four of them turned and walked in the opposite direction.

Hannah was pleased with the verdict. Guilty. But the sentence was important, as well. Two years in prison, suspended only if Lyle would enroll in a psychiatric-counseling program that would evaluate his problem and offer treatment for as long as deemed necessary.

She'd gotten lucky. Preparing for the case, she'd located two other coeds who today had come forth and testified that Lyle had also date-raped them. "I'm not utterly convinced a man who's raped several women can truly be cured, but I'd like to think so," Hannah commented.

"I've revised my opinion of you, Ms. Richards," Bill Tompkins said. "Something I rarely do, since I consider myself a fair judge of people. You handled a touchy situation very professionally. My friendship with Lyle's father clouded my vision, I'm afraid. You were right and I was wrong." He touched his niece's arm. "I owe both of you an apology."

"Oh, Uncle Bill," Lisa said, hugging him tightly. "Thank you for that."

"I thank you also, Mr. Tompkins," Hannah added. "It means a lot to me."

"Well," he blustered, "when you're wrong, I always say, be man enough to admit it." He kissed Lisa's cheek, then slipped his arm around his sister-in-law's waist. "What say we all go have a celebration lunch? My treat. You're invited, too, Ms. Richards."

"Sounds good to me," Lisa's mother said, dabbing at her eyes.

"Thanks for the invitation, but I'll have to take a rain check." Hannah shook hands all around and left them. She had something important to take care of, something she'd put off too long already.

Noticing a Christmas wreath hanging on the front door of the office brought Hannah up short. It was only the first week of December. The holiday had sneaked up on her. Of course, she'd been hearing carols on the radio, but disk jockeys began playing Christmas songs earlier each year. Time surely was zipping by, she thought as she walked over to Marcie's desk.

Waiting for the secretary to finish her phone call, she removed her coat, laying it across the chair by the reception desk. Since she'd parked in front, she didn't know if the other two attorneys were in. Will's door was closed, but Joel's was ajar. She was about to walk over when something Marcie said grabbed her attention.

Pausing, she waited until Marcie hung up, then stepped closer to the secretary's desk. "Did I hear correctly, that Joel is involving himself in a food-stamp fraud case?"

"Yes, indeed," Marcie replied. "The plaintiffs are six separate families, all living in the neighborhood of Mac's Market. The owner is accused of cheating them on the food-stamp program. Joel's investigated and believes they're telling the truth. That was Mac's lawyer on the phone, wanting to postpone the preliminary-hearing date."

It wasn't Joel's usual thing, Hannah thought. Maybe he was expanding his client list.

Marcie made a notation on her pad, then smiled up at Hannah. "How are you feeling these days? We haven't seen much of you."

She'd avoided coming in the past few days, doing much of her telephoning and research at home. But avoidance in a small office building could only go on so long. She'd finally come to grips with her problem and decided to do something about it today. "I'm fine." She handed the folder she'd been holding to Marcie. "This is the Tompkins file. Would you close it out, please?"

"Did you win?" Marcie asked, her eyes wide with curiosity.

Hannah smiled. "We sure did."

"Good for you. That young girl's got guts to take on a family with clout."

"Yes, she does." Hannah glanced down the hallway, trying to work up her courage. "Anything else going on around here since I've been out?"

Marcie looked up. "Joel's new clients surprise you?"

"To say the least."

The secretary leaned forward confidentially, her back-combed blond hair shiny with lacquer. "Not only that, but Will told him about a tenement that had a fire due to the landlord's neglect, and you should have heard Joel! He did some digging and learned that a local city councilman owns the place. He marched right over to his office." Marcie chuckled. "I'd love to have been asked to take notes at that meeting."

"Did anything happen?"

"Not yet, but you can bet it will. When Joel gets his dander up, the fur flies."

Yes, and she'd best be prepared for it. She hadn't seen him since Thanksgiving night, when she'd deliberately hurt him. She'd felt rotten about it ever since. She was about to eat some crow. "Is he in?"

"Sure is. He's not really that tied up. Just doing some research, so he asked me to take that call for him."

Hannah squared her shoulders and took a deep breath. "Good, because I need to talk with him." She walked purposefully toward Joel's office. At the open doorway, she paused. He was making notes on a yellow pad, his head bent, several law books open on his desk. She knocked lightly.

He looked up, his expression inquisitive but far from warm and friendly.

"I won the rape case today," Hannah said.

"Congratulations." Joel didn't move, didn't put down his pen or lean back. Didn't invite her in.

She walked in anyway. "You may remember I mentioned that the victim had an uncle who'd warned her not to bring the boy to trial, that she couldn't hope to win?"

He nodded noncommittally.

"After we left the courtroom, the uncle apologized to his niece and to me. He said something that impressed me. He said that when you're wrong, you should be man enough to admit it." She walked closer, until she was standing right in front of his desk so that he had to sit back to look up at her. He still didn't speak, didn't encourage her.

"I was wrong, Joel. I lashed out at you cruelly. I said you were more like your father than you thought—and you're not at all, from what I can see. I was hurt because you forced me to...to face my feelings. I'm ashamed to admit that I felt cornered and I reacted badly. I'm sorry."

His eyes warmed as he rolled his pen between his fingers. "It's hard, isn't it, apologizing?"

She let out a long breath. "Very. But I mean it. I never meant to hurt you."

"I knew that. I figured that, in time, you'd come around." He pushed back his chair, rose and walked over to shut his office door. Then he went to her and took her in his arms, hugging her fiercely. "I've missed you."

Hannah closed her eyes, more relieved than she'd anticipated. "I missed you, too." It was nothing but the truth. Not that much time had passed, and yet it felt as if she'd been away from him for ages. What was she going to do about this incredible need?

He eased back from her and searched her eyes. "Friends again?"

She nodded, her eyes just a little bright.

"Can I kiss you?"

"Please, allow me." Rising on tiptoe, she reached to kiss him, to hold him, to welcome him back. The kiss went on and on, yet wasn't long enough.

The phone rang. Joel lifted his head and shouted through the closed door. "Take a message, Marcie." And returned to her waiting mouth.

Finally, she eased back and smiled up at him. "That call might have been important."

"Not as important as this." He nuzzled her neck, inhaling her scent. "Mmm, you smell good."

She thought the same about him. And he felt good back in her arms. Too good. She stepped away. "I understand from Marcie that you've taken on that grocery swindling case. Aren't you a little off your specialty?"

Joel shrugged, leaning against the edge of his desk. "I take on what interests me."

Hannah sat down in one of the comfortable chairs facing his desk. "I thought you told me there was no money to be made representing *causes*."

He nodded, crossing his ankles. "I did, and there isn't. But I made plenty of money on the Fowler case. I can afford to do one just because."

"Just because?"

He might have known she'd question him on this. No matter. It felt good to be explaining his feelings on this one. "Because those people really need help. Mac has been cheating them for years. Imagine, most of the folks who live around his store barely scrape by, and yet he adds to their problems. It's like stealing the church offering."

She almost smiled at how righteously indignant he was. "How'd you hear about it?"

"I was working late one evening and got to talking with the woman who cleans our building. Dorie's sister shops at Mac's and had told her. I promised I'd look into it. What I found surprised me. Not just that lady, but fourteen other families so far. He's got a real scam going."

"I understand if you report grocers like that, the government will take away the food-stamp privileges."

Joel shook his head. "Not good enough. These folks work hard, most don't even own cars and live too far to walk to the larger markets. We want Mac to repay them for their losses and to be fined. Then we put together a citizens' committee to police him and make sure he stays on the straight and narrow."

Pleased, Hannah cocked her head. "They really got to you, didn't they?"

He crossed his arms over his chest. "I went to see Dorie's sister. Her name's Betsy, and she's not even twenty-five yet. If you could see how she lives. Four kids crammed in one bedroom, three in a bed and one in a flimsy cradle. It's the kids who got to me. Big eyes, thin little bodies, clean clothes but nearly threadbare. Betsy cleans office buildings at night. A teenage girl stays with the kids." Joel shook his head, still angry at the poverty he'd witnessed. "And then Mac steals from her!"

There was hope for Joel Merrick yet, Hannah thought. "And I understand you're also upset about some tenement housing."

He raised a questioning brow. "You've been talking with Marcie?" He didn't care. He was so glad she'd come to him. He'd been hoping she would, but he knew how difficult apologies were. And he'd been more than a little afraid she'd written him off. Hannah Richards was a hard woman to figure.

"Guilty. Did you get the councilman to listen?"

"Hell, no, he wouldn't. I thought if I gave him a list of all that needed doing and told him I was sure he hadn't intended to let things get so run-down in his building that he'd be too embarrassed not to make the repairs. Not so. They even had a fire there about a month ago, and that apartment hasn't been fixed."

Hannah frowned. "You mean he simply refused?"

"More or less. Told me he owns it through a limited partnership and that the actual running of the building was left to a management company. Conditions and maintenance were their problem, not his. I wanted to punch him in his jowly face."

She almost laughed aloud.

"What makes it worse is that he's Clement C. Brown, a friend of my father. He kept trying to divert me with the good-old-boy stuff—how's your dad, I miss seeing him at the club—that sort of thing. He's a smoothie, all right."

Hannah leaned back, curious. "So what are you going to do?"

"I've already done it. Filed a class action suit against him and all his partners."

She knew her face looked shocked. "You honestly did?"

Joel wondered why she was surprised. "Well, wouldn't you have? That building isn't even up to minimum safety standards. Someone has to do something. It's full of young children. Someone's bound to get seriously hurt sooner or later." He saw her expression change to bemused. "What?"

"I'm having trouble seeing you as Joel Merrick, crusader for the poor and disadvantaged."

He straightened, returning to his desk. "I'm not on any crusade. I know better than most that cases like that net you nothing but trouble. But I can afford to do an occasional one because of the others that pay well. You, on the other hand, can't."

"Who said? Am I behind in my rent? Am I starving?"

"Maybe not, but you're driving a car that's six years old and I noticed that your apartment is somewhat sparingly furnished."

He wasn't going to make her defensive. Not today. She felt too good, having won a tough case and making up with Joel. "I happen to like my car. And I want to go slowly in furnishing my apartment, chasing down just the right piece, decorating exactly as I've always wanted. That takes time."

All right. He'd buy her explanation because he knew he couldn't change her mind about her client list. Leaning forward, elbows on his desktop, he smiled at her. She was wearing a pale yellow wool suit with a black blouse and accessories. Her hair was down past her shoulders and had his palms sweating with the need to touch her. "Yellow's really your color, you know."

She smiled at his neat conversation switch. "I thought you told me green was?"

"Yeah, that, too." The phone rang, and he frowned but continued to study her. "Let's go have lunch somewhere."

"Aren't you going to answer that?"

"Only if you go to lunch with me."

How could she refuse? Besides, she really was pretty well caught up just now. "Okay, you win."

He grinned as he picked up the receiver. "Merrick." His frown returned as he listened. "I don't know where you got your information, Mrs. Lang," Joel said into the phone, "but I haven't agreed to represent Rusty."

Hannah got up, reluctant to eavesdrop again, and strolled over to gaze out the window. The sky was cloudless, but it was cold and the sun's rays weren't strong enough to melt the accumulated snow. She hated to think of the long winter stretching ahead. Boston would be lovely in the spring and summer.

"No," Joel went on, "I'd rather you didn't send anything over on Rusty right now. The truth is, my caseload is pretty heavy and . . ." He paused, listening to the anxious woman plead on behalf of her husband.

Chelsea Lang had called him earlier in the week, asking him to represent Rusty, accused of murdering his brother, Tom, in cold blood. The father of the two men had passed away in January and left a brand-new will that Rusty felt Tom had coerced the old man into sign-ing. Rusty had challenged the will, but the courts had decided in Tom's favor. Left out in the cold and in debt over the court case, Rusty had snapped, according to Chelsea. She wanted Joel to represent Rusty with a tem-porary-insanity plea.

"Insanity pleas are seldom believed by juries, Mrs. Lang. And the fact that Rusty hid in Tom's garage and basically ambushed him seems very premeditated, even to me."

For another few minutes, Joel listened to her speak of how much Rusty had loved his brother, but how the in-justice of the inheritance division had changed him into someone obsessed. "I admire your loyalty to Rusty, Chelsea, but I can't accept your word. I'd need to talk with him, check out everything, research the case, etc. I simply don't think I have the time right now for all that would be required in order to represent him fairly."

Joel was getting annoyed as she persisted. He had to end this now. "Listen, here's what I'm willing to do. I need some time to see if I want to take on this case. Meanwhile, you interview other attorneys and hire one if he seems enthusiastic." He made an instant decision, one he felt in his bones was the right one. "I'll be out of town for a few days. When I return, I'll get in touch with you and we'll talk again."

He knew she wasn't happy, but she had little choice but to accept his decision. Chelsea hung up and so did Joel, swinging his chair toward Hannah. He brushed a weary hand across his eyes, then along his chin. He needed to get away. Law was a difficult taskmaster. The need for a change of scene, to clear his head and refresh his spirit, came over him infrequently. But when it did, he knew better than to ignore it.

"Tough decision?" Hannah asked, turning toward him. She'd heard his comments, of course, and didn't envy Joel's dilemma.

He rose, walking to her. "Not really." He'd always felt that every person deserved fair representation, and still did. But the only argument he could see for Rusty would be temporary insanity. It wasn't a defense Joel was comfortable with. "I don't think I can take the case, feeling as I do about Rusty Lang's guilt. Maybe, if I were to talk with him, I'd feel otherwise, but I doubt it."

Placing his hands on her arms, he let his eyes roam over her lovely features. He wanted to get away, but not necessarily alone. The idea washed over him, and he liked it a lot. "How's your calendar looking for the next few days?"

"Not too crowded, why?" Surely he wasn't going to ask her to help him with a murder investigation, especially when he didn't believe in the client's innocence.

"I think I mentioned that I'd been planning to go to Montana to visit my uncle's ranch after the holidays. I've decided to go now instead. Come with me." Before she could recover from the invitation that he could see surprised her, he forged on. "Bart will send his private plane for us. Montana's so beautiful, the sky so vast. We can ski or horseback ride. Do you like horses?"

"Well, yes, but . . ."

"Of course you do. You grew up on a farm. You'll love this place. Acres and acres of cattle and horses and clean, fresh air. Bart's Terry's father, you know, and a great guy."

"I'm sure he is, but I can't just up and leave. I've got clients and . . ."

"You just told me you were caught up." He squeezed her arms. "I know you're not an impulsive person. But do it, this time, Hannah. Come with me. You've been working hard. We'll just sit by the fire, relax, eat lots and forget the law.''

Oddly, the invitation sounded appealing. No, she wasn't impulsive. But she'd never fully rested up from her illness, and she hadn't had a vacation, short or otherwise, in years. ''How long a stay did you have in mind?''

She was weakening. He smiled. ''I'll call right now. Bart will have the plane here tonight. We'll be there by morning. We can stay three days, max. Back by Tuesday morning in time for court, if necessary.''

She didn't have a court appearance until Wednesday. She'd have to make a few calls, check with a couple of people. Suddenly, it sounded like fun. Wasn't it about time she had a little fun?

There was one thing. ''How large is this ranch house?'' she asked.

Joel's smile widened. ''Six bedrooms. That enough for you? You'll have your own room and bath.''

That did make her feel better. ''Are you sure he wouldn't mind your dragging me along?''

''Positive.'' He kissed her quickly, thoroughly. And walked to the phone before she'd find reasons not to go with him.

She'd never even seen a private plane up close, much less flown on one. At Logan Airport at the hangar used by private licensees, Hannah stood in a blue parka and watched the small Learjet taxi to a stop on the lighted runway. Alongside her, dressed as warmly as she, Joel waved to the pilot as he turned off the engines. She had to admit that her heart was pounding with excitement.

In her wildest dreams, she hadn't thought she'd be flying almost across the entire country in a luxury aircraft.

"It may not be exactly as you imagined," Joel said, taking her arm to guide her to the descending staircase. "Planes in Montana are used to haul livestock at times, so there's a cargo section that's strictly utilitarian. The people section is quite small."

Ducking her head into a chill night wind, Hannah hurried to keep up with him. "Why would you fly cattle somewhere?"

"There could be a prize bull at a distant ranch, so you might take some cows over to be impregnated. Or to breed horses to a prime stallion. Or to complete a sale." He helped her up the stairway. "Hey, Fred," he called out to the pilot. "How's it going?"

"Can't complain, Joel." Fred acknowledged the introduction to Hannah, then moved past them to the door. "I'll see to the refueling, and we'll be taking off in about half an hour."

Joel introduced the copilot, as well, and waited until he'd walked out before ushering her into the main cabin. "Well, what do you think?"

It was more spacious than she'd imagined, and nothing like a commercial airliner. There was a table with four swivel chairs around it, all anchored to the floor. And three sets of large reclining chairs, all upholstered in gray. The curtains over the small windows were in maroon, and the carpeting and walls carried the color theme through. In the back, she could see a small galley and two bunk beds with railings along one side. A television set was mounted over the front entrance, and a stereo was playing softly in the background. Yes, she could handle this nicely.

"It's wonderful." She turned to him, eyes shining. "This must be how the rich and famous live, eh?"

"Believe me, in Montana when winter closes off even the main roads sometimes for weeks at a time, a plane is a necessity, not a luxury." Joel took his sheepskin jacket and her parka and hung them up, then walked her down to the door at the far end. "This is the cargo section, empty right now." He heaved open the heavy door.

The faint odor of animals and antiseptic lingered in the stale air. Hannah checked out the stalls outfitted with guide straps to keep the animals anchored and the bins for hauling hay and other grain. The entire area was of stainless steel and spotlessly clean. "So then Bart's ranch has a runway on it, or do you have to land at the nearest airport?"

"They have two runways, one by the hangar and a landing strip out in the grazing area to distribute food bundles to the cattle in winter." He led her back into the main cabin and saw that the pilots were checking their instruments in the cockpit. "Take any chair you like and make yourself comfortable." He went up front to talk with Fred.

Hannah settled herself in a chair by the window and fastened her seat belt. A half moon cast a silvery glow on the tarmac. She glanced at her watch as she struggled with a yawn. Just after five a.m. Joel had told her he preferred flying at night. With the three-hour time difference, they'd be arriving at about sunrise.

Sighing, Hannah stretched out. Who would have thought she'd be streaking across the night sky on her way west to a place she'd scarcely imagined ever visiting? It must be wonderful to be wealthy enough to snap your fingers and have jets waiting to fulfill your every whim. She'd never be in such a position, not with the legal specialty she'd chosen. But she had no regrets, since she loved her work. And, amazingly, Joel was beginning to see the value in helping people who had nowhere else to turn.

He'd surprised her by considering refusing to represent a man whose innocence he didn't believe in. He hadn't changed as much as become more aware of his own feelings about the people he represented. Hannah felt it was a positive step.

Joel stepped past the curtain separating them from the cockpit, then pushed the button that retracted the stairs. He closed and latched the door before walking over and sitting down alongside her. "Almost ready for takeoff," he said, fastening his seat belt. "After we're at cruising altitude, I'll see what's in the galley. I'll bet you were too rushed to eat before I picked you up."

She had been, first going over some things with Marcie, who'd seemed almost more excited about her trip than Hannah. Then she'd driven home and packed, taking longer than she should have in deciding what to take. It was only a friendly trip, she'd reminded herself. Not a romantic adventure. She didn't want that, and Joel knew it. Separate rooms, time to sit and relax by the fire, no demands on her. She would keep her distance, keep her resolution to stay uninvolved.

The pilot fired up the engines, and the lights in the cabin dimmed. Slowly, the plane began to push away from the gate. Hannah couldn't help but be excited. She wondered what Joel was thinking.

As she completed the thought, he took her hand in his, lacing their fingers together. She turned to him. His eyes were dark blue, his look intimate. He was wearing jeans and a white V-neck sweater, the sleeves pushed up on his strong arms. Black hair curled around the opening, inviting her touch. Her pulse picked up its rhythm.

"I'm glad you decided to come with me," Joel said softly.

She returned the pressure of his fingers, forgetting everything she'd resolved not to do just moments ago. "Me, too."

"I asked Fred to overfly Red Lodge because just a little west of there is the Beartooth Wilderness. The Absoraka mountain chain extends all the way to the eastern crest of Yellowstone. It's a fantastic sight." Joel leaned toward Hannah so he could point things out to her through the window.

She was awestruck by the colors—gold and red and orange—the rising sun in a sky so pure a blue it looked fake. And far below were rugged-looking canyons and dark forests sprinkled with patches of snow. The plane dipped, the pilot allowing the passengers to get a better view. "I can't believe it. The snow looks pink the way the sun hits it."

"A lot of people have thought so. There's an explanation—something about pigmentation. I've never seen it anywhere else."

Her nose nearly pressed to the glass, Hannah was totally absorbed. "I suppose there're wild animals down there."

"Oh, yeah. Grizzlies, although not as many as there used to be. Bighorn sheep, elk, bull moose. And, of course, coyote, fox and mountain lions. Not a good place to go climbing without a big gun."

She turned back, blinking from the bright sunshine. "Are you a hunter?"

"No, but Bart is. You'll see a couple of heads in his den." When the plane straightened out, he got up. "I'm going to make some coffee. They probably could use some up front."

Hannah thought she wouldn't mind a cup herself. She stretched lazily. It had been a pleasant flight, very smooth. She'd fallen asleep after they'd eaten a snack earlier, her hand wrapped in Joel's. That was twice now that she'd slept with him. She was beginning to like the feeling. Too much so.

She returned her attention to the window, noticing that the pilot was turning the plane in a wide circle, heading them back to Red Lodge and Bart's ranch. Maybe back on terra firma, she'd be able to keep her distance from Joel more easily.

She almost believed she could.

Hannah was afraid to move, to breathe. She stood peering over the stall door at the mare lying on a bed of clean hay while three men stood ready to assist her with the birthing. The foaling barn was heated, yet Hannah felt a chill run up her spine. The mare moved her big head, snuffling out through distended nostrils. Her dark, expressive eyes watched the humans closely between contractions. The atmosphere was tense, the air heavy with the scent of leather and animals. Hannah leaned closer.

Johnny, the seasoned vet, crouched down. Bart Merrick, a taller, craggy-faced version of his older brother, stood behind Johnny. And by Domino's head sat Joel, murmuring gently to the straining mare. Despite having grown up on a farm, Hannah had never witnessed a birthing, since her father hadn't bred his stock. She'd been thrilled when Bart had suggested she come along.

The old vet squatted on his haunches, his weathered face wearing a frown. "I think we've got some distress here," he told Bart as he removed the stethoscope from the mare's belly. "I don't get a fetal heartbeat."

Bart leaned down. "I thought you said earlier everything's okay?"

"Earlier, it was. Don't know what happened. Too late for an ultrasound. We'll just have to see what happens."

Hannah saw the concern on everyone's faces. She'd been told coming in that Domino had been in labor for hours now. She knew precious little about equestrian pregnancies, but in humans, that usually meant problems. Leaning on the stall door, she watched the mare strain through another pain. The minutes passed slowly.

"I think we're almost there," Johnny finally said. Reaching in, he punctured the amniotic sac. A surge of liquid gushed forth. "Here comes the front feet and head. Step back, Bart."

Bart did just as the foal, in a diving position with head tucked between front feet, emerged. Domino gave another big push, and the foal was born. The mare let out a low whinny of relief.

"Damn!" Johnny exclaimed. "Cord's around his neck."

"Is he breathing?" Bart asked.

At the mare's head, Joel stroked the mare while the other two worked on her foal.

Hannah couldn't take her eyes from Johnny as he cut the umbilical cord and twisted it free. Moments later, she saw him turn to Bart and shake his head.

"Stillborn. Sorry, Bart." Johnny let out a disappointed whoosh of air, then quickly went to work cleaning up.

"Not your fault," Bart muttered as he bent to help the vet.

Hand to her mouth, Hannah looked at the mare as she shifted her snout toward her son. She sniffed once, twice, then deliberately turned away. Was she grieving inside, knowing her baby had died before it had had a chance to live? Hannah felt tears well up in her eyes for the mother's loss.

Even after the stall was cleaned out of all traces of the birth, the mare showed no signs of concern. As Joel stepped out to join her, Hannah turned to him. "She must be hurting but pretending it doesn't matter, right?"

He'd witnessed too many birthings to agree. "No, it's not like that with animals. If a foal is stillborn or born defective, the mother turns from it and goes on as if the birth had never taken place."

Hannah was shocked. "You're kidding?"

Joel shook his head. "It's the same with dogs and cats. If one from a litter is blind or deformed, the mother ignores it and puts all her energy into the remaining live ones. In the animal world, it's survival of the fittest."

"That's so cruel, so unbelievable. A mother turning her back on her baby." She pressed her lips together, struggling with suddenly overwhelming emotions. Oh, God, she shouldn't have watched, but then, she'd never dreamed this would happen. She couldn't let these people see how upset she was. "I need a little air." Turning, she set off down the walkway.

Perplexed, Joel followed. At the far end of the barn, few stalls were occupied, the horses in the corrals or out on the range. A door was open, letting in a shaft of light and fresh air. There was an old wooden bench that had been there as long as he could remember. He drew her down to sit with him, watching her. "Are you okay?"

Hannah felt the walls closing in on her as memories flooded her. She was going to make a fool of herself, and there was nowhere to hide. She felt the tears begin and did nothing to stop them. She had to ride this out, she knew.

Worried, Joel offered his handkerchief. "What's wrong?"

Hannah dabbed at her cheeks and placed a hand on his arm. "It's just...nothing. I can't explain." She closed her eyes, willing the emotional turmoil to pass.

He slipped his arm around her, cradling her head against his shoulder. The only thing he could think to do was to let her cry it out. Then maybe she'd tell him, if she could. Gently, he stroked her back, wondering what had set her off.

They'd arrived early that morning and received a warm reception from Bart, as Joel had known they would. Everyone, from the housekeeper to the ranch manager to the hands that he introduced to Hannah, had been welcoming. The three of them had shared a big breakfast in the country kitchen, he and Bart catching up on some family news. Then he'd taken Hannah horseback riding for about an hour only, since he didn't want her to be sore. When they'd returned, Bart had asked her if she'd ever seen a foaling. Excited, she'd all but run to the barn.

And now this reaction.

Finally, the turbulence slowed, then came to an end. Hannah wiped her face and blew her nose. Embarrassment flooded her, pinking her cheeks. "I'm so sorry," she said, her voice quavery.

"It's all right. I'd just like to know what that was all about."

Staring at his handkerchief as she worried it in her hands, she wouldn't look at him. "It just sort of comes over me at times. Odd times. Emotions build up, and I can't seem to control the tears for a short time. I'm sorry. You must think I'm a nut case."

"Never." He touched her chin, forcing her to face him. "Did you ever try to find out what brings on these bouts?"

She knew exactly what had set her off today. But she couldn't tell him. She'd have to skirt the issue. "The doctor I talked with in Michigan said it was a reaction triggered by buried memories. Today it was probably the barn smells, the horses, the foal being stillborn. I don't remember a lot from those early years, but the feelings break through." That part, at least, was true.

Will had said she'd had a disturbing childhood. "You've said you were orphaned. How old were you and how did it happen?"

She supposed she owed him some explanation after her embarrassing outburst. This story was far easier to tell than the other one. "We lived in Frankenmuth, a farming community not far from Detroit. We didn't have much, but I remember we were really happy. My mother sang while she worked, and Dad was a tease. I was eight when he was killed in a tractor accident. My brother, Michael, was fourteen, and my sister, Katie, was just six. Mom tried to keep things going, but there was so much work and she was crying all the time, missing Dad. Then she got sick. I never knew what she had, only she seemed so weak and she was always coughing. One day, the ambulance came and took her away. That same day, the Child Protective Services picked us up and took us to separate foster homes."

Joel heard the remembered pain in her voice and took her hand, wishing he could erase all she'd suffered. "That must have been awful."

"It was. No one would tell me anything, not how my mother was doing or where Michael and Katie were. I cried a lot in those days, and the foster parents weren't too happy with me. I went from one home to another, always unhappy. In looking back, I think the fault was more with me than the foster parents. I wanted things to go back to the way they were, and that couldn't happen. There was no one who really cared about me, and the natural children in the homes where I lived resented me being there."

Hannah looked up then, noticing his expression and unwilling to allow him to pity her. "I figured out how to survive, though. I wasn't beautiful like Katie, but I had two things going for me—my brains and good behavior. Studying came easily, thank God. I learned to behave so as not to draw attention to myself. I managed all right. Then one day, they told me that my mother had died of tuberculosis. I really fell apart after that."

"No one could blame you." Joel's heart ached for the child she'd been.

"But I soon realized that crying did no good, nor did self-pity. I learned to rely on myself. By then, I was beyond the age when most people want to adopt children. When I turned fourteen, I got lucky. The Murrays took me in, and we moved to Lansing. They'd lost a daughter to cancer and seemed to want a child in the house. I knew they didn't love me, but at least, they were kind. I stayed with them until after high-school graduation. Mr. Murray helped me to apply for and win a scholarship to Michigan State."

"Do you still keep in touch with them?"

"Mr. Murray died two years ago, and Mrs. Murray moved to California to live with a sister. We write occasionally."

So she'd lost them, too. So much sadness. Leaning toward her, he framed her face with his big hands. "You have no apologies to make for getting emotional occasionally. You had a rotten break, losing both parents and your siblings. But lady, look what you've made of yourself despite all that!" He smiled at her. "You should be proud." Gently, he kissed her.

Proud, Hannah thought, sliding her arms around him. That wasn't at all how she viewed the situation. But how nice that Joel had seen it that way, wanting to make her feel proud. If he knew the whole truth, she wondered how he'd feel. However, she wouldn't worry about that today.

She returned his kiss, feeling something inside shift for her.

Chapter Eight

It was early when Hannah woke on Monday morning. She stretched under the marvelous feather bed that Eudora, Bart's housekeeper, had told her she'd made herself. She'd never slept better.

Pushing the heavy coverlet aside, she got up and shivered. Ranchers apparently kept their bedrooms cool at night, which was why the feather beds came in handy. She went to the window and saw the sky just beginning to lighten. It seemed to go on for miles, pale blue and gold, finally meeting the snow-covered land way in the distance. Not a sound could be heard.

Joel had been right about Bart's ranch. It was peaceful.

She usually preferred a shower, but last night, she'd indulged herself and soaked in the deep, claw-footed bathtub, something she hadn't done in years. Heavenly.

But now, she hurried to pull on clean jeans and a heavy turtleneck, feeling chilled in the morning air.

Eudora might already be up, Hannah thought as she tiptoed downstairs. None of the other bedroom doors were open. She knew from what Bart had said that the ranch hands were usually out early tending to the livestock, but her window faced the front and the barns were all to the back.

At the foot of the stairs, she heard voices coming from the direction of the kitchen. Deep male voices, two of them. She'd been about to step in when she heard her name mentioned, and paused.

"Hannah's different from any other woman I've known," Joel was saying as he wrapped his hands around his coffee mug. "I've known my share of women, but there's something about her that keeps her on my mind, even when we're not together."

There was amusement in Bart's voice. "Better watch out, son. That kind of talk is what got me married."

Joel looked up at his uncle. The man was nearing sixty yet still strong as an ox. His wife, Elizabeth, had died the summer Joel graduated high school. Joel had cried almost as hard as Bart, who'd never remarried. "And did you live to regret it?" he asked, knowing full well the answer.

Bart sobered and his eyes grew misty. "Not one day." He cleared his throat, yanking his thoughts away from Elizabeth. Gone thirteen years, and he still missed her as if it were yesterday. "You think you love Hannah?"

Joel let out a long breath. "I care about her more than I've ever cared about a woman."

That wasn't news to Bart. He'd watched the two of them together both days. There was attraction there, certainly, but he sensed deeper feelings. In both of them. "And how does she feel?"

"Good question. She cares about me, I think, although she doesn't want to. How much, I can't say. She's very distrustful of men. Something happened a while back, I'm not sure exactly what. Some guy hurt her badly, that much she's told me. We'd have to get past that. I want her to trust me, but so far, it hasn't happened." He took a taste of coffee and found it oddly bitter. "One thing I'm certain of—she's not after my money. Hell, I don't know what I'd be offering her, even if it came to that."

Bart stretched out his long legs sideways to the table. His one knee was always stiff on these cold mornings. He felt good most of the time, but the years were catching up with him. "I don't know what you mean by that. You're a fine man with a good career. You come from good stock—I ought to know. What are you worried about?"

Joel stared into his cup. "I don't know where I fit in, not to this day. I tried corporate law, like you did, and I hated it. Dad's never forgiven me for that and probably never will. I came out here to be with you and loved that. But I got restless and went back."

"Restless, or were you feeling guilty on account of Jason?"

"Maybe a little of both. Now, I'm in criminal law, which I really thought I'd like. But it doesn't feel quite right, either." He sent Bart a crooked smile. "What do you suppose is wrong with me?"

"Just growing pains, son."

"I'm thirty-two. I should be on track by now. Look at Todd and Sam, even Regan. And Terry. Yet here I am, floundering."

Bart frowned thoughtfully. "Not everyone knows what he wants to do with his life early on. Nothing wrong with trying this and that till you find where you belong." He leaned forward, his lined face serious. "Ask yourself, if nothing stood in my way, what would I want to do with the rest of my life?"

Blue eyes so like his own didn't waver as Bart stared at him as if demanding an answer. Joel shifted in his chair, asking himself the same, all-important question. "I'd have to give that some thought."

"You do that. Be honest with yourself and you'll know which way to go." He rose and went to pour himself a refill.

Joel got up, needing some time alone to think. He grabbed his sheepskin jacket from the back hook. "I think I'll go out into the barn for a while."

"See you later," Bart said, sitting back down. He'd already been out once this morning with Craig, his manager, going over some things. He'd earned a second cup of coffee. Stretching out his bad leg and propping it onto an empty chair, he made himself comfortable.

A sound from the archway had him glancing up as Hannah came into the kitchen. "Good morning. You're up early."

Hannah saw by the big clock on the wall that it was barely seven and still not fully light. "I feel thoroughly rested. That's a wonderful bed."

He grinned. "Eudora's feather bed gets most of the credit. She made breakfast for Joel and me a while ago. I can round her up for you and . . ."

"No, please don't. Coffee will do for now just fine." She found a mug on the counter and poured herself a cup, then wandered over to join him at the table.

She was still digesting all she'd overheard. Eavesdropping had her feeling contrite. Yet she'd probably learned more about Joel in that brief conversation than in several much longer ones they'd shared. Thoughtfully, she sipped her coffee, hoping she didn't look as guilty as she felt.

Bart knew Joel and Hannah planned to leave tonight. Over the rim of his mug, he studied her, as he'd been doing for two days now. She was lovely with that great hair and big eyes, though a little too thin. He'd seen the intelligence, the meditative manner, the melancholy mood that would overtake her, like that first day in the barn. And he'd seen her fierce independence.

He wondered if she was a good match for Joel, who was as close to him as his own son, if not more so, for they were kindred spirits. Maybe he'd do a little gentle inquiring.

"I hope you've enjoyed being with us," he began.

"I have." Hannah set down her cup. "It's so beautiful here, the mountains, the peace and quiet. I can see why Joel loves coming to visit."

"His reasons for coming here are more than all that."

Hannah sensed that beneath Bart's casual manner, he was trying to tell her something. "Do you know what they are?"

"I think so. Because here, there's no pressure. On your ranch, you're your own boss. No one breathing over your shoulder. If you've got a good crew like we do, every man knows what has to be done, and he does it. No one stands on ceremony. At the end of the day, you're tired, but you feel good. You have pride in what you've accomplished."

Hannah wished she knew what Bart was getting at. "I suppose that's true. But don't you think Joel has pride in what he accomplishes as an attorney, in the cases he wins, the people he helps?''

Bart narrowed his gaze. "You tell me. Does he?"

"I guess only he could answer that." She was silent several moments, sipping coffee, thinking over what she'd heard and what Bart had said. "He does seem happier here than back in Boston. But if that's so, why doesn't he just quit the law and move here? I have a feeling you'd welcome him."

"Damn right I would. I'd try to coax him here if I thought that was best. But no man's comfortable with a decision he didn't come to on his own. I was in Joel's position once. A hotshot Boston lawyer, fancy suits, fast cars. Didn't have time for my family, my friends. I was on the fast track heading nowhere. I didn't wake up until my wife threatened to leave me if things didn't change."

"That's when you moved here?"

"Right. Elizabeth's father owned this ranch and he was in poor health. We moved here with Terry when he was only seven, same age as Joel. The place was getting rundown because the old man had run out of steam and money. I took over and worked like three men. By the time he died, we were on our way. He was grateful enough to leave everything to us."

"Those must have been hard years."

"Not as hard as lawyering in Boston. I never really loved law the way Jason does. I like the outdoors, a more simple life. But, like Joel with Jason, I wanted to please my father, who started the Merrick firm. I didn't realize until it was almost too late that I was a round peg trying to squeeze into a square hole. Elizabeth straightened me out. A good woman can usually do that for a man." His eyes flickered over her face, and he wondered how much she was reading between the lines.

"Joel spent a lot of time here in his teens, I understand."

"Sure did. He worshiped Elizabeth. Lois and Jason are good parents, provided you do as they see fit. Elizabeth and I believed that a child has to find himself, to walk his own path in order to be all he can be. Naturally, I'd have been pleased if Terry would have wanted to ranch here with me. But from the time he was small, he wanted to be a doctor. So I let him go, with my blessing. I didn't want him feeling the guilt I carried around with me for years over disappointing my father."

Hannah watched him closely and knew he was speaking from the heart. "I've met Jason. I was surprised that he's disappointed in Joel simply because he didn't stay in the firm. I've seen Joel in action in a courtroom, and he's very good. And I've watched him while we've been here. Do you feel he'd be better off living in Montana?"

"Not necessarily. I think he should be where he feels he's happiest. If it's Boston, fine. If here, that's okay, too. But *he's* got to decide. Jason's influence runs deep in that boy. He has it in mind that he'd be a quitter if he gave up the law and chose ranching, like I did. Jason still thinks of me as a quitter."

She'd had a little taste of Jason's philosophy. "Jason seems to want to control the entire family."

Bart chuckled. Hannah was all right. It had taken her only one Merrick dinner to get old Jason's number. "That he does. It's not enough he's got two out of three sons turned into clones, he's still after Joel." He shifted his gaze to Hannah. "What Joel wants, I believe, is the kind of family life we had here before Elizabeth died.

What Joel needs is a good woman to help him decide where he belongs."

She kept her eyes on his. "If that's so, I hope he finds the one right for him."

No one would ever accuse Bart Merrick of subtlety. "Are you sure he hasn't already found her?"

"If he hasn't, it's not for lack of trying. Rumor has it he's dated nearly every woman under the age of thirty in Boston."

"A man has to kiss a lot of frogs before he finds the one who turns into a princess," Bart said, unabashedly revising the fairy tale as he gave her a wink. "Besides, I don't know as though we can trust those rumors. He's young, handsome and he's got a bank account. Naturally, people are going to speculate, but not necessarily truthfully."

The kitchen wall phone rang just then, cutting off Hannah's need to reply. As she watched him rise to answer it, she was glad for the interruption. She hadn't pegged Bart as a matchmaker. Then why did she get the impression he was trying to pair them? Or was he just poking around, looking for answers?

"Slow down, Marcie," Bart said into the phone, "I can't make out what you're saying." He listened as the distraught woman repeated her message. "All right, I've got it. I'll tell Joel and Hannah. They'll get the plane gassed up right away." He hung up and turned around.

"That was Marcie. Will's had a heart attack." Bart reached for his jacket.

"Oh, no!" Hannah whispered, her hand fluttering to her throat.

"I'll go get Joel." Bart hurried out the back door.

* * *

Massachusetts General was a very large, very modern, efficient hospital. Joel felt uncomfortable there anyhow. He hadn't had much experience hanging around hospitals and was glad of it. He'd sweet-talked the nurse into allowing both of them into Will's intensive-care unit cubicle, provided they didn't disturb him. As he stood at the foot of Will's bed, where the older man was hooked up to half a dozen monitors and tubes and machinery, he realized that no amount of rehearsal could prepare a person for the trauma of a life-death situation.

It was painful watching someone you cared about on the brink of death. Struggling with his emotions, Joel decided he didn't want to think about his life without Will in it. He'd played a big part when Joel had been a child, serving as a surrogate for the father who was always working or away on business, and constantly critical when he was home. Will, like Bart, had never been that driven, that intense. Will should have had children, Joel had often thought, for he'd have made a marvelous father. Joel had been crazy about Emily, too.

It wasn't fair, he thought, stepping a little closer to the bed. Good people shouldn't be snatched from us before we're ready to say goodbye. Yet he knew deep inside that the day would never come when he'd willingly bid his old friend farewell.

Joel looked at the frighteningly still form on the bed. Will was sleeping, his breathing a bit labored even with the oxygen cannula running beneath his nose. His normally ruddy cheeks were as devoid of color as the stark white pillowcase. Something was attached with tape to his neck with wires running beneath the sheet. A blood-pressure cuff on his arm tightened at regular intervals, the readout on the machine changing as it did.

A hell of a way for a man to be seen, Joel thought.

He shifted his gaze to Hannah, who'd pulled a chair close to the bed on the opposite side. The nurse had warned them that Will needed his rest, so they were both quiet. He'd seen Hannah struggle not to cry several times, her control over her emotions finally winning. But now he saw silent tears slide down her cheeks as she pressed her hand to her lips to keep from making a sound.

On the long flight home, she'd sat quietly staring out the window. She'd withdrawn, and he'd felt he should try to get her to talk about her feelings. He hadn't had much success. All she'd told him was that she'd loved three men in her life. Both of the other two had left her. She couldn't lose Will, too.

If it were possible to keep someone alive by sheer force of will, Hannah was going to do it. She didn't touch him, didn't want to wake him, didn't say a word, but instead let her eyes speak for her. Maybe in that netherland where he'd gone, he could hear her, she thought. Maybe he knew she was here, helping him fight to stay alive.

The doctor had said the heart attack had been serious, but that he'd managed to get help quickly. The next twelve hours were critical. He had a chance, albeit not a very good one due to his age, his weight and the fact that he'd already suffered a mild heart attack two years ago. Will hadn't told her about that one.

He couldn't die, Hannah thought, he simply couldn't. Not now when she'd uprooted herself and traveled hundreds of miles to be with him. He'd been the main reason for her move, to be with someone who was more like family than anyone else she knew. He was the reason she'd succeeded in law school, the driving force behind her need to excel. He was like the grandfather she'd never known.

Immediately, she felt contrite at thinking only of herself when Will was struggling to live.

"Please don't die, Will," she whispered softly. "I need you so much. We all do." She bent her head and took his hand into hers, choking back the tears. "I'm so sorry I haven't had you over for that dinner yet. You were going to bring the wine, remember? And you asked me to go ice fishing, but I turned you down. I want to go, Will. Please get better so we can go together."

She bent her head in prayer. *Please, God, don't take still another person from me.*

Joel swallowed around a lump in his throat, then walked over and placed a hand on Hannah's shoulder. He couldn't do anything but pray for Will. And he couldn't do anything for Hannah except let her know he was there for her, as well.

It was eight in the evening. He had a feeling it was going to be a long night.

Hannah leaned back against the soft leather upholstery of Joel's Mercedes. "Out of danger. The three most beautiful words I've heard lately, wouldn't you say?"

"I agree." Joel pulled out of the hospital parking lot and turned onto Charles Street. It was barely six in the morning, still dark out, the streetlights on.

Bone weary but enormously relieved, Hannah closed her eyes. She'd catnapped a little in the chair in the small waiting room next to the intensive-care unit, but she'd been too worried to really sleep. Now she felt tired but not really sleepy. "Are you sure we can trust Dr. Bailey?"

"Franklin Bailey is a well-known cardiologist, the best in the city. If he can't call 'em, who can?" Joel came to a decision and swung onto Embankment Road, heading for Beacon Hill.

"Marcie was pretty cute on the phone," Joel said, recalling their conversation. He'd called from the hospital and told her not to expect either of them in the office today. She'd been with Will when they'd arrived, but noting her exhaustion, they'd sent her home. "She said, 'Thank God he's going to be all right. I'm too old to spend this much time on my knees praying.' She also said she'd hold the fort while we got some rest."

Hannah brushed back her hair, realizing she must look bedraggled from lack of sleep and from being in the same clothes for what seemed like days. "I've got so much I should do, but I don't think I have the energy right now."

"What you need is a good meal first and..."

"No, a shower first, then maybe something to eat." Straightening, she glanced out the window. "Where are we going? This isn't the way to my apartment."

"You're right. I'm taking you to my place, where I plan to fix you the best breakfast you've ever had."

"Oh, Joel, I'd really rather just go home. I'm not very good company when I'm tired and..."

"No arguments, Red. If I don't feed you, I know you won't eat, and you can't afford to lose more weight. Besides, the only meal I know how to make with pizzazz is breakfast. How does a cheese omelet and fresh coffee sound?"

Her stomach gurgled at the thought. "Pretty good, although I'm not sure I can handle more coffee." They'd been drinking what passed for coffee from a machine most of the night, which was probably why she felt a little wired. "You've been away. How do you know you have eggs and such in your apartment?"

"Because Bessie was there today. She's worked for my mom for years and comes to my place once a week. She knew I was coming home and so she's stocked the fridge. I leave money for her, and she shops when I get too busy. Bessie's a sweetie and knows all my favorite foods."

A maid who cleaned and shopped for him. Probably did his laundry, as well. Must be nice. "That's great, but honestly, I can feed myself. I need a shower badly...."

"I've got a big bathroom with lots of towels." He glanced over at her as he swung into the parking lot of his apartment building. "And I've got your suitcase in the back. You can clean up while I cook."

Too exhausted to argue, Hannah gave in. "Such a deal. How can I refuse?"

She might have known his apartment would be wonderful. Ten stories up, with wide windows that looked out on the Charles River Basin. Big, comfortable furniture, warm woods, thick wool carpeting you all but sank into. Yet very masculine, using shades of blue from Wedgwood to navy, and browns from tan to rust. Finally, a bowl filled with yellow mums was on the entryway table. That had to be Bessie's touch.

He'd given her the tour, then carried her bag into his bedroom, pointing out the connecting bath before making his way to the kitchen. She'd closed the door with a heavy sigh.

Such an intimate thing, taking a shower in someone else's home. Her hair smelled of his shampoo, her skin wore the scent of his masculine soap. His towel was damp from her body. His fragrance was the one that lingered, exciting her senses.

She dressed in his room, unable to ignore his big king-size bed with its navy quilt. How many women had he brought here? she wondered. None of her business, Hannah told herself as she pulled on the last clean thing in her bag, green sweatpants and shirt. Curiosity got the better of her, and she looked around, searching for the key to the man out there fixing her breakfast.

On his dresser was a framed snapshot of the Merrick clan—parents, kids, spouses, grandchildren and pets—taken on a recent summer day at Hyannis. Standing next to his father, Joel looked unusually sober, or was he just squinting into the sun? Another photo was of a much younger Joel astride a black stallion, a big grin on his face. Probably taken in Montana on Bart's ranch.

Brushing her hair, she wandered to his nightstand and found a Grisham novel and a black address book. Hannah smiled. What would she find in that? No, she wouldn't snoop that far. Leaving her hair to air dry, she finished repacking her bag and left the bedroom.

"I've got everything ready to go," Joel told her. "I'm just going to take a quick shower before I put it all together. Help yourself to orange juice in the fridge." He left her there.

The juice was cold and tart and just right. Hannah carried it into the living room and stood looking out the windows. A cold and dreary day, but inside, it was warm and cozy. She swung around and checked a couple of titles in an overflowing bookcase, then walked over to turn on the stereo. Elton John came on, low and sad. She was just checking out the fireplace when Joel came back out.

She turned around, then stopped. He was barefoot, wearing a pair of gray drawstring pants and a white T-shirt, his black hair still wet from the shower and curling onto his forehead. Her breath backed up in her throat. He was beautiful.

Noticing her look, Joel frowned. "What?"

Hannah shook her head. "Nothing. Nothing at all." Why was her voice so husky? Oh, Lord, she never should have let him talk her into coming here. She'd been shocked emotionally by Will's near-fatal heart attack and sleep deprived until she had no defenses left. And she needed plenty to deal with her chaotic feelings for Joel Merrick.

Following him into the kitchen, she decided she'd eat quickly and grab a cab home. They'd been together too much; that was all. She was, after all, a woman with normal needs that would surface at the most inconvenient times. That didn't mean she'd act on them. Impolite though it was, she'd eat and run.

"Can I do anything?" she asked as he poured batter he'd already prepared into the omelet pan.

"Not a thing. Just sit down. Everything'll be ready in a couple of minutes." He slid the split bagels under the broiler. "Sure felt good to shower, didn't it?"

"Mmm-hmm." Hannah poured herself a cup of coffee. She didn't need more caffeine, but it might snap her out of this strange mood.

Joel placed small smoked sausages on a serving plate, then dished up hash browns. But his mind was on the woman sitting so nervously at his table. They'd spent a good deal of time together recently and had even slept together twice, though not in the way he'd have liked to. He didn't know if it was fatigue or jet lag or just her presence here in his home, where he'd pictured her many nights as he'd lain in his bed alone. But somehow, today, right now, his awareness of her, his need for her, was at the straining point.

And he could tell she was as affected as he.

In minutes, he had the rest of the meal on the table. He sat down opposite her. "I hope you're hungry."

"You made enough for a starving family of four." He'd gone to so much trouble. She'd been hungry on the way over. What had happened to her appetite? It had been replaced by another kind of hunger, one that was making her edgy.

The fork fell from her hand onto the tabletop with a clatter. Embarrassed, she picked it up and sent him an apologetic smile. Terrific, now she was clumsy, too. She took a bite, found it wonderful and told him so.

"Thanks. Breakfast is my favorite meal of the day. Sometimes I have it for dinner."

"Me, too. I guess people who live alone do that sort of thing." Inane. Her comments were absolutely inane. Next thing, she'd begin babbling. She tore her bagel in half and took a bite, hoping to forestall that possibility.

Funny how his soap smelled different on her, Joel thought. The warm scent drifted to him, and his palms began to itch.

A safe topic—that's what they needed, Hannah decided. "Do you think we should call the hospital and make sure Will's still doing okay?"

"Sure, we can. I'll call when we finish."

"This omelet's wonderful." It really was. If only she were hungry.

"It's the cheese. Dofino."

"Ah, yes." She couldn't keep this up another minute. Slowly, she set down her fork. "Please don't think me terrible, but I think it's all caught up with me. I'm not so much hungry as tired.'' She looked up, tried a smile. ''Thanks so much for all this, but I really need to go home.''

His appetite had faltered, as well. ''You can sleep in my bed. I'll take the couch.'' He had a feeling she wouldn't invite him to lie with her, even if nothing happened. Probably because this time, it was highly possible that something would.

''No, really. I need to get home, check my mail, the answering machine.'' She rose, hoping he wouldn't make this too difficult. ''You finish eating. I'll just slip out and grab a cab.''

''You will not. If you insist on leaving, I'll drive you.'' He stood up, watching her closely.

Why did she feel so terrible? ''I'm sorry, Joel.''

He stepped closer, took her hand. ''For what?''

She felt confused, twitchy. ''I'm not sure.''

He lifted her hand, turning it, and bent to place his lips gently in her palm. His thumb on her wrist, he felt her pulse scramble. She tried to pull her hand back, but he held on, his eyes rising to meet hers. The look held, speaking volumes.

''Joel, you said all you wanted from me was friendship, remember?''

''Friendship, for now, I said. And I told you we'd worry about later later.'' He tugged on her hand and brought her body close up against his. ''Later's here, Hannah.''

''Joel, I think...''

He touched a fingertip to her lips. ''Shh. You think too much.'' His eyes locked with hers, he ran his fingertip over her top lip, then traced the fullness of her lower lip. Her mouth trembled open as her breath hitched in her throat. He kissed the corners, then placed feathery kisses on her cheeks, on her eyelids, which closed as if too heavy to stay open, and moved down to taste the sweet column of her throat. He didn't rush, didn't demand. Just moved lazily, letting her needs build.

Finally, he settled his mouth on hers while his hands moved to the back and slipped under her sweatshirt. He felt her shiver as he stroked the soft skin there, moving to the sides along her rib cage, then shifting to the front and closing at last around her breasts. She moaned low in her throat at the contact as he deepened the kiss.

Her breasts were small and firm, fitting perfectly in his hands. His fingers traced the sensitive skin as he felt her grip his upper arms. She didn't resist but didn't participate wholly either. It was as if she were fighting an inner battle, unable to make up her mind to take part or take flight. Patiently, Joel waited, his tongue mating with hers.

As before, he sensed a passion within Hannah that she seemed to struggle against, to want to deny. Why would a beautiful, desirable woman fight her own sexuality? he wondered. Scars from the past, undoubtedly. Maybe he could make them disappear.

His mouth pressed down on hers, coaxing a deeper response, urging her without words to touch him, to give in to her own needs, to answer his. Her breathing was ragged, her knees shaky. His body's demands were making him desperate. Her special taste had him throbbing, her clean scent robbing him of all coherent thought. He wanted her *now*.

Slowly, so as not to frighten her, Joel slipped his hands beneath the waistband of her slacks, then inside the last satin barrier. With a groan, his fingers reached her. Soft, warm and wet, she was as ready as he. He stroked once and felt her convulse against him.

Stunned, breathing hard, it took Hannah a few moments to recover. Trembling, she stepped away from him, shaking her head. "No! No, I can't do this."

It wasn't the reaction he'd expected. Joel moved to her, urging her back into his arms. "Why not, Hannah? You must know how much I want you. I won't hurt you."

Yes. Yes, he would. It would happen again, the way it had the last time, if she gave in. "Please, let me go." She shoved against him, turned and left the kitchen.

He went after her, angry, confused. "What's wrong? What are you afraid of?"

She couldn't, wouldn't, answer him. On the chair was the jacket she'd shed earlier. She struggled into it, then picked up her shoulder bag. "I'm sorry" was all she could think of to say as she yanked open the apartment door.

"Wait! Your suitcase. Damn it, let me drive you." He looked around for his shoes.

"No. I'll get it another time." She rushed across the hallway and punched the button for the elevator.

In his doorway, Joel jammed his fists onto his hips. "I'm not him, Hannah. Not like him at all. I wouldn't hurt you."

The doors opened, and she stepped inside. Then she turned and looked across at him. "Yes, you would. Maybe you wouldn't plan to, but you would."

The doors slid silently shut as Joel stood watching. "Damn whoever hurt you," he whispered, then closed his door with a resounding thud.

Chapter Nine

"This time, Ms. Richards, I promise to follow through," Ellen Baxter said. She sat at the big dining-room table at Sanctuary, holding her daughter, Carrie, on her lap. Her hand shook as she smoothed the blond hair back from the child's thin face. An ugly bruise stained Carrie's left cheek, and there was a bandaged cut above her right eye. "This time Rod's gone too far."

Seated across from her, Hannah wasn't sure if she believed Ellen. It had been her experience in these battering cases that the women usually didn't take action until the husband involved the children. But Ellen's history of leaving, then returning to Rod was long and depressing.

"I hope you mean it, Ellen," Hannah said, taking out her pen. She glanced through the archway where Carrie's brother, Ryan, was watching cartoons, his cheeks still red from the slaps he'd endured. Their outer wounds would heal, but what internal harm had Rod Baxter inflicted on his children?

"I believe your restraining order is still valid," Hannah went on, rummaging through her briefcase for the copy she'd made. She found it and checked. "Yes, it is. Now, Ellen, do I need to tell you again that you must not go to him and give him access to you and the children?"

Lee Stanford, seated next to Ellen, jumped in. "I talked to Ellen before I called you. She promised me she'd stay here until this thing is settled." From the candy dish on the table, she picked out a red lollipop and held it out to Carrie. "Here, sweetie. I'll bet this'll make you feel better."

Carrie stared at Lee with her big eyes, but didn't make a move to take the sucker.

"It's all right, honey," Ellen said, taking the candy and removing the wrapper. "I hate to see her like this, afraid of everyone."

Hannah took out a yellow pad. "All right, Ellen, tell me exactly what happened."

Speaking through puffy lips, Ellen told her story. It wasn't a pretty one, especially concerning the children.

Ellen pressed a tissue to her damp eyes with her free hand. "They wanted a snack, some cookies and milk, but Rod hadn't given me any money in a long while, so I hadn't shopped. I asked him for a couple of dollars so I could go to the store. That's when he blew." She sniffled into her tissue. "He's never hit them before. It's just the job loss, you know. He feels like a failure."

Hannah stopped writing. "Ellen, don't make excuses for him. There are no acceptable reasons for a man who strikes his wife and children. Not a job loss, not a lack of money, nothing justifies what Rod has done."

Ellen nodded, her eyes downcast. "I know."

She knew intellectually, but was she really convinced? Hannah wondered. "How did you get away from him?"

"I did a terrible thing. I reached behind me and grabbed a skillet from the stove. I . . . I hit him with it."

Hannah was surprised. "What did he do?"

"He fell backward. It sort of dazed him. If he'd have been sober, it probably wouldn't have, you know, 'cause he's real strong. He was cursing and swearing, so I grabbed Carrie and ran to the car. Ryan was outside, and I hustled them both in and we drove off. Rod was on the porch by then. I could see him in the rearview mirror. He was furious, but I had to do it, don't you see? I couldn't let him hurt the kids no more."

Lee reached over and patted the woman's thin shoulder. "Of course you did the right thing, honey."

"What do you want me to do?" Ellen asked her attorney.

"Well, for starters, all three of you must not leave the premises. Lee, I know you won't let Rod in if he should somehow find Ellen. And don't accept calls from him. Can you take Ellen and the children to the hospital to be thoroughly checked out? I want their injuries on record."

"Right after lunch," Lee said.

"Good. You still have the camera I brought over?" Hannah saw Lee nod. "Terrific. I want pictures of all the injuries on all of you."

"Then what?" Ellen wanted to know.

"We're going to charge Rod with assault and battery."

"Will I have to testify?"

"Probably. Do you think he's still at the house? Does he have relatives he might go stay with?"

"I don't know if he's at the house. We don't have relatives here, none at all. Rod's father lives in Tennessee, but we never hear from him."

Hannah slipped her pad and pen back into her briefcase. "I don't want you to worry. We'll get him this time, as long as you don't back down again." She rose as the front doorbell rang and Lee went to go see who was there.

Ellen looked at her two children sitting close together on the floor watching television. "I won't, I swear."

Hannah gathered up her things as voices in the front foyer came nearer. She looked up and saw Lee carrying several boxes of diapers. Following behind her was a familiar tall figure.

"Look who's here," Lee said, setting down her bundles on the table. She turned to the man with a smile. "Joel, thanks so much for all this. And thank your mother for me. It's so sweet of her to help out. Baby food, canned goods, flour, sugar. Cookie's going to be thrilled."

Joel set the large box he'd brought in on the table, his eyes on Hannah. It had been two days since she'd left his apartment upset and trembling. He hadn't seen her since and noticed that his unexpected arrival had unnerved her.

"I didn't know you knew Lee," Hannah said. She'd been avoiding him again, her feelings still in a jumble. Perhaps it was best that she ran into him here with others around instead of alone. Perhaps if she made no reference to their last time together, he wouldn't, either.

"Oh, Joel's been bringing us supplies for a couple of weeks now," Lee explained. "His mother's been doing some fund-raising for us, as well."

Joel picked up the explanation. "I told Mom about Sanctuary after she met you on Thanksgiving. She belongs to several organizations that do fund-raising, so I had no trouble persuading her to include this place on their lists."

"I see," Hannah murmured, though she really didn't. There were a dozen or more shelters in and around Boston. Why had he directed Mrs. Merrick to this one?

"Mom got hold of a sewing machine, Lee," Joel went on. "It's used but works just fine. I couldn't fit it in my car, but I can have someone drop it off later, if you could use one."

"Wonderful," Lee said. "We often get donated clothes that need repairs. And we have several bolts of cloth in the closet that someone gave us. Maybe one of our residents can sew."

"I'm a fairly good seamstress," Ellen said shyly. "My mother taught me. I make most of the children's clothes."

Lee gave her a grateful smile. "That's wonderful."

Hannah put on her jacket. "I've got to run. Ellen, I'll be in touch. Lee, thanks for calling me. I'll see you both later." She looked up at Joel, at a loss as to what to say. His eyes were so blue today, but not smiling. "I guess I'll see you at the office."

"I'm leaving, too." He turned to Ellen and Lee. "Ladies, I hope you can make use of all that stuff." He trailed after Hannah toward the door.

"Yes, indeed," Lee called after him. "Thanks again."

Outside, a chill wind had Hannah turning up her coat collar as she went down the porch steps heading for her car parked at the curb. Maybe Joel would walk on to his Mercedes in front of her Volkswagen without another word.

The day pigs fly, she thought as he came up alongside her.

"How've you been?" he asked, wishing she didn't look as if she wanted to bolt.

"Fine, thanks." She unlocked the passenger door and tossed in her briefcase and shoulder bag.

Joel stopped by her open door. "I went to see Will a while ago. He told me I just missed you."

"Yes, I was there early. He looks so much better, doesn't he?"

"Yeah, he does." He decided to jump in and test the waters. "Do you have time to go somewhere and have a cup of coffee? I'd like to talk with you."

Hannah made a great show of checking her watch. "I'm afraid not. I've got too much work to do." She shut her car door and pulled her keys from her jacket pocket. "Besides, I've just had coffee with Lee. But thanks, anyway." She started to walk around to the driver's side.

Joel touched her arm. "Are you angry with me?"

He wasn't going to let it go. Hannah shook her head. "No. If I'm angry with anyone, it's me. I should never have let things go as far as they did. I don't want a relationship. If I did something to make you believe otherwise, I apologize."

"Why? I don't understand. You're attracted to me— you've already admitted that, not that I couldn't see for myself. I certainly am to you. We're both free. What's holding you back?"

She felt cornered. "Look, Joel, I don't want to go into this now, here on a cold and windy street. I . . ."

"Then when? When do you want to discuss it?"

"Actually, I don't. Friends, that's all I want us to be. I can't handle anything more than that. I have my reasons, but I don't want to go into lengthy explanations. Suffice it to say that I'm perfectly content with having you as a friend. Period."

She was hiding, running from her own feelings. He had to know why. "I care about you, Hannah. Doesn't that matter to you?"

His persistence was annoying her. "You care? I thought love-'em-and-leave-'em was more your style. Get them in bed and then move on. Tell me that isn't so."

There was some truth to what she said. "I used to be like that, I admit. Until I met you."

She gave him an incredulous look. "Right. I came on the scene, and bingo! Suddenly, you're a changed man. Because I'm such a beauty, so irresistible. Is that what you want me to believe?"

"You are beautiful, and I do find you irresistible. Why can't you believe that?"

"Because I'm a realist and I can't be won over by smooth flattery. I'm average, Joel, not a stunner. I don't set men's hearts to beating wildly. I . . ."

He grabbed her arms and yanked her to him, taking her mouth with his. He kissed her deeply, passionately, lengthily. When he let her go, he saw the glazed shock in her eyes. Taking her hand, he placed it under his jacket on his chest over his heart. "Can you feel that wild beating? Do you think I can fake that? Maybe you need to reevaluate your effect on men. Maybe you should stop hiding behind something that happened in your past and open your eyes to the present. You might very well be passing up the best thing that's ever happened to you."

He let her go then and marched to his Mercedes, more angry than aroused. Without a backward look, he climbed in and took off with a juvenile squeal of tires on damp pavement.

Hannah Richards had to be the most obstinate, exasperating woman he'd ever met. Why he wanted her was a mystery to him.

Yet he did.

Hannah was having a good day. First, she'd been to see Will and he was out of intensive care and sitting up in bed, looking so much better. The doctor had said he planned to release his patient in a day or so. And she'd had a marvelous day in court with Dawn Carruthers at her child-support hearing.

Her footsteps light, Hannah entered her office building the back way and hurried to Marcie's desk. "Did you hear? Will's going home soon."

The older woman stopped typing. "Oh, that's wonderful news. I was planning on visiting him after work."

"You'll probably find him strolling up and down the hall. They've got him up walking, he's eating regular food and his color's good." Hannah removed her coat and opened her briefcase. "And wait'll you see this." She handed the folder to Marcie.

Pleased at Hannah's buoyant mood, Marcie opened the folder and glanced at the top paper. Her face broke into a big smile. "You nailed him, eh?"

"Sure did." Hannah sat down on the vacant chair and leaned forward. "I can hardly believe how arrogant Adam Carruthers is. He came in the courtroom dressed in what had to be a five-hundred-dollar suit, with imported leather shoes and a gold Rolex watch, carrying a hand-tooled briefcase. And he was there to get his child-support payments *reduced* when he's seven thousand in arrears. Do you believe the nerve of the man?''

Marcie shook her head. "Some people. Who was the judge?''

"Judge Bannister, and I thought we were sunk. He's a tough old bird, or so I'd been told. He listened patiently to Adam pleading poverty, saying he'd had to turn in his BMW for a Ford because he couldn't keep up the payments, that he was representing himself because he couldn't afford an attorney. And so on. Meanwhile, we pointed out that Adam had let the kids' health insurance lapse, that Dawn couldn't afford to buy new winter coats for them and that they usually ate pasta without meat three times a week for lack of money.''

Waiting for the punch line, Marcie leaned forward. "So what'd the judge do?''

"He called Adam up to the bench and asked him to empty his pockets onto the clerk's desk. Adam objected, but the judge insisted. In his gold money clip was over eleven hundred dollars. Judge Bannister handed the money to Dawn right then and there, and told Adam he had until five today to get the balance of the seven thousand arrearage to the clerk or go to jail. And he increased his future child-support payments.'' Hannah laughed out loud. "You should have seen the big jerk's face. He was absolutely stunned. When he tried to object, the judge looked pointedly at his own watch and said he'd better hurry because he had only three hours to cough up the money or get his jammies for a night in the clinker.''

"In just those words?''

"That's right.''

"You win again. Congratulations, honey.''

Hannah sobered. "I'm not the winner, Marcie. Those two little kids are. They shouldn't live practically in poverty while their father carries around a wad of twenties that would choke a goat."

"Yes, you're right. I'm glad for them. But you made it happen. I'll update the support papers." She set aside the file, then glanced toward Joel's office. "I wish he was having as good a day as you."

"What happened?"

Marcie wouldn't have said a word if she didn't honestly think that Hannah could make Joel feel better. Since the week she'd taken chicken soup to Hannah's when she'd been ill and seen the concerned way Joel took care of her, she'd realized that there was something between these two. She'd mentioned her suspicions to Will, and the old man had just smiled knowingly. They both seemed to be fighting the attraction, and she wondered how long that would continue. "First, his father called and tried to strong-arm him into dropping the lawsuit on that tenement owned by Jason's friend, the city councilman."

That didn't surprise Hannah. "I'd wager Joel said no."

She smiled. It was gratifying to know that Hannah believed in Joel's innate goodness. "You're absolutely right, but I could tell from Joel's expression that his father's really annoyed with him this time. And then that Lang woman showed up, insisting she see Joel. She's hell-bent to hire him to represent Rusty Lang for killing his brother."

"That's a messy one. Is he going to take the case?"

"I don't know. She left about half an hour ago, and he's been mighty quiet in there. Told me to hold his calls. What do you think?"

Hannah shrugged. "The ones involving moral dilemmas are always tough. It appears as though Rusty shot Tom Lang in cold blood. But did he? Or was he set up? If so, why and by whom? And even if he did, doesn't he deserve fair representation?" She glanced toward Joel's office door, standing ajar. "I don't envy him his problem."

Marcie looked up hopefully. "Why don't you go see him? Problems often seem more solvable if you talk them over with someone."

Hannah looked hesitant, remembering how they'd parted just yesterday in front of Sanctuary. Joel had been angry; she'd been stunned. But then, his kisses always left her feeling overwhelmed. And needy. He'd said he cared for her, and she longed to believe him.

Because she'd done some soul-searching of her own since then. She knew she cared for Joel Merrick more than she should. She didn't want to believe he'd tire of her and walk away, hurting her badly. But she feared that he would. And, caring so much this time, she wasn't sure she would recover. "I don't know...."

"Go on, honey. He doesn't have Will to confide in these days." That should do it, Marcie thought. Tug on the old heartstrings.

Marcie was right. Joel had been her sounding board more than once. "All right, I'll try." She left her things on Marcie's desk chair and walked toward Joel's office.

As Hannah reached Joel's halfway-open door, a paper airplane came zooming out, arcing up, then zeroing down and crash-landing. Amused, she shoved open the door. "I hate to interrupt you when you're obviously very busy."

In the process of forming another airplane, Joel glanced up. "Damn right I am. It's not easy folding these so they'll fly." Scattered about the floor were a dozen or more paper aircraft.

Hands in the pockets of her gray wool suit jacket, Hannah strolled in. "I think I was out the day they taught airplane folding in law school."

"Too bad. You don't know what you're missing." Putting the finishing touches on the tail, he then lifted his newest creation to eye level and examined the sleek lines. "You've got to take into consideration wind velocity, structural soundness, air speed—all that."

"I'm sure you do."

Taking careful aim, Joel launched the plane. It sailed through the air, going high then curving into a loop before spiraling to the floor. "Not bad," he announced, checking his watch. "Five seconds." He picked up another sheet of paper from a stack on his desk.

Uninvited, Hannah sat down opposite him and crossed her legs. The stack, she noted, had at least fifty pages to go. "Do you plan to spend the day in aeronautical comparative studies?"

He made a face. "As good a way to pass the time as any."

"Does this have anything to do with avoidance, or are you mentally going over a puzzling case while perfecting your planes?"

He shot her a quick glance. "Avoidance is your specialty. And yes, I'm trying to decide whether to represent a client or recommend another attorney to his somewhat aggressive wife."

She caught the avoidance barb and decided to ignore it. "The Lang case. I heard she was in."

"Oh, yeah, she was in." He busied himself folding.

"I thought you were fairly certain you weren't going to take the case."

"I did say that, didn't I?" Losing interest in playing with paper, Joel tossed aside the half-finished plane. "My problem here is that I can't really empathize with the guy. So his father favored his brother and left him out in the cold. That's life. You've got to accept certain things."

Hannah thought she knew where this was going.

"For instance, if my father died tomorrow," Joel went on, "I'm sure he'd leave the practice to my brothers. But I'm not going to go shoot Todd or Sam over it."

"I doubt that he would. Jason may be annoyed with you about not staying in the family firm, but he wouldn't disinherit you."

"You don't know him like I do." He didn't say it angrily or with self-pity, but just stated a fact.

Hannah had a feeling this strange, melancholy mood had more to do with Joel's phone conversation with his father over the tenement case than over the Lang decision. "Joel, why don't you take up ranching and give up law, like Bart did? You seemed so much happier in Montana. Then you wouldn't have to wrestle with moral decisions like the Langs and you wouldn't have to contend with your father's interference."

Funny, he'd been thinking along those lines himself. Yet he wasn't entirely sure that such a move would make him happy, either. Something was missing from his life, but was the location the key? Maybe it had more to do with people. Or a certain person. "Would you come with me if I did?"

Her shocked expression was quite genuine. "Go with you? I..."

A knock at the door had Hannah looking over her shoulder, grateful for the interruption. "Hannah, Judge Eastman's on the line about Sheila Barns. He says he can

spare you ten minutes if you'll hurry on over to his
chambers right now.''

"Great." Hannah got to her feet. "Thanks, Marcie.
Tell him I'm on my way."

"What's that all about?" Joel asked.

"I haven't got time to explain, but it's really important. I'll tell you later."

"Okay. Your place. Seven o'clock. I'll bring the
pizza."

In the doorway, Hannah paused. "As friends and no
pressure for anything more?"

He affected an innocent pose. "Who, me? Pressure
you? Never!"

She didn't have time to argue. "You'd better mean
that," she said over her shoulder as she hurried off.

Smiling broadly, Joel picked up his discarded plane
and went to work perfecting it.

At five to seven, Joel pulled into Hannah's driveway
and parked behind her Volkswagen. It was snowing
heavily again, and by the slight accumulation on her car,
she hadn't been home long, either. He stepped out,
grabbed the pizza box and hurried up the back stairs.

She pulled the door open before he had a chance to
knock. "It seems you're always feeding me," Hannah
said, standing back to let him in. "Mmm, that smells
heavenly."

Joel stomped snow from his shoes and stepped into
her kitchen. He saw that she'd set the drop-leaf table
with blue place mats and napkins, and two tall white
candles were waiting to be lighted in brass holders. She
never ceased to surprise him. He hadn't known if she'd
be welcoming or feisty or just plain not interested in
sharing a meal. He wondered if she meant to keep him

on edge or if this ambivalence was part of her personality.

Hannah took the pizza to the counter while Joel removed his coat. "Would you like beer or wine with your pizza? Or I have soft drinks and coffee made. I've also got a gooseberry pie I baked yesterday."

"I haven't had gooseberry in years." He pulled a slim paper bag from his coat pocket. "Wine. I remembered you like Chardonnay." He held up the bottle.

"Great. The corkscrew's in the second drawer, glasses up above." While he served the wine, she dished pizza onto two large white plates, then decided to zap each in the microwave for a minute or so. The drive over had cooled them.

He found slender wineglasses, set them on the table and poured the cool wine in both, then turned to her. She was wearing a white blouse with the same gray skirt she'd had on, obviously not home long enough to change. Except she'd removed her shoes and put on red slippers. Her hair had been up earlier, but now hung past her shoulders, looking as if she'd recently brushed it. She was a knockout and didn't even know it.

"So, have you decided whether you're going to tackle the Lang case?"

"I have." He sat down. "I called and told her I pass on this one. I don't believe in his innocence and wouldn't be doing him justice."

Hannah carried their plates to the table and sat down. "I'd bet she wasn't too happy."

"You'd be right." He noticed that her dark eyes were bright with excitement. "Are you going to tell me what has you so keyed up?"

"Patience, patience." She held up her glass. "Here's to good days. May we have more of them."

"I'll drink to that." Joel touched his glass to hers and took a long swallow. "I hope you like everything on your pizza, because that's what you have."

Suddenly starving, Hannah took a bite. She rolled her eyes in appreciation. "Wonderful. Double cheese, too. I love it."

"Maybe you're part Italian," he said, digging in.

"Actually, I have some Spanish blood. My grandparents married young and migrated to New Mexico, where my mother was born. Later, they all moved to Michigan where work was more plentiful. My grandmother was a wonderful cook." She hadn't thought of that in years, Hannah realized.

She'd actually volunteered some information about her background, Joel thought with surprise. "Then you knew your grandparents before your folks died. What happened to them?"

Hannah finished chewing. "My grandfather died before I was born, but my grandmother lived with us. The social workers told us that when they took my mother to the hospital, Grandma went back to New Mexico, where she had some cousins. She wasn't well and needed to live with someone who could help her."

"Later, when you were older, did you ever try to find her?"

"Yes. Mr. Murray, from the last foster family I lived with, helped me. We wrote to all kinds of agencies and finally learned that she'd died two years after leaving Michigan. By then, the cousins had scattered, and we couldn't find any family members." Remembered frustration washed over Hannah, but she was determined today to not let the past drag her down. "Let's not talk about that now. I want to tell you about Sheila Barns."

Joel got up to get himself a second helping. "All right, tell me."

"She's twelve with long black hair and these huge dark eyes. Not much to look at, but one day, with the proper care, she's going to be lovely. She was picked up for shoplifting. Not clothes or jewelry. Food, because she was hungry. I just happened to be in the courtroom when they brought her in before Judge Eastman. My heart went out to her. Thin, dirty, scared. She'd just run away from her fourth foster home." Hannah leaned back in her chair, her expression melancholy.

By now, knowing Hannah, he could guess where this was headed. "Don't tell me, let me guess. You talked the judge into letting you take over."

"Well, of course I did. I couldn't let them lock her up. It's a first offense."

"That we know of."

She hadn't planned on eating more, but it was so good. She got up for another piece. "Listen, no child should have to be locked up for stealing food because they're hungry. There's something wrong with the adults in this world if we can't feed our kids."

Joel sipped his wine and grinned at her. "Spoken like a true bleeding heart."

Narrowing her eyes, Hannah sat back down. "I am *not* a bleeding heart. You don't know anything about it. You've never been in foster care—often scared, ignored, lonely. You're a ward of the state, and they look out for you. But you can't talk to them, explain how you feel. The state can't hug you and make it all better. I have a feeling, if you'd been in that situation, you might have run away a time or two yourself."

Propping his elbows on the table, Joel leaned forward. "You're right. But what are you going to do about

Sheila now that you got her released to your care? Where did you put her, and how are you going to keep her from being a repeat offender?''

''I've already taken care of that, smarty. Lee told me about this halfway house for teens. I checked it out, and it's not bad at all. I took Sheila there for now. They gave her a clean bed, a change of clothes, a hot shower. Monday, I'm going to see about getting her back in school.''

Joel studied her, his face serious. ''You've taken on an awful lot here, Hannah. A kid like that needs so much. Counseling, probably. A medical exam. Maybe a...''

''What Sheila needs most is a big sister. A friend. That's where I come in.'' Her eyes took on a sadness. ''I keep remembering the way she looked when I left her just a little while ago. She looked so small, so young sitting on that cot, with all her worldly possessions in a paper bag. 'Are you sure you're coming back?' she asked me. She thinks I'm going to abandon her like everyone else has.''

Like everyone abandoned Hannah, Joel thought, whether by death or design. ''What about her last foster family?''

Hannah pushed back her plate. ''That's the one that really put her on the run. The teenage son tried to molest her.'' She drew in a shaky breath, feeling Sheila's pain.

''Is that why you relate to her? Did that happen to you?''

''No, thank God. Plain girls are usually left alone.''

Finishing, Joel folded his napkin. ''Are we going to have this discussion again? You are *not* plain.'' She'd brought this up once too often. He got to his feet, took hold of her hand and all but dragged her out of the kitchen. "Come with me."

"What are you doing?" Hannah asked, wondering if he'd lost his mind.

He'd been in her bedroom when she'd been sick. He remembered a cheval mirror by the window. Pulling her along, he stopped to turn on the bedside lamp, then turned her so she was facing her own image. "There. Take a good, long look. What do you see?"

Memories resurfaced reluctantly. Her grandmother saying what a sweet girl she was, so good with a needle and in the kitchen. Not pretty like Katie, but smart in school. She remembered foster parents, several of them, whispering when they thought she couldn't hear. *She's so plain that at least we won't have to worry about boys coming around.* And none had. She would tell him, and then he would know. She didn't want to point out her shortcomings, but she wanted to end this.

"I see an average woman with eyes that are too big for her face and cheekbones that are too prominent and hair that can't make up its mind whether to be red or brown, curly or straight, and . . ."

"That's enough." He was standing behind her, his arms encircling her. "I see perfect golden skin so soft my hands itch to touch it. I see hair so beautiful I want to lose myself in it. I see a slender nose and gorgeous deep brown eyes that have seen too much and yet still crinkle up at the corners when you laugh, which isn't often enough. And I see a mouth made for kissing, made for loving."

Hannah watched him silently, wanting desperately to believe he was telling the truth, yet afraid to.

"Now look at me," Joel said. "Do you remember what you told me once? That I'm easy on the eyes, have a terrific career and money to burn, or words to that effect. Is that what you think?"

This, she was certain of. "Yes."

"If that's so, do you think I'd have a hard time finding a woman, Hannah? Tonight, even within the hour?"

The truth of that brought a lump to her throat. "No," she whispered.

He turned her around to face him, his expression gentle. "But I'm here, aren't I? Why is that? Why do you think?"

His nearness here in her own bedroom, with the soft light playing across his strong features, was making her head swim. She struggled to find a way out. "Honestly, what I think? I think you want to get me into that bed. Put another notch on the scoreboard. I've heard that women who are reluctant become a challenge. You want me so you can say you've had me."

He was angry at her assessment but not surprised. Someone had apparently sweet-talked his way into her life, used her and then left her. Left her feeling abandoned, unwanted, alone and unable to trust again. He had to prove to her that he wasn't like that someone. He drew in a deep, calming breath, his hands resting lightly at her waist. "There's usually a time in the early years of most men when getting women into bed is high priority. But I long ago outgrew meaningless sex."

She watched him carefully. He seemed so sincere. Could she let herself believe?

"I want you. Not anyone else. You. Because I care about you, a great deal." He dipped his head to kiss her gently, oh, so gently.

Hannah closed her eyes and sighed. Her limbs felt heavy, but comfortably so. He was seducing her. She wasn't fighting him, but it was a seduction nonetheless.

She felt as if she'd drunk the entire bottle of wine instead of half a glass. She felt his lips move to her ear, his warm breath causing her to shiver.

Joel leaned back and watched her eyes flutter open, saw the hazy beginnings of passion in their dark depths. "But I won't push you, Hannah. I won't do anything more unless I know you want me as much as I want you. Unless I hear the words." He eased her body close to his and felt her breasts yield against his chest.

Fear and uncertainty mingled with need inside Hannah. "You should go now," she whispered huskily.

"You're right," he answered, but made no move to leave her embrace. His hands wandered into her hair, the pads of his fingers slowly massaging her scalp. He heard her struggle to suppress a moan.

She was drowning in desire, going down for the count. His clever hands drifted down her back, caressing, stroking. His lips settled at her throat, and Hannah knew she was lost. "You can't stay," she murmured feebly. And her arms lifted to draw him closer.

"I know." Her blouse buttoned down the back. His fingers fumbled with the closures, slowly opening each one.

"This can't happen," Hannah sighed, then her lips sought his as an overwhelming need overcame her good sense. Drugged in pleasure, she let the kiss go on and on.

Joel was the first to pull back. He wanted her so badly he was hurting. But it had to be her call. "Well?"

Her mouth was moist from his, her heart thundering its message to her foggy brain. "I can't afford to get involved with you, Joel." There, she'd told him. Now he would leave.

"So you've said before." The blouse was open. He slid the soft fabric over her shoulders, down her arms and tossed it aside. Beneath the thin chemise, her pointed breasts beckoned him. Unable to resist, he pressed his mouth to her.

A sound came from low in her throat as Hannah buried her hands in his thick hair, urging him closer to her yearning flesh. Physical pleasure was a temptation she'd ignored for years. But she could no longer fight this. She stepped back, breathing hard, fighting for a control that was no longer within her grasp.

"If you don't want me, I'll go," Joel said, his voice unsteady. "Tell me what you want."

She, who had never clung to a man in her life, clung to him now as she looked up. "You. I want you."

Chapter Ten

She'd said exactly what he'd been hoping to hear, that she wanted him. He would take her at her word, Joel thought.

The light was shadowy, soft and hazy. The room smelled of her cologne, something fresh and floral. Only the sound of their breathing could be heard in the silent room. His heart was beating rapidly, his pulse pounding. He promised himself he would go slowly, think only of her. He prayed he could keep that promise.

Her luminous eyes watched him, hesitant and aware. His hands moved around back and eased down the zipper of her skirt, letting the garment fall to the floor. Her gaze never left his face as she stepped out of her slippers and kicked the skirt away. But he saw her lower lip tremble and recognized a case of nerves he shared.

She wanted him desperately, Hannah thought. But could she go through with this? What if she froze as she had before? "Joel..."

He kissed her then, not wanting to give her time to overthink her decision, to change her mind. Shifting them both, he lowered her to the bed and followed her down. Murmuring softly, he undressed her slowly, his words soothing, reassuring.

Hannah watched while he stood to hurriedly rid himself of his clothes, then fumbled in his wallet for protection. She'd put herself on birth-control pills for health reasons years ago, but she appreciated his added thoughtfulness. As he turned around, she kept her focus on his broad shoulders, his hard chest matted with dark hair, his narrow waist and strong legs. This was what she wanted, she reminded herself. She wasn't afraid, only a little nervous. It was just that it had been so long and she was so needy. It had to be better this time. Silently, she prayed she wouldn't disappoint him, that he wouldn't walk away pitying her or, worse yet, laughing at her.

Joel returned to kiss her again while his hands stroked, calming her fears, arousing her everywhere.

Hannah's fingers trembled as she touched his bare back, uncertain what she should do, what he'd want her to do. She should have explained, should have told him she wasn't good at this. Then, as his lips moved to her breasts, she drew in a stunned breath and lost her train of thought.

Hesitancy fueled by desire changed her from languid to urgent as she felt his hungry mouth trail over her body. Suddenly, she was no longer wavering, her actions no longer timid. She arched into his touch as his hands skimmed along the insides of her thighs. She felt a rush of heat as he maneuvered further, then a surge of passion as he drove her up and higher yet. Cresting fiercely, she clutched at his back as the waves broke over her.

Jolted by feelings that buffeted her unmercifully, she opened dazed eyes and saw that slow, killer smile on his face. Then he slid down her, his hands leading the way, followed by his mouth, tasting, teasing, tantalizing. No small spot was too insignificant for his loving attention. The satin of her shoulder, the sensitive inside of her elbow, the curve of her waist. Moving with purpose, he trailed lower until he found his target. In moments, he had her whirling over the edge again as she let out a strangled cry.

Joel was sure he'd never known a woman so responsive, so naturally sensual yet seemingly unaware. He heard her whisper his name, and desire for her raced through his blood. He wanted to show her everything, all that could be. But his own body begged for release as he returned to crush her mouth with his.

Steeped in passion, Hannah could scarcely think, could only feel. And no man had ever made her feel like this—so alive, so feminine, so desirable. She returned his kiss, wrapping herself around him, letting him know in the only way she knew how that he'd given her a marvelous gift. And he'd yet to get equal time.

She eased back, wanting to fulfill his needs, as well. All shyness was gone, all reserve shattered. Eyes locked with his, she reached down and guided him inside her. She closed her eyes and tightened her hold on him as he began to move.

She wouldn't have believed there could be more awaiting her than he'd already shown her. She felt his muscles tense and bunch beneath her fingers as he took her deeper, took her further than she'd dared hope. More than willing to let him lead, she followed him into an explosion that rocked her to her very soul.

Joel lay, holding her close, not wanting to lose the closeness of aftermath. He'd guessed from the earlier kisses they'd shared that the tight control Hannah held herself in by day was a facade. He'd felt that inside her was a passion waiting to be set free. He'd been right. But what he hadn't known was how deeply moved he would be in releasing that passion, in watching her face as she abandoned herself to the moment.

He smoothed back her hair and saw the light flush on her face as she eased onto the pillow. When her eyes opened, he wasn't sure what to expect: embarrassment, regret, a need to withdraw from him. What he saw was her slow smile as she looked up.

"Are you all right?" he asked, needing to hear her say it.

Hannah let out a shaky breath. "A long time ago, I saw this movie, a beach scene where Deborah Kerr said something to Burt Lancaster that I wasn't sure I understood. She said, 'I never knew it could be like this.' Now, I understand." She reached to touch his face, thinking how much he'd changed her world today. "Thank you. I didn't know, either, not until you."

Joel found himself deeply moved. What kind of men had she known in the past? Still, he had to admit it pleased him to be the one to show her more. "I'm glad." He touched his lips to her mouth, still moist from his kisses.

Hesitancy crept back into her suddenly wavering gaze. "Was I . . . that is, was everything all right for you?" Lord, but this was awkward. Maybe she never should have asked. Would he even tell her the truth? "I mean, I know I'm a long way from being an expert and..."

"Who said? Honey, making love has a lot more to do with feelings than technique. I care about you and it shows. And I believe you care, too, but you're afraid to admit it."

He was right. She did care and she didn't want to admit it. But she was still worried. She searched his eyes, wondering what he was really thinking.

"What is it, Hannah? Certainly, after what we just did, you can ask me anything."

"No, just forget it." Shifting from him, she sat up, pulling the sheet around her, feeling suddenly exposed.

"I'm not going to forget it." He touched her chin, forcing her to look at him. "What did you mean?"

It amazed her that he could be so boldly naked and yet unconcerned about it. She shrugged. "It's not important. It happened a long time ago."

If a memory could so easily overshadow the obvious glow of their lovemaking, then it damn well was important. "I want to know. Tell me."

Hannah ran a hand through her hair, shoving it back, then rearranged the pillows behind her head and lay back. "I don't know if I can."

"Yes, you can." He shifted closer to her. "You can tell me anything, and it won't change how I feel about you. Don't you know by now that I love you, Hannah?"

Her eyes widened, then looked frightened. She sat up again, shaking her head. "Don't! Don't say that. I don't want you to say things like that when I know you don't mean them."

"I do mean them. Why are you afraid to hear them?"

She covered her face with her hands, but there was nowhere to hide. "Because men say those words too casually just to get what they want. Then, when things get sticky or they're ready to move on, you realize it's all been a lie." She lay back down, feeling drained. She should have known this would happen, should never have let things go so far.

Joel leaned over her, his face inches from hers. "I *never* say what I don't mean. I've *never* told another woman that I loved her. Do you believe that?"

She blinked up at him, desperate to believe him but afraid. "I want to...."

"You should." He took her hand, held it in both of his. "I've wanted you since the day I walked into Will's office and you were so spitfire angry beneath your good manners because I hadn't told you who I was. Maybe I didn't fall in love with you that day. Maybe it was a week later when I saw you fighting so hard to get justice for that girl who'd been raped. Or the evening I found you buying diapers for kids whose father couldn't seem to bother. Or the night I spent holding you in this very bed when you were too sick to object. I don't know what day it happened, or what instant. I only know it happened, lady. I love you, and you're stuck with that."

She couldn't say a word, couldn't. She hadn't counted on this, afraid of still another disappointment. Now that he'd said words that should have cheered her, she felt like weeping. "You'd be better off with someone who wasn't so screwed up inside," she said softly.

Propping himself on one elbow, Joel frowned. "How are you screwed up? I've told you how much I care. Now, it's your turn. Talk to me, Hannah. Tell me about the man who hurt you."

Could she? She hadn't talked about Paul in years. It was such a risk, opening herself up like that. "There's something about me, something that happened, that I never speak of. If I tell, you might not understand, might not believe me."

He curled his fingers around hers. "Take a chance, Hannah. Trust me to understand. I love you."

Maybe he would understand. Maybe he, too, would leave her. Having come this far, she would have to take that risk. Better now than later, when her feelings for him would be so strong she might never recover.

She stared at their joined hands as she began. "I was nineteen years old, in my junior year at Michigan State on scholarship, living on campus except summers, when I went back to the Murrays. I met this fellow, Paul Lawson. He wasn't particularly handsome, though he was tall and had nice brown hair. He didn't have pots of money and he wasn't a jock. His mother was on the faculty, an assistant professor, and his father was an accountant. But he had one thing going for him that I couldn't resist—he seemed to like me a lot."

She sent him an embarrassed look. "I hadn't dated much. I worked two jobs and with school, that didn't leave much time. I turned him down at first, but he persisted. Finally, I gave in. We went to a concert, then movies, a local play. Paul was fun to talk with and quite intelligent. I guess I was a case of arrested development. I fell like a ton of bricks. It didn't take much for him to talk me into his bed."

"That was the first time for you?" Joel asked.

"Yes, the first time. I didn't get much out of it physically, but I liked being wanted. He told me repeatedly that he loved me, and, sap that I was, I believed him. Paul had his own apartment, and I'd skip a class and meet him there. I convinced myself I was in love, and maybe I was. With love, not with Paul. A big difference."

"You wouldn't be the first, nor the last."

"Sad, but true. At any rate, after a couple of months, I realized I was pregnant." She looked at him. "Yes, I knew about birth control, but I was naive enough to trust him to take care of it. I was too timid to go to a doctor and get on the Pill. I don't know what happened, really, because he used condoms."

"Nothing's foolproof."

"I found that out the hard way. When I told Paul I was pregnant, he changed into this person I didn't recognize. He became hard, even cruel. He said he'd always used a condom so I had to have been with another guy. I swore I hadn't, which was the truth. He wouldn't believe me."

Joel clamped down on a rush of rage at a man he'd never meet, the one who'd turned his back on Hannah and his unborn child.

"After that day, Paul stopped calling me. I finally phoned him, desperate enough to swallow my pride. He told me it was my problem and if I brought him into it, he'd have his mother use her connections to see to it that I lost my scholarship and his father would back her up."

"Nice family."

She seemed not to hear him, lost in the past. "I didn't know what to do or where to turn. I couldn't tell the Murrays. They'd been the only two people who'd been kind to me. How could I disappoint them like that? So one night, I poured it all out to my roommate at the dorm. Connie and I weren't really close, but I guess I just had to tell someone. She told me she'd get the name of a doctor who did abortions. But I'd need four hundred dollars. It might as well have been four million."

Hannah drew in a deep breath, hurrying now to get past the worst part. "Connie tried to be a good friend. She borrowed the money for me, but by then, I'd changed. I wasn't even showing yet, but the baby had become real to me. I decided that, somehow, I'd find a way to raise my child if I had to scrub floors to do it. Connie was upset that I wouldn't go through with the abortion. She'd had one the summer before, and it was no big deal, she said. But I knew it wasn't right for me. All I could think of was that, despite the way the baby had been conceived, this was *my* child, my flesh and blood."

"So what did you do?" Had she given the baby up for adoption? Was that why she'd said she didn't want children now, because out there somewhere was her own growing up without her?

"I know now that I wasn't being very realistic, but I was determined. I made all these plans—quit school at the end of the semester, get a better job, a place to live. But the Fates weren't through with me yet." Hannah couldn't prevent the bitterness from coming through. "A week later, I started to bleed badly. The pain was awful, and I was so scared. Connie had gone home for the weekend, which I seldom did. I've been alone so much of my life, but I'd never felt so alone as that night."

Joel scooted up to her and took her in his arms. "I'm so sorry you had to go through that by yourself. Paul's a bastard who didn't deserve you."

She wasn't crying, had already shed so many tears over the child that would never be that she had none left. Nevertheless, her voice was shaky. "I thought God was punishing me. I sat up all night, holding that bloody towel and just rocking, wondering if I'd make it through.''

Hannah felt Joel's strong heartbeat under her hand where it rested on his chest, and took comfort in his closeness. She took a moment longer, then went on. ''I did something then that now I realize must have come from being totally exhausted, drained, half out of my mind with fear and grief. About three in the morning, I went outside into the yard behind the dorm. It was spring and the ground was soft from a recent rain.''

She remembered the heavy scent of lilacs from a nearby bush, the bark of a dog from some distant house, the moon lighting her path. She remembered everything as if it were yesterday. ''I fell to the ground and dug a hole under this old maple tree and buried the towel there.'' She choked on a dry sob, her breath hitching out. ''I buried my baby there. I know it was just a bloody towel, but not to me. Not to me.''

He pulled her closer, kissing the top of her head, wishing he hadn't asked her to relive such devastating memories. Hot, scalding tears finally fell onto his chest. He hoped they'd cleanse her, heal her.

''I wanted to die so I couldn't feel so much pain. I wanted to crawl right in that hole with my child who'd never had a chance. I couldn't tell anyone, couldn't yell and scream at the Fates, couldn't weep except behind closed doors. No one understood, no one could help.'' She held on to him and waited for the waves of remembered pain to pass.

He understood so much now. ''That's what bothered you so much that day in the barn on the ranch, isn't it? It brought everything back, the colt dying, the mare's cool indifference. It was your miscarriage, not memories of your childhood, that upset you.''

She was surprised he understood so well. ''Yes. I can go for days, even weeks, when I don't think of that time. Then suddenly, something triggers a memory, and I go into such a black mood that I scare myself.''

Joel tightened his arms around her. ''You don't have to be afraid anymore. You don't have to face anything alone anymore. I'm here.''

After long minutes, Hannah straightened, needing to end this unexpected confession. She swiped away the tears and leaned back. ''The following year, at graduation ceremonies, which the Murrays insisted we attend, I watched Paul go up and receive commendations for his scholarly achievements, and I wanted to throw something at him. But I didn't. It wasn't all his fault. It takes two. You're only a victim if you let yourself be one.'' She raised her eyes to his. ''That's when I decided I'd never again let myself be a victim, not for anyone.''

''And why you fight so hard for women who are victims,'' he added. ''I knew there had to be a serious reason behind your dedication.'' His thumb caressed her wrist as he held her hand. ''I didn't guess how terrible it was. You're a hell of a woman, you know. To go through all that and instead of turning bitter, you help others.''

''I do it for *me,* Joel, as much as for them. I need to do something so others won't have to pay such a high price for youthful stupidity, for making the wrong choices, as I did. And maybe one day I can stop wondering what my baby would have looked like, would have been like.''

He squeezed her hand. "Is that why you said you didn't want to have children, because of the one you lost?"

She dropped her gaze to the sheet. "Not altogether. I should have gone to a doctor after the miscarriage. But I was too ashamed. Finally, much later, when I did, I found out there'd been complications internally. I might never be able to have children. As a precaution, I still take birth-control pills, but I know it wouldn't make any difference." The eyes she turned to him were bleak. "So I go on paying for trusting a man."

"Not just a man, Hannah. The *wrong* man. I've known men who've trusted the wrong woman, too, and been scarred for life. This works both ways. You made a mistake and you've paid for it. But that doesn't mean that all men are like Paul." He tilted her chin up. "I'm not Paul, Hannah. I've said it before, but it bears repeating. I won't ever hurt you."

More than anything in the world, she wanted to believe him. But if she allowed herself to trust again, she'd be vulnerable once more, opening herself up to possible pain once more. The fear and the doubts lingered. Yet intellectually, she knew that Joel wasn't anything like Paul. If only she could convince her heart.

"I can't get over years of fear and mistrust in a few weeks, Joel. I don't believe you want to hurt me, but I need time."

He kissed her forehead lightly. "I can give you time. Just don't shut me out. Don't back away from me. I love you, and that makes me pretty vulnerable, too."

She angled to look at him, at his wonderful blue eyes. "No, not you. You're strong."

"Not always. Men can be hurt, too."

"I believe that. And I know there are many good men—my father, Mr. Murray, Will, you. I don't want to hurt you, either, which is why I said you'd be better off with someone who isn't so screwed up inside."

"We're all a little screwed up, Hannah, some more than others. I don't want someone else. I want you."

How could she turn away from that? "I want you to know that I do care about you, but love isn't something I'm prepared to consider right now. Perhaps one day, perhaps never. There's so much I have to work through. I don't know if I'll ever get rid of all that baggage."

"I'm willing to wait. I'm in no hurry."

Maybe then, maybe this time. Hope. She'd been without it for so long that it was heady just to contemplate hoping again. She placed her hands on his face, on his beautiful face. "I *do* care, Joel." And the feeling was so brand-new, so frightening.

That would have to be enough, for now. He kissed her, deeply, softly.

Hannah settled back into his arms, feeling an unexpected rush of contentment. Another sweet feeling.

"We started this conversation because you said you weren't very good at making love. Was it Paul who made you feel that way?"

Another memory, this one no less bitter. "He used to call me 'little girl,' not because I was so small, but because I was so inexperienced." Now, after what she'd experienced in Joel's arms, she knew that there was a great deal Paul had lacked, too. "He wasn't a man who cared much about the before and after, just the moment itself. But when he left that final time, he said that I'd never been very good in bed anyway and he was glad to get me out of his life."

Joel ground his teeth, his anger rising. "And you believed him?"

"Of course. I had no basis of comparison. About two years later, I did have a brief relationship, but by then, something had happened to me. When it came right down to it, I froze and couldn't go through with it. We tried twice, but I simply couldn't respond. I was too honest to fake it, and he became furious." She sighed audibly. "So I gave up on sex." She glanced at him, wondering what he was thinking. "That's why, that first time you kissed me and I felt so much, I was truly stunned."

He let go of the useless anger at the men who hadn't cared enough to take care of her, and smiled. "Maybe your heart was telling you that here's a guy you can trust."

She returned his smile. "Maybe."

"Have you looked out the window lately?" Joel asked. "It's still snowing like mad. You wouldn't want to send me out in a snowstorm, would you?"

She snuggled down more comfortably. "Of course not."

Sometime during their discussion, the sheet had slipped down. Joel gazed at her breasts, moving gently with her breathing. He circled each with just his fingertips and saw the pulse in her neck begin to pound. He touched his tongue to that throbbing center, then skimmed up to whisper in her ear. Sweet things, wild suggestions, sensual needs. And felt her shiver as he returned to take her mouth.

He'd heard her say that only with him had she been able to respond, to leave this world and enter one of their own making. He wanted to see her lose control again, to watch her climb and know he'd been the one to send her off the edge.

His mouth went on a mad journey of her, ravishing her flesh with teeth and tongue, feeling her quiver, hearing her moan. She felt boneless as she arched to accommodate his roving lips, his searching hands that had her skin rippling under his touch. This time, there was a wildness in him that wanted to push her to the limits, to send her soaring over and over again. He wanted to indelibly imprint his actions on her memory so that, even in quiet moments, when she thought of him, she would ache with longing for only him.

Hannah whispered his name, unable to believe that passion could have her so helpless, have her straining again so soon. His hands knew exactly how to touch her and where. His smoky male taste lingered on her swollen lips as she shifted, her entire body humming. Need for him was like a drumbeat playing loudly in her ears as her mouth reached for his. The desire to possess him and be possessed was like a heady drug in her bloodstream, making her crazy, making her wild beneath him. Unable to bear the wait, her hand sought him and her fingers curled around him.

He took her then as if it had been weeks, months, since they'd last made love instead of mere minutes ago. Frantic, desperate, he drove her up and up still higher. The flush of desire on her face pushed him on, his breathing labored, his heart pounding within his heaving chest. Still, he held off, until finally he felt her shudder of surrender and he was able to let himself join her.

When it was over and she was limp in his arms, Joel cradled her against his spent body and closed his eyes.

* * *

The ringing of the bedside phone woke both of them, Hannah more quickly than Joel. Reluctantly, she reached for the receiver and cleared her throat before murmuring a hello.

"Is this Hannah Richards?" a harsh male voice asked.

She frowned, trying to identify the caller as she shifted from Joel's embrace. "Yes, speaking."

"Listen, bitch, if you know what's good for you, you'll call off the cops," the man snarled.

Fully awake now, she felt a shiver of alarm. "Who is this?"

"Rod Baxter. You bad-mouthed me to my family. You took them away from me. I can't go home because of you. Call off the cops or you're going to be one sorry dame."

Hannah sat up, her mind clear now. "Mr. Baxter, your behavior drove your family away and brought you to the attention of the police. Turn yourself in and accept the counseling they offer. You need help to—"

"Shut up." Impatience and rage had his voice raspy. "I don't need your advice. Everything was all right between me and Ellen until you started filling her head with filthy lies. I want my wife and my kids back."

She felt Joel's hand on her arm and turned to see his concerned expression. She shook her head. She would handle her own clients. "So you can beat them up again, break Ellen's other arm? I don't think so. Maybe one day, if you'll submit to counseling to deal with your anger—"

"I'm angry, all right. I'm telling you once more. Get the cops off my back and send my family home. If you don't, you're going to wind up with a lot more than a broken arm." The phone clicked, and the line went dead.

Swallowing hard, Hannah slowly hung up, then fell back against the pillow.

"Baxter, the wife beater, right?" He'd heard enough to recall the pale woman he'd seen at Sanctuary, her arm in a cast, her eyes frightened and defeated.

"Yes." How had he discovered her phone number? Perhaps Ellen had left one of her business cards at the house.

"What did he want?" Joel thought he had a pretty good idea.

Hannah drew up the sheet, suddenly chilled. "He wants his family back and the police called off. He blames me for all his problems."

He watched her face. "Did he threaten you?"

She ignored his question and reached for the phone. "I need to call Lee at Sanctuary and warn her that Rod might try something."

The fact that she didn't answer was answer enough for Joel. "You also need to alert the police. Maybe they'll look harder if they know he threatened you."

Hannah glanced at the clock and saw that it was nearly ten. But Lee picked up on the third ring. First, she asked if Ellen and the children were all right. Determining that they were, she quickly told Lee about Rod's call, skirting over the threat. "Has he tried to contact Ellen there?"

"He called twice, but Daisy wouldn't give him any information as to her whereabouts."

"Good. I don't have to remind you to be sure you keep the doors locked, even during the day. And when you or anyone else leaves, check the area carefully. I don't trust Rod Baxter. He's mean and he drinks, as you well know."

Lee's voice was calm, as always. "Yes, I've seen proof of his handiwork."

"Probably you should alert the staff, but I see no purpose in telling Ellen. She'll only get upset."

"I agree."

"I'll stop in tomorrow. And thanks, Lee." Wearing a concerned frown, Hannah hung up.

"Are you going to call the police, get a restraining order?" Joel asked.

"What for? Rod Baxter's out of control. He'll only ignore it."

"Damn it, Hannah, you're in danger, too. The cops need to know that they have to find this guy."

It was happening already, Hannah thought. He was interfering in her case, trying to call the shots, overriding her objections. That's what happened when you let someone into your life.

Why was she so damn stubborn? Joel forced her to look at him. "I don't want to lose you. Please."

It cost him to ask, she knew. Because of that, she picked up the phone.

Finally, I'm out of the hospital. Two full years of my life, gone without a thing to show for them. Except that they say I'm well now. I do feel better, a little stronger. But my heart aches far more than my body ever did.

I have a little money that they'd put into a bank account for me from the sale of the farm after all the bills were paid. Not much, but a start. I bought a used car and rented a small apartment. I don't need much. I drove to Frankenmuth and stopped in front of the farm. It's thriving now with another family living there, working the fields. So many memories. Heartbreaking. I couldn't stay.

The social worker told me my mother has died. I weep for her, for all of us. So much sadness. Why did this have to happen? But crying will not bring back my children. I must find them. I get tired easily and have to be careful not to get sick again. But I go out every day. I visit agencies, adoption centers, orphanages, homes for runaways. I talk with the police, with an attorney one of the nurses recommended. No one gives me much hope, not after two long years.

Faith. My mother had so much. I must have it, too. God will not let me fail this time. I will search everywhere, go anywhere, follow even the smallest lead. I will keep myself strong so I can reunite us. I live for that day.

Oh, God, where are my children?

Chapter Eleven

Sheila Barns sat on the bed in the cubicle at the half-way house where Hannah had taken her and looked up at her benefactor with eyes bright from unshed tears. "They're mine to keep? Really mine?"

Taking the chair alongside the single bed, Hannah smiled at the young girl. "Yes, absolutely. Yours alone to keep."

Sheila ran a hand over the winter jacket, two pairs of jeans and sweaters, the package of brand-new underwear, then glanced over at the shoes still in the box. "I . . . I don't know what to say."

Hannah watched the girl struggle with her emotions and smiled. "Your expression has said it all." She'd gone begging, something she never minded doing on behalf of someone in need. The clothes donated to Sanctuary were mostly for adult women and small children. So she'd finagled some donations and picked out the things for

Sheila herself, making up the difference when the money ran out. She had a feeling the child couldn't recall the last time she'd owned new clothing.

"I've got you enrolled in the elementary school not far from here, for now. You'll start classes after the Christmas holidays, but I've made an appointment to take you in for testing next week, so they'll know what grade to put you in." Hannah softened her voice. "Sheila, when were you last in regular classes long enough to finish out the semester?"

The young girl dropped her eyes to where her hands were stroking the soft sweater fabric. "Finished all the way? Fourth grade, I think. I'm not sure."

That would put her two years behind kids her own age. But Hannah had a feeling that Sheila would catch up, for the conversations they'd had indicated she was quite bright. Moving from one foster home to another, bouncing from school to school, had put her behind. And she'd missed a lot of school due to illness. "We'll find where you belong after the testing. How are you feeling?"

Sheila blinked away the tears, determined not to cry in front of this wonderful woman as she placed a hand on her thin chest. "A lot better. I'm not coughing anymore."

Hannah had called Dr. Terry Merrick, hoping he would take a new patient. Joel's cousin had been wonderful, seeing Sheila that very day. He'd found she had bronchitis and the beginning of an ear infection, which hadn't surprised either of them, given the fact that the girl had been wandering the streets and sleeping in the bus station and God only knew where else. When Hannah had tried to pay Terry, he'd refused, endearing him to her forever, Hannah decided.

"You keep taking the medicine Dr. Terry gave you until it's all gone." Hannah glanced around the big room, past the curtain that separated each small cubicle from the others. The place was clean and neat, if not terribly homey. "How is it here? Are they nice to you?"

"Maggie's real nice, and the food's good." Again, Sheila looked away, hesitant about saying more. It felt good to be out of the cold, to eat well and to have a clean bed and clothes. But she was scared and lonely. Still, she couldn't criticize anything here at Maggie's Haven, as the place was called. She didn't want Hannah to think she was ungrateful for saving her from juvenile detention.

Hannah watched the emotions the girl was unable to hide come and go on her expressive face. She'd been in situations similar to what Sheila was facing, though she'd never had to steal to eat. But she'd felt the bone weariness, the fear, the hunger for love.

"I know it's not home, Sheila," she said, leaning forward. "This is only temporary, you know. I'm looking for another place for you."

Home. Sheila wasn't sure she'd ever really had one. Alcoholic parents who drank up all the money and scarcely knew she was around. She'd run away from them and landed in a system that shuffled her from one family to another until she'd run from that, too. "I've never had a real home," she admitted. It was something she wouldn't have confided to anyone else. But this woman had done more for her in the short time she'd known her than anyone else she'd ever met.

Hannah felt her chest tighten at the sad confession. "You will, Sheila. Give me some time and you will." If it was the last thing she ever did, she'd see to it. No child's eyes should look so hopeless.

She'd gone out on a limb, with Judge Eastman's permission, and gotten in touch with a local television anchorman, Curt Wheeler. A few weeks ago, she'd caught a new program Curt had begun, called "Wednesday's Child." That one evening a week, he'd feature a child in need of adoption, showing films he would take earlier of them at play, perhaps reading, taking a walk and chatting with him. Hannah felt that Sheila would make an excellent subject. Maybe out there somewhere in the viewing audience was a couple able to tackle a young lady who needed a great deal of TLC, but would give a lot of love back in return.

Rising, Hannah brushed back a lock of Sheila's lovely black hair. She'd taken her for a haircut just yesterday and thought she looked awfully cute with the stylish trim. "I have to go now. Enjoy your new things. I'll be back soon."

At first, Sheila had been afraid to believe Hannah when she said she'd return. But she knew now she could trust her. She gave her a shy smile. "Okay." She reached under her pillow for the red leather book. "And thanks for this, too."

Her mother had always written in a journal, as she herself had. Hannah had thought perhaps Sheila would enjoy recording her thoughts. "You're welcome, sweetie." She gave the child a fierce hug, then left the room, hurrying as she glanced at her watch. She'd stayed longer than she'd intended, but then, Sheila seemed to look forward to their visits so much that she hated to cut them short.

She would be a little late, but her two favorite men wouldn't mind, Hannah hoped. At that thought, she found herself smiling as she started her VW.

* * *

"A little more to the left." Hannah cocked her head to one side. "A bit too much. Back to the right just a wee bit." She stepped back, surveying from another angle. "Yes, that's it. Perfect."

"Okay, then," Joel said. "You come hold the stem still while I tighten the bolts in the stand."

Hannah did as he requested and watched him flatten himself to the floor and inch his way under the full Douglas fir that was filling Will's living room with a marvelous scent. "What do you think, Will?"

From his easy chair across the room with his feet propped onto a broad footstool, Will grunted. "I think you two have gone to an awful lot of bother for an old man. I told you I have a small ceramic tree put away in the attic that would do."

"You can't *not* have a real Christmas tree," Joel muttered from underneath as he turned screws so the tree would stand straight. "It's downright un-American."

"Right," Hannah agreed, smiling at Will. "And besides, you're not an old man. You're merely in the twilight of your years, a lovely place to be, where you needn't work if you don't feel like it, where you can fish when you want and let others do things for you now and again."

"Well said by a woman who hardly lets a man pour her coffee, so independent is she," Will said by way of counter.

"Touché. One for your side, Will." Joel crawled out from under. "Do we have a watering can or something?"

Hannah let go of the tree. "I'll look. In the kitchen, Will?"

"Under the sink," he called to her. With longing, he eyed his pipe sitting in the big ashtray on the end table. Damn doctors. Took away every pleasure a man had on account of a couple of chest pains.

Hannah returned with the can and bent to hand it to Joel, then walked over to Will. "Would you like me to make some tea?"

"Only if you're going to lace it heavily with whiskey. I hate tea." He looked up hopefully. "The Jameson's on the top shelf. I keep it for medicinal purposes only, of course."

"I didn't see Jameson's on the list of doctor's orders." She smiled at him affectionately. "I'm so glad you're looking so good." And he was, his color once more healthy looking, his eyes bright, his orneriness back to let them know he was on the mend. The only evidence of his illness was a slight weight loss and the fact that he still tired quite easily.

Will folded his hands and rested them on the belt of his robe. Never before could he remember entertaining in his robe, but first Joel and then Hannah had surprised him, dropping in and insisting on decorating his home for the holidays. He was secretly pleased, despite his grumblings, not only to have a little Christmas spirit in evidence, but at the easy rapport he could see between the two of them.

They'd shared more than good rapport would be Will's guess. They hadn't done anything overt, hadn't kissed at the door when Joel had opened it to let Hannah in, nor so much as touched hands while the three of them had shared the Chinese dinner Hannah had brought. Yet Will knew. Love was a difficult thing to hide from a man who'd seen the many sides of it for nearly seven decades.

The knowledge warmed his heart more than even the Jameson's would have. Briefly, sadly, Emily's face came into focus in his mind's eye. Ah, that first bloom of love, that first realization that there is another human being you care for more than your biological family. Far more than for yourself. More than life itself.

So wonderful, so heady. He closed his eyes a moment as they became moist. Must be getting old, or perhaps it was the medication causing him to get so sentimental so often lately. Or maybe it was just the season. The Christmas season. The season of love.

Will saw Hannah looking at him kind of funny and realized he'd been so lost in his thoughts he'd missed what she'd said. "I'm sorry, honey. Off in my own world, I guess. What did you say?"

"I asked if you like tinsel on your tree or not. I brought some, but it's sort of a personal choice."

He glanced over at his aging cat curled up near the hearth, where the fire Joel had built was blazing nicely. "I never use the stuff. If Benjamin ate a strand or two, he'd choke. I can't risk it." His look was filled with tolerant affection. "Poor old Benjie's bones are as creaky as mine these days."

"No problem, then." Hannah shoved the icicles back into the sack. Straightening, she saw that Joel had finished stringing the lights. "Looks good already," she said, reaching for the first box of bulbs. They'd found six boxes neatly labeled and stocked in the attic. "But wait until we finish."

"The angel's in that red box," Will directed. He hadn't put up a tree the past several years, accepting holiday invitations from friends so as not to spend much time at home alone. But this year, the doctor had warned him to stay put, especially during the cold weather. He didn't like it, but he'd do it.

Carefully, Hannah removed the angel, smoothed the wispy yellow hair and straightened the filmy white dress. "She's lovely."

"Emily made her," Will said. "Even painted the china face. She's old but still as good as she was that first Christmas."

Hannah handed the angel up to Joel, who was waiting on the footstool, and watched him put her in position with care. Traditions were lovely, she couldn't help thinking. Emily and Will with their angel. Joel's family probably had ornaments handed down through several generations now that there were grandchildren. Just one of the things she'd missed out on.

What, she wondered, had become of the things in the farmhouse where she'd been born? All the furniture, the personal possessions. Who'd taken them or sold them after her parents were gone and the three of them had been scattered?

Absently, she handed ornaments to Joel to hang near the top, but her mind was back in Michigan seeing long-ago Christmases when she and Michael and Katie had helped Dad trim the tree while Mom had made hot chocolate for them and strung berries to hang and played carols on the phonograph. They'd had fun together and laughed a lot in those days. How few were the good years they'd been able to share. The ache of that terrible separation seemed worse at holiday times.

Deliberately forcing a smile, Hannah set down the empty box and picked up another. Moving to the far side of the tree, she turned to see Joel watching her, his eyes soft with understanding. As she handed him a delicate ornament in the shape of a teapot, he captured her hand in his.

"We'll make new memories," he said softly, for her ears only.

Surprised that he could read her so well, she could only stare.

The three of them were having a cup of tea laced with honey rather than whiskey and gazing at the completed tree when the phone rang. Since it was on the end table next to Will's chair, he answered it.

"Well, hi, Marcie. You should get yourself over here and see what a wonderful tree I have in my living room."

"Invite me over next week and I'll check it out, Will." A note of anxiety crept into her voice. "Is Hannah still there? She told me she planned to help trim your tree tonight."

"She sure is. Just a minute." He held out the phone. "Marcie for you, Hannah."

Frowning, Hannah took the receiver, thinking it had to be important for the secretary to call at Will's. "Yes, Marcie."

"I got a little piece of news I think you ought to know. Lee from Sanctuary called me. It seems they had a little problem. Rod Baxter tried to break into Sanctuary. One of the women identified him for sure, but Ellen didn't see him. They called the police and they caught him several blocks away. But somehow, there was a scuffle and he got away."

"Oh, Lord. Is Ellen all right, then? And the kids?"

"Sure. That place is like a bloody fortress, according to Lee. Between Cookie, Lee and Daisy, no one can get in. It's not them I'm worried about. The cops came back to tell Lee something Rod said."

Hannah braced herself. "What was it?"

" 'Tell that lawyer of Ellen's I'm going to get her for taking away my family,' is what he said. Hannah, why don't you come spend the night with me? I don't like the sound of that lunatic." Marcie's voice trailed off.

She didn't, either. "Thanks, but that won't be necessary, Marcie."

"This is no laughing matter, honey."

"I'm not laughing, I assure you. But he's threatened me before. He doesn't even own a car. I'm very careful, so don't worry. And thanks for calling." Thoughtfully, she hung up.

Joel had been listening intently to her end of the conversation, well aware that Marcie wouldn't have phoned unless something was fairly urgent. "Rod Baxter again?"

Sighing, Hannah nodded as she resumed her seat and took a sip of her tea. The man was obsessed and drunk most of the time. How was it that he managed to get away from two police officers?

"What's this all about?" Will asked.

Very concisely, Hannah filled him in, downplaying the aspect of danger for herself. "They'll pick him up soon, probably later tonight. They're watching Sanctuary and his home. He's on foot with probably very little money. How long can he evade them on a cold, wintry night?"

"You can stay here with me, honey, in my spare room," Will suggested. "I'm not much of a bodyguard these days, but I've got good locks, and two pairs of eyes and ears are better than one."

She sent him a grateful smile. "Thanks, but don't worry, please. I'll be fine. They'll get him by morning."

Joel came to a decision as he stood. "We're not going to wait for that. You're coming to my place tonight."

She sent him an annoyed look. "By now, I'm sure you must know how very fond I am of being told what I'm going to do, right?"

"This is different." His concern for her safety had his voice harsher than he intended. "The man's a loose cannon. We can't take the chance that they'll nab him right away. Rod's crazy enough to take all sorts of risks a smarter, more sober man wouldn't. Don't be unreasonable with me about this, Hannah."

She wasn't stupid; she knew what men who had little else to lose might do. And certainly, she didn't want to get hurt. But she also didn't like him telling her what she must do. "I'm not trying to be unreasonable. But I have no intention of going into hiding until Rod Baxter gets caught." She also stood and began picking up the tea things. "Thanks for your offer, but I'll be careful."

His teeth clenched, Joel watched her take the full tray into the kitchen. Exasperated, he looked at Will, who was watching him.

"I believe I told you early on that she was stubborn and independent," Will said calmly.

"Truer words were never spoken."

After loading the dishwasher, Hannah returned and went to the closet for their coats. "Will, I'm sure you're ready for some rest. We'd better get going." She leaned down to hug him. "Is there anything you need before I go?"

"No, honey, I'm fine. Thanks for everything." Will watched Hannah put on her coat, then her gloves, while Joel shoved his arms into his jacket. "You, too, Joel."

Joel shook hands with the older man. "Enjoy your tree."

He can't fool me, Will thought. He's fuming inside. He wondered what Joel was going to do once they got outside. He didn't know, but even money said that his young partner was definitely going to do something. As they closed the door behind them, Will hoped Joel could do what no other man had yet been able to do: make Hannah listen.

He stayed several blocks behind her, after having said good-night by the curb and lingering a bit before starting out to give her a head start. Stubborn female. She absolutely wouldn't listen to reason. All right, fine. He would have to take matters into his own hands.

A lunatic on the loose, looking specifically for her, one who knew where she lived, where she worked, the places she frequented, like Sanctuary and, of course, the courthouse—and yet Hannah said she'd be all right. Sure, she'd be all right. Because Joel was going to make damn sure she was.

A block from her place, he sped up, pulling in behind her in the back driveway. Jumping out, he saw her surprised expression when she noticed him. She'd probably been so lost in thought she hadn't spotted him following behind. "Hold it right there," he ordered.

Hannah curled her gloved fingers around her keys in frustration. She should have known he'd given in too easily back at Will's to be believed. "What do you want?"

"You're coming with me," Joel said, his voice firm.

"No, I'm not," she answered, her voice equally as firm.

Joel watched his warm breath curl up in the cold night air. It was silly standing out here arguing. "You have two choices—you can go upstairs, pack an overnight bag and then come along with me like a civilized person. Or you can fight me on this. If you choose door number 2, I'm going to throw you over my shoulder, cram you into my car just as you are, with no clean undies, and drive off. Either way, you're coming with me tonight. What'll it be?''

Planting both curled fists on her hips, she glared up at him. "You have no idea what a turnoff these caveman tactics are to me. I am not—I repeat *not*—going anywhere with you."

"Door number 2 it is."

Faster than she could ever have guessed, Joel scooped her up, flung her over his shoulder, marched around to the passenger side of his car, opened the door and unceremoniously deposited her on the leather seat. Breathless, she tried to raise her arms in order to bat him away, but before she could get off a punch, he'd already fastened her seat belt tightly around her. While she struggled with that, he rushed around the front, slid behind the wheel, shoved the gearshift in reverse and squealed out of the driveway. They were speeding around the Common, down Charles Street, heading for Beacon Hill before she managed to free herself.

"Damn you, Joel Merrick, you're going to pay for this," she all but hissed at him.

"You're probably right," he said quietly, trying desperately to keep all traces of humor from his voice. If he laughed at her now, she'd probably punch him in the jaw.

"*Why* must things always go your way? *Why* can't you believe that my decision might be right for me? *Why* must you act as if I were a child and you were a Neanderthal? Which, by the way, you are."

He appeared to consider that. "I am something of a Neanderthal at times, but you're definitely not a child."

He dared glance at her, but only for a moment. She was glaring fiercely. He pressed his lips together.

She could jump out of a speeding car, Hannah supposed. Naturally, all the lights were with him, so he scarcely slowed even for turns. She could make a try for the ignition keys, but he'd probably grab her hand before she could connect. She could punch him hard and... No, she doubted if he'd even feel it through that heavy leather jacket. Damn!

Minutes later, he pulled into his regular parking space, turned off the ignition and placed a finger on the door-lock button before turning toward her. In the shadowy lot, he stared into her angry eyes. "I want you safe because I love you. Is that so terrible?"

The steam whooshed out of her rebellion. How was it that he knew exactly what to say to make her drop her defenses immediately? "It's the *way* you go about things, Joel. You don't ask. You command."

"Hardly ever. Only when it involves your safety. I would have bound your hands and feet and carried you off rather than allow you to place yourself in danger." He grinned. "Love makes you do stupid things."

"Apparently." She let out a ragged sigh. "I don't want to fight with you. But I honestly can't go into seclusion every time one of my clients or their batty husband threatens me. You ought to know. Lawyers get threats all the time."

"Just until he's caught. That's all I ask. If this car wasn't so cramped, I'd get down on my knees. Please come upstairs with me, Hannah. Please."

She wouldn't give him the satisfaction of the smile that was just about to break free. Instead, she turned her head. "All right, but I don't even have anything to sleep in."

''I like it best when you don't have anything to sleep in.'' Before she could react, he stepped out and hurried around to help her. If it was the last thing he did, Joel vowed, he'd make Hannah forget about the madman out there somewhere gunning for her. And he knew just how to do it.

Chapter Twelve

Joel locked the door of his apartment behind them, but didn't turn on the lamp. Ten stories up, moonlight drifted in through the wide living-room windows. He turned to Hannah and held her captive there with just a look, his hands at his sides.

He didn't touch her, didn't speak, but instead let his eyes do the asking. He could see she understood, could almost see the wheels of her mind turning, considering, rethinking. He did a great deal of negotiating in his work and knew that the first one to break the silence or make the first move in a tense situation was the one to give in. So he waited, wanting this to be her call, her decision, made willingly.

Hannah studied Joel's face, that wonderfully familiar face that monopolized her dreams, awake or sleeping. That she wanted him wasn't the question. That accepting his invitation might move them to a new plateau might be. She sensed that he was asking more this time, more than a physical expression of their feelings. He wasn't demanding, something she would have known how to deal with. He wasn't even using his considerable powers of persuasion, by word or touch. He was doing something far more deadly.

He was allowing her to see the need in his eyes.

She could deny her own, could turn from it and walk away. But the raw need, the sudden vulnerability she saw in Joel, pulled her in neatly, completely. Surrendering, she went on tiptoe and pressed her mouth to his.

Joel's heart leapt as if released from a taut spring. His arms enfolded her as his tongue met hers in a mating dance as old as time. He scooped her into his arms and carried her to his room, then let her slide down his body before switching the bedside lamp on low.

Urgency, desire, need screamed inside him as he quickly undressed her while Hannah's impatient fingers tugged at his clothes. Shoes dropped, shirts were flung aside, slacks slipped to the floor. A button popped as haste made way for passion. He had to be flesh to flesh with her, had to see and taste and touch before he went mad.

Finally, no barriers stood between them, and he paused, for just a moment, to fill his eyes with her beauty, to fill his hands with her breasts, heavy with arousal. Then he backed her up to the bed and followed her onto the navy quilt.

She was on fire. Whispers of heat skittered over her skin where he touched, across her lips where he kissed, in her ear where his warm breath had her shivering. Restlessly, Hannah arched, needing more, impatient for fulfillment, yet wanting to prolong this delicious torture. His mouth moved to her breast, and she felt the tug deep inside.

She was naked in his bed, where he'd wanted her to be since that first day, Joel realized. Her eyes as they stared up at him were misty with the first flush of passion as her restive fingers moved to fist and bunch at his back. She was everything beautiful, everything lovely, everything he'd ever wanted.

He watched dim light play across her lovely face as she waited, still hesitant to take the lead, the shadow of that other man's words controlling her memory. Anger at what he'd done to her rose in Joel, hot and fierce. He wanted to remove all traces of anyone who'd ever touched her, anyone who'd ever hurt her.

"If Paul didn't find pleasure with you, it was his fault, not yours. Know that. Always know that." His eyes bore into hers, wanting to brand her mind with new memories, new pleasures. "Do you believe me?"

She did. She could see the truth in his eyes. Her hand on his heart could feel what she did to him. He'd been aroused before they'd stepped in the door. Because of her, of what she could do to him. The knowledge warmed her, made her bolder.

"Yes," she answered, then touched her mouth to the pounding pulse in his neck while her hands stroked, searching for his weak spots, his pleasure points. She heard him draw in a quivery breath and felt the power of making him tremble. For her.

His reaction gave her confidence, so she pushed him onto his back and sent her lips on a journey of him, letting his special male flavors seep into her. She felt his heartbeat go wild under her roaming mouth and discovered a new high. Nothing in her limited experience had prepared her for this kind of feeling. So much feeling in this freedom to do what she would to his magnificent body. Moving back up him, she took his mouth, desperate for that state of euphoria only he could bring to her.

This kiss was savage in its intensity, both of them running out of patience and edgy with need. She'd wanted to savor, to go slowly, but it was too late. Her body demanded, and she had no choice but to drag him closer, wrapping herself around him. For Hannah, for the first time, the world had zeroed down to one man, one bed, one room. Nothing else mattered. Nothing else was real except the way he made her feel, the way she could make him react.

Joel was lost in her, totally absorbed. No other woman had ever been able to make him want this way. His mouth still on hers, he shifted their positions, then slid into her so easily, as naturally as if they'd been lovers for years.

He'd wanted this, needed this, and now strove to make it the best for her. She was so ready that in moments, he felt her swirl away to a place only he had ever taken her. Feeling powerful, he let go of the world outside the one of their own making.

Hannah had no idea how much time passed before she became aware again. Limp and utterly spent, she lay with her eyes closed, absorbing the aftershocks. She didn't mind the weight of him pressing on her or his skin damp beneath her touch. Instead, she was comforted by his solid presence. A feeling of peace stole over her as her heart slowed. She sighed, feeling wonderfully replete.

Hannah raised her hand to brush back Joel's hair from where his head lay on her shoulder. It was so new, this desire to caress, to stroke, to explore this beautiful man who seemed more than willing to let her. Her fingers slipped down along his neck, then trailed across his broad shoulders and finally settled at his back. How steadfast he was, how strong.

She felt her blood humming, satisfaction causing her to wiggle and squirm like a contented cat. She wasn't surprised when he lifted his head to look at her. She smiled at him lazily.

Joel couldn't take his eyes from her. He wondered if she'd ever believe how lovely she looked, the blush of passion still on her face, pleased with her own sensuality. "I love you, Hannah. So very much."

She sobered immediately, wariness tensing her. "Joel, don't. I don't need those words. I . . ."

He eased back from her, shifting to his side. "I've never known anyone who needed them more. But that's not why I said them. I said them for me, because I'm so full of the feeling, and because it's true."

She pulled back, needing some distance. Saying the words meant moving into commitment. There was so much in her past to remind her of the risks involved with commitment. She'd become truly intimate with him, allowing him to get closer to knowing her than anyone before him. She'd let him become too important to her. That made her vulnerable, made her frightened.

Once before, she'd thought herself in love, and had come to realize she'd been too trusting and naive. Time had made her infinitely more cautious.

Joel saw her withdrawing, not just physically. He had to assure her, to reassure her, that he wasn't like the man who haunted her nightmares. "I know what you're thinking, but it's not going to happen. I love you. I want to be with you for all time. Marry me, Hannah."

Her gasp of surprise was audible as she swung back toward him. "You don't mean that. I know you don't. You're caught up in the moment and . . ."

"I've never meant anything more in my life." Joel sat up, twisting around to face her. "You asked me recently why I didn't just move to Montana since I seemed happier there. I did that once, and still something was missing. I thought my career was the problem, but I realize now that it's not that, either."

"What is it, then?"

"I want a home, Hannah, one like Bart and Elizabeth had. All along, I've been thinking home is a place. It's not. Home is a person, the person who shares your life, the place you live in and everything else. We could live in Boston or Montana. Or Bora Bora, Iceland, the dark side of the moon. I don't care as long as we're together. Home to me is you, Hannah. Marry me, please."

Hadn't she been searching for a home all her life, as well? But commitments scared her. What if she disappointed him?

They came from vastly different backgrounds. His ancestors had probably come over on the *Mayflower*. Hers had been farmers, and all of them were gone now. How could she even think that the well-heeled Merricks would want to taint their pure bloodline with the blue-collar likes of her family tree?

She remembered something else. "I probably can't have children," she said quietly.

"You don't know that for sure. If you can't, we'll adopt." He watched her carefully as she slipped back into silence. Again, he waited.

She'd been quiet so long he couldn't help but wonder what was going on behind those suddenly hooded brown eyes. He'd stated his feelings, hopefully made his case.

He wouldn't rush her, wouldn't try to win by more persuasion. She had to want this as much as he, or nothing would work out.

Finally, she looked up. "It's not that I don't want to, but..."

"But you're afraid to trust me," he finished for her.

"Yes, that's part of it. And then, there's your family. Your father wasn't terribly impressed with me in our brief meeting. How would he feel about your marrying a farmer's daughter who came from nothing?"

"Now you're really reaching. You're a beautiful, successful, dynamic attorney with a great future. Educated, funny, charming. And besides, what's wrong with being a farmer's daughter?"

"*I* don't think there's anything wrong with it, but your father—"

"Has nothing whatsoever to say about my choices. I think I've proved that by leaving his firm, by spending time in Montana, by taking a stand against him if I thought I was right and he was wrong." He was doing what he'd sworn he wouldn't, trying to win her over by persuasion. Joel sucked in a frustrated breath.

"I know you've opposed your father several times. But you're not comfortable with the way he views your decisions or the way he treats you because of them. If we married, there'd be more of that, and on a more personal level. I don't want to come between you and your family." That said, she pulled the sheet about her protectively.

"You're not. You wouldn't be." Joel shoved a hand through his hair, wondering what in hell he could say to convince her. "Look, our families, dead or alive, aren't important to this decision. We are. I've already told you how I feel. You have only one question to answer. Do you love me?''

Did she? Time to face the truth. Hadn't she known it for weeks now? Perhaps she'd been expecting love to announce its arrival in some dramatic fashion. She'd discovered it was far more subtle.

If loving was wanting, needing, to share each little victory, each terrible disappointment, with only him, then she had a bad case of it. If it was having his face intrude on her thoughts hourly, his comments coming to mind frequently, his pleasure becoming more important than hers, then she was surely there. Yes, she loved him. Indisputably. Irrevocably. Undeniably. Did that change anything, remove her fears, assure them a bright and happy future?

Unfortunately, no.

Hannah couldn't meet his eyes as emotions twisted and churned inside her. She moved into his arms, clutching at him, wishing she could be all that he wanted, everything he needed. "I care about you and . . . and I'm beginning to need you. Far too much. That frightens me terribly. I've lost so many. I don't think I can survive another loss."

He held on to her, spoke into her hair. "Not everyone you love leaves, Hannah. I won't. Not ever. You couldn't chase me away with a stick."

Dare she believe him? Oh, God, she wanted to. Her life had been so serene before Joel had entered it. Boring, lonely, dull—but not filled with emotional turmoil as it was now. A part of her longed for that peace again. The other, larger part longed for him.

"I don't know, Joel." She sighed deeply and pulled back. "I don't think I can do this. You deserve better."

His patience was strained to the limit. "That's ridiculous. You need me and I need you. What could be better?"

Needing someone. The whole concept had her mind whirling. Slowly, she shook her head. "I think you should find someone who's whole and problem free. I'm just not ready to trust, to love again. All my life, people have..."

"Abandoned you. Yes, I know." His eyes reflected his disappointment in her, in himself for not being enough for her. "Your father, your mother, your grandparents, Paul, the Murrays—they all left you. Ergo, everyone else will, too. No exceptions." He slipped out of bed and reached for his pants, his movements abrupt and choppy. "Okay. So run away. Pack up and move. Back to Michigan or some new place. Or stay here and steer clear of anyone who dares to care for you. Help total strangers, but don't get too close. Don't let yourself care. Walk alone. Love no one and, for God's sake, don't let them love you."

Hannah could see he was more than a little angry. She couldn't blame him. Woodenly, she picked up her clothes and began dressing.

Over. It was over. He was going to let her go. Wasn't that what she wanted?

No! It wasn't, not really. She wanted things to stay the same. To remain friends, loving friends. She wanted him in her life, but she wasn't sure she could handle more. Marriage. Lord, she'd never once considered it, removing the word from her vocabulary years ago. Marriage was for others, normal people who had no trouble trusting, loving.

Hannah stepped into her slacks, then slipped her sweater over her head. Why couldn't he be content with a caring friendship? Why did he have to complicate things? Now he'd never want to see her again, probably. He'd find someone else, laugh with them, make love with them.

Shoving back her hair, she walked to stand and look out the window. But she didn't see the view, looking instead inward, seeing her life stretching out ahead, vast and empty. Without Joel in it, her days would be bleak, colorless. Her nights would be a living torment. Tears she couldn't seem to prevent came rolling down her cheeks. Bending her head, she muffled out a sob, struggling with the reality of still another loss.

And this time, she had no one to blame but herself.

Joel shoved his feet into his shoes, his thoughts dark. There for a minute, he'd thought they were in agreement. Then she'd retreated into her fears again, her mistrust leading the way. How could he fight that unseen enemy?

Sighing, he decided he'd take her home, make sure the apartment was secure and let her be. He couldn't push, not more than he already had. Turning, he looked over at her. To his surprise, he thought he saw her shoulders moving slightly, the thick curtain of hair hiding her face. Was she crying?

Slowly, he walked over and turned her around to face him. He saw her damp cheeks, her downcast eyes, her trembling lips. Hope flared within him as he pulled her into his arms.

With a moan, Hannah clung to him. "I don't want to lose you. I *can't* lose you. But I…I need some time." She hiccuped around a shaky breath. "I won't blame you if you can't wait."

"Take all the time you need," he said into her hair, his voice husky. He could wait, knowing this was how she felt. He could be patient a while longer. He eased back and wiped away her tears with his thumbs as he smiled into her damp eyes. "Just don't take too long, please."

"I'll try not to. I just need to think things through, to get used to these brand-new feelings."

He kissed her eyes, then gently kissed her mouth. "I'll try to be patient. I love you, Red."

At last, she could smile. "Thank you."

It was Wednesday, a little past five, and everyone at Maggie's Haven was gathered around the small donated television set in the rec room. In a moment, after the headline news, Curt Wheeler would be on the air with his "Wednesday's Child" portion of the program. This week, his featured guest was Sheila Barns.

Seated on the floor next to Sheila, Hannah felt the young girl's hand creep into hers. She gave it an encouraging squeeze. "It's going to be wonderful, just wait and see."

Nervously, Sheila chewed on her lower lip.

Seven assorted teens and two younger new arrivals, all current residents, crowded around as Maggie passed out homemade cookies. A heavy-set jovial woman, Maggie walked among her young charges. "Take a couple, kids. There's milk in the kitchen." Dinner had been served early tonight so they could all watch together.

The news segment ended, and the camera closed in on Curt's pleasant face. The father of four teens himself, Curt was well-known in the Boston area for his commitment to helping kids of all ages. "Now it's time for this week's 'Wednesday's Child,'" he began. "Our special young lady is Sheila Barns, who is twelve years old. I spent a fun afternoon with Sheila last week and I can personally tell you she's quite an ice skater."

The scene shifted to an outdoor rink where Curt and Sheila, along with the usual assortment of weekend skaters, made their way around the perimeter. Curt was a little wobbly, but not Sheila. She was steady and unafraid, even shifting to skate backward for a bit.

"Hey, where'd you learn to skate like that, Sheila?" a freckle-faced boy about thirteen asked, squinting at her through thick glasses.

"I don't know," Sheila answered, her eyes riveted to the screen. "I just picked it up." She leaned closer to Hannah. "Do you think my hair looks funny?"

Hannah smiled. "Your hair looks lovely. The wind's just blowing it around."

Curt's voice went on to explain a little about Sheila's background, leaving out the rough parts, mentioning that she'd tested as having quite a high IQ, that she loved sports, movies and puppies and hoped to be adopted by a family who liked those things, too. Next, they showed the two of them, man and young girl, building a snowman in the park, then drinking hot chocolate at an outdoor stand. Curt ended with a close-up of Sheila smiling shyly into the camera while his voice-over repeated the phone number appearing at the bottom of the screen and urged anyone interested in the young girl to call him.

The entire segment had lasted only about four minutes, yet the residents gathered around Sheila cheered and applauded as if they'd just finished watching their favorite movie. Hannah was warmed by their reaction, knowing full well that most of these kids could use a similar boost. She'd gone with Sheila during the filming and had already talked with Curt about selectively supplying him with more candidates for "Wednesday's Child" specials.

Now she looked down at the blushing girl so unused to being the center of attention. "You were perfect, simply perfect."

Wide eyes looked up at her. "Do you think anyone will call Mr. Wheeler about me?"

"Honey," Maggie interjected, "I'll bet those phone lines are already lit up like that Christmas tree over there."

Hannah slipped an arm around the thin shoulders and hugged Sheila. "I agree." Getting to her feet, she prayed she was right. Noise and confusion reigned as the residents scattered, some to the kitchen and others taking the stairs, two at a time. She turned back to Sheila. "I've got to get going, sweetie." She reached for her jacket from the pile on the chair and was putting it on when Curt's deep voice suddenly drew her attention back to the television.

"This just in, a late-breaking story. In central Boston, a man armed with a gun is holding a secretary in a law office hostage while demanding that the female attorney who represents his wife show up so he can talk with her."

Law offices. Secretary. Oh, God, not Marcie. Hannah's heart skipped a beat as she moved closer to the small set, praying she'd guessed wrong.

Curt's serious voice went on. "The police are on the scene and have surrounded the building, talking to the man on the bullhorn, urging him to surrender. But so far, he's refused. Our sources tell us that one of the male law partners is inside the building, as well, though we don't have a name for you. Stay tuned to this station for updates."

Joel! And Rod Baxter. Oh, no! Grabbing her purse, Hannah headed for the door. "Sheila, Maggie, I'll talk with you later." And she raced to her car.

"Everything's gone. My wife, my kids, my job. Got no home to go to. Nothing!" Rod Baxter's whiskey voice was whiny and grating. He swiped at a drippy nose with the back of one hand while his other held a Smith Wesson .38 Special to the back of Marcie's head. "That fancy lawyer took everything from me."

Joel stood about six feet in front of the secretary's desk, his mind racing as he kept his steady gaze on the crazed man. Finished for the day in court, he'd left his car out front and run in the front door to sign a couple of letters. Marcie's scream had stopped him in his tracks. She was seated at her desk, her eyes still wide with fright, but he could see that she was trying not to let her captor see her terror. She was smart enough to know that men like Rod were egged on by a woman's fear.

Joel assessed the man as he muttered on. Baxter had thinning blond hair, watery blue eyes and he hadn't shaved in a while. His plaid jacket was old and frayed, his navy pants dingy. He looked to be about five-seven. Joel thought he'd have no trouble disarming Rod as soon as the opportunity presented itself. The smell of unwashed body and beer drifted to him, yet Rod's eyes were bright. Was he also on drugs?

Even so, he'd been alert enough to sneak in through the back way and surprise Marcie at her desk, then force her to phone around looking for Hannah, leaving messages demanding that she come straight to her office. His addled mind hadn't figured that someone would alert the police. Joel had heard them arrive minutes ago, then listened to Rod talk with them on the phone, insisting that Hannah show up or he'd kill Marcie. Through the bullhorn, they'd urged Rod to surrender, but that had only made him angrier.

"Put the gun down and let's talk this out calmly, Rod," Joel said, his voice calm. There had to be a way to get through to the guy. "I'll help you explain your position to the cops if you'll come outside with me. We can settle this without anyone getting hurt. You don't want to add a shooting to your other charges, do you?"

"What do you know?" Rod screamed, his hold on the gun at Marcie's back tightening. "You lawyers are all the same. You don't care about a working stiff. You'd turn me over, just like she did. That Richards dame. Where is she?"

He continued ranting and raving, a cigarette in one hand while his bony fingers kept the gun rammed into Marcie's neck. The thing to do was to keep him talking, Joel thought, to let him run out of steam. The guy was filled with rage—at Hannah, at Ellen, his wife, at the system. Undereducated and not terribly bright besides, he couldn't seem to fight his way out of poverty. So he'd given up trying and turned to drinking, which made him mean and dangerous.

"It's all her damn fault," Rod snarled. "Are those cops trying to find her?"

Tension made Joel's palms damp as he took a small step closer to the secretary's desk. "I told you, we don't know where Hannah is. Let Marcie go, and I'll track Hannah down for you." Like hell he would, but telling him that might buy some time. He sent an encouraging look to Marcie, whose eyes were pleading with him to do something.

"You get that bitch here, and I'll let this one go." Rod drew deeply on his cigarette, then tossed the butt on the floor, stomping it out with a snowy shoe. "Tell them cops out there I got nothing to lose by killing you both, but *she's* the one I really want. Wrecked my whole life, is what she did. She's got to pay."

Joel watched the man lick his dry lips, his eyes getting wilder. An idea came to him, and he wondered if it would work. It was worth a try. "I can see you're thirsty. I've got a bottle in my desk. Why don't you let Marcie go and you can hold the gun on me instead? We can have a drink and talk. Twelve-year-old Scotch. Good stuff."

He could see that he had the man's attention. Again, Rod licked his lips, considering.

Hannah stood next to the sergeant in charge by the police car in the horseshoe driveway in front of the law offices. "Let me go in, Sergeant, please. This is *my* problem, not Joel's and certainly not Marcie's. Rod Baxter wants me and . . ."

Sergeant James Watkins spared her an impatient glance. "I can't let you do that. We've already got two people at risk. We don't need to make it three."

With difficulty, Hannah kept hysteria from her voice. "But Rod's demanding to see *me*. Call him back and tell him that if he lets those two go, I'll walk in." She had to make him see. Joel was in there in danger.

"And then what? Do you think he just wants to have a friendly chat with you?" Watkins's tone left no doubt as to the absurdity of her request.

Oh, God! What was happening inside? Rod Baxter was, as Joel had said, a loose cannon. He'd been pushed to the brink. She had no idea if he was capable of killing, but she feared he was. Poor Marcie. She was an innocent bystander. And Joel. What if something happened to him and she hadn't even told him how much she loved him?

Why, oh why, had she been so stubborn, so foolish, so blatantly stupid? Yes, loving was a risk. But, as this afternoon was proving, merely living was a risk. Who was she to turn from the happiness he offered because she was afraid he'd leave? He might leave her today, unwillingly, at the hands of a madman.

Glancing over her shoulder, Hannah saw a television crew arrive and begin to set up, a newsman hurriedly testing a microphone. She had to try to get through to the sergeant. "Please, I'm a trained negotiator. Let me talk with him, at least."

A tall, burly man with over twenty years on the force, Watkins turned to her. "Listen, lady, you're a civilian and you're not calling the shots here. Step back and let me do my job."

Just then, the front door burst open and Marcie stumbled out.

Joel poured a generous amount of Scotch into a glass and placed it on the desktop. Rod held the gun aimed at him in his right hand, but his left snaked over and grabbed the glass. He gulped the amber liquid down quickly.

Joel watched, waiting for the right moment. He wasn't a fool or a hero. He didn't want to die. He had too much to live for. Hannah's face swam into focus in his mind's eye as he refilled Rod's glass.

The gunman narrowed his eyes. "You think you're going to get me drunk, then take away my gun?" He gave a bark of laughter. "I could finish that whole bottle and still have a steady hand." He reached for the glass.

Sure he could, Joel thought. Carefully, he shifted closer to the man, ignoring his rank smell. "What happened to things, Rod?" he began, using a conciliatory tone. "I know you lost your job. Is that when things started to fall apart at home?" He knew that wasn't it, that the man had been beating on his wife and even his children way before his job loss. But if he could get him talking . . .

Rod sat down heavily in Joel's desk chair, but kept the gun steadily aimed. "Yeah, that was it. Ellen, she's always naggin' at me, you know." He took another long swallow. " 'Don't stay out late. Don't go out with the boys.' Hell, a man's got a right to relax after a hard day's work, right?" He considered the near-empty glass. "This is good stuff."

Joel poured again.

Hannah stood with her arm around a trembling Marcie, who'd just told her story to the sergeant. Watkins was in a huddle now with members of the SWAT team, who'd just arrived. Apparently, they were planning on entering from the back and setting up some sort of ambush. Hannah's heart was firmly entrenched in her throat at the thought.

She knew they had to do something. But what if the wrong man got shot?

Marcie squeezed Hannah's hand. "Joel's going to be all right, honey. He's got Rod drinking by now, I'm sure. I know he's just waiting for the right moment and he'll grab the gun."

"Drinking makes men like Rod Baxter worse." She clutched Marcie's hand and prayed as she'd never prayed before.

Moment's later, a single shot rang out, the sound coming from inside the house. Hannah cried out. The SWAT team hadn't gone in yet. "Oh, God, no!" she screamed as several policemen raced toward the door. She felt her knees give and would have crumpled if Marcie hadn't held on.

"Come on, honey," Marcie said, her own voice shaky. "Let's get you into the car and..."

"No!" She wouldn't leave and she wouldn't pass out. She had to find out, to see for herself. Drawing in a breath, she let go of Marcie and started toward the door. With a touch of his hand on her arm, a policeman held her back. Anxiously, she waited.

And then Joel was coming outside, walking toward her, straight and tall and looking wonderfully alive.

Hannah broke free of the cop's hold and ran to him, right into his arms. Blinking back tears, she clutched him to her as relief shuddered through her.

"It's all right, Red," Joel said, holding her tightly. He hadn't been a hundred percent sure himself, not until Rod had tilted his head back to drink more deeply and Joel had grabbed his gun hand. The shock of it had the man squeezing the trigger, the shot going wild into the ceiling. Then the gun was in Joel's hand as, with a well-aimed shove, Rod fell, collapsing into a heap on the floor.

"Yes," Hannah said, raising her damp face to his, "finally, it is all right. Have I told you lately that I love you, you big jerk? You scared me silly. Don't you *ever* do that to me again."

He grinned down into her beautiful brown eyes. "I promise I won't." He leaned closer. "What was that you said?"

Her smile had her heart in it. "That I love you. I have for a long time. I was just too stubborn to admit it."

"Better late than never, Red. Does that mean you'll marry me?"

"Tonight, if you want."

"I definitely want." And then he kissed her.

Epilogue

The wedding had taken place over two years ago, Hannah recalled as she finished her tepid tea. Her life with Joel had been everything she'd ever dreamed of and never thought she'd have. In each other, they'd both found a true home. They still lived in Boston, and both still practiced law, but only the cases that truly interested them. And they still visited Bart's ranch in Montana frequently.

She glanced at the pad with the phone number from the television show. And now there was this. Her mother was alive and searching for her. And maybe Michael and Kate had seen the show and would call the 800 number. Why not? Hadn't she already experienced one or two miracles?

Hearing a sound, Hannah glanced up, and her heart turned over. Standing in the doorway was Joel, holding a wide-awake baby boy wearing corduroy pants and a plaid shirt. Nine-month-old William Joel Merrick, dressed the same as his father, grinned at her and waved a chubby arm. "Look who's up from his nap," Hannah said, smiling at the two of them.

"You bet, and probably hungry." Joel sat down on the couch and watched Will scamper over to his mother. The child Hannah had thought she couldn't have was a daily joy to both of them. After minor surgery, she'd had no trouble conceiving. Fear had kept her needlessly worrying all those years.

He'd been doing some paperwork in the den when he'd heard the baby awaken and begin chattering to the stuffed animals in his crib. He noticed Hannah's eyes light up as she hugged their son, and he felt a rush of warmth. At long last, the restlessness was gone, and he was a contented man.

"Are you feeling any better, honey?" he asked his wife, worried about her lingering cold.

Hannah nuzzled the wonderfully soft baby neck. "Yes, much." Glancing at the phone number on the pad, she rose with Will in her arms. "Come with me while I fix Will a snack. I have something I want to talk over with you."

A chilly winter wind dashed snow against the windowpanes as the small family walked to the kitchen. But they didn't mind the outside cold or the storm. They were together inside, where their love would forever keep them warm.

* * * * *

Where are her children? Julia's search continues next month in MICHAEL'S HOUSE, coming in September from Silhouette Intimate Moments.

The dynasty begins.

LINDA HOWARD
The Mackenzies

Now available for the first time, Mackenzie's Mountain and Mackenzie's Mission, together in one affordable, trade-size edition. Don't miss out on the two stories that started it all!

Mackenzie's Mountain: Wolf Mackenzie is a loner. All he cares about is his ranch and his son. Labeled a half-breed by the townspeople, he chooses to stay up on his mountain—that is, until the spunky new schoolteacher decides to pay the Mackenzies a visit. And that's when all hell breaks loose.

Mackenzie's Misson: Joe "Breed" Mackenzie is a colonel in the U.S. Air Force. All he cares about is flying. He is the best of the best and determined never to let down his country—even for love. But that was before he met a beautiful civilian engineer, who turns his life upside down.

Available this August, at your favorite retail outlet.

Who can resist a Texan...or a Calloway?

This September, award-winning author
ANNETTE BROADRICK
returns to Texas, with a brand-new
story about the Calloways...

SONS OF TEXAS

Rogues and Ranchers

CLINT: The brave leader. Used to keeping secrets.

CADE: The Lone Star Stud. Used to having women
fall at his feet...

MATT: The family guardian. Used to handling
trouble...

They must discover the identity of the mystery
woman with Calloway eyes—and uncover a
conspiracy that threatens their family....

Look for **SONS OF TEXAS:** Rogues and Ranchers
in September 1996!

Only from Silhouette...where passion lives.

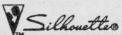

**You can run, but you cannot
hide...from love.**

OUTLAWS
and Lovers

This August, experience danger, excitement and
love on the run with three couples thrown
together by life-threatening circumstances.

Enjoy three complete stories by some of your
favorite authors—all in one special collection!

THE PRINCESS AND THE PEA
by Kathleen Korbel

IN SAFEKEEPING
by Naomi Horton

FUGITIVE
by Emilie Richards

Available this August wherever books are sold.

Silhouette®

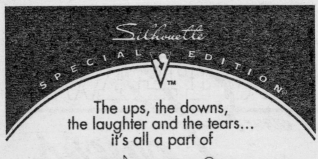

Silhouette

SPECIAL EDITION ™

The ups, the downs,
the laughter and the tears...
it's all a part of

PARENTHOOD
Diana Whitney

Stories that will touch your heart and make you
believe in the power of romance and family. They'll
give you hope that true love really *does* conquer all.

DADDY OF THE HOUSE (SE #1052, September 1996)
tells the tale of an estranged husband and wife, who can't
seem to let go of the deep love they once shared...or
the three beautiful—and mischievous—children they
created together.

BAREFOOT BRIDE (SE #1073, December 1996)
explores the story of an amnesiac bride who is discovered
by a single dad and his two daughters. See how this
runaway rich girl becomes their nanny and then
their mother....

A HERO'S CHILD (coming March 1997)
reveals a husband who's presumed dead and comes home
to claim his wife—and the daughter he never knew he had.

You won't want to miss a single one of these delightful,
heartwarming stories. So pick up your copies soon—only
from Silhouette Special Edition.

Look us up on-line at: http://www.romance.net   PARENT

There's nothing quite like a family

REUNION
HANNAH · MICHAEL · KATE

The new miniseries by
Pat Warren

Three siblings are about to be reunited.
And each finds love along the way....

HANNAH
Her life is about to change now that she's met
the irresistible Joel Merrick in HOME FOR HANNAH
(Special Edition #1048, August 1996).

MICHAEL
He's been on his own all his life. Now he's
going to take a risk on love...and
take part in the reunion he's been
waiting for in MICHAEL'S HOUSE
(Intimate Moments #737, September 1996).

KATE
A job as a nanny leads her to Aaron Carver,
his adorable baby daughter and the
fulfillment of her dreams in KEEPING KATE
(Special Edition #1060, October 1996).

Meet these three siblings from

Silhouette SPECIAL EDITION®
and

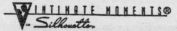
INTIMATE MOMENTS®
Silhouette

Look us up on-line at: http://www.romance.net

REUNION

SILHOUETTE... Where Passion Lives

Add these Silhouette favorites to your collection today!
Now you can receive a discount by ordering two or more titles!

SD#05819	WILD MIDNIGHT by Ann Major	$2.99 ☐
SD#05878	THE UNFORGIVING BRIDE by Joan Johnston	$2.99 U.S. ☐ $3.50 CAN. ☐
IM#07568	MIRANDA'S VIKING by Maggie Shayne	$3.50 ☐
SSE#09896	SWEETBRIAR SUMMIT by Christine Rimmer	$3.50 U.S. ☐ $3.99 CAN. ☐
SSE#09944	A ROSE AND A WEDDING VOW by Andrea Edwards	$3.75 U.S. ☐ $4.25 CAN. ☐
SR#19002	A FATHER'S PROMISE by Helen R. Myers	$2.75 ☐

(limited quantities available on certain titles)

TOTAL AMOUNT	$_____
DEDUCT: 10% DISCOUNT FOR 2+ BOOKS	$_____
POSTAGE & HANDLING	$_____
($1.00 for one book, 50¢ for each additional)	
APPLICABLE TAXES**	$_____
TOTAL PAYABLE	$_____
(check or money order—please do not send cash)	

To order, send the completed form with your name, address, zip or postal code, along with a check or money order for the total above, payable to Silhouette Books, to: **In the U.S.:** 3010 Walden Avenue, P.O. Box 9077, Buffalo, NY 14269-9077; **In Canada:** P.O. Box 636, Fort Erie, Ontario, L2A 5X3.

Name:_____

Address:_____ City:_____

State/Prov.:_____ Zip/Postal Code:_____

**New York residents remit applicable sales taxes.
Canadian residents remit applicable GST and provincial taxes.

Silhouette®
TM

SBACK-JA2